"I'm far too normal."

"Outwardly, perhaps." Connor's eyes darkened. "Except I've already figured you out. You're a happy, singsong Marian the Librarian to all appearances, but inside, beneath the cocoon of small-town life, is another person waiting to burst free. Like a butterfly."

The muscles in Tess's stomach clutched, even though he was getting carried away. She really was the nice, normal person she claimed. She didn't need to be set free.

From what? she silently scoffed. Her life was her own. Entirely her own.

"Well, Connor, that sounds nice, it really does. But on the other hand, I'm pretty certain that you just called me a caterpillar."

He smiled, but his gaze was even deeper and softer than before. It enfolded her. "By any other name…"

Dear Reader,

Hello from the North Country!

As I'm writing this letter, it's a beautiful summer day with breezes playing through the trees and sunshine glittering on the lake. But by the time you read this, I'll be plunged into the dead of winter with snowdrifts up to my eyeballs. The Upper Peninsula of Michigan is a land of extremes, where only the tough survive—as long as the tough have a good heating system and a snow shovel.

In this story, the second in my NORTH COUNTRY STORIES miniseries, Connor Reed comes to the wilderness to escape his notoriety as a true crime writer. Is there anywhere more remote or romantic to escape to than a lighthouse, seemingly at the edge of the world? Small-town librarian Tess Bucek is certainly intrigued by the stranger in town, and it's not long before truths of the heart are revealed....

Look for my next NORTH COUNTRY book in November of this year. And please visit my Web site at www.carriealexander.com for news of future books, contests and "North Country" photos and map.

Sincerely,

Carrie

Three Little Words
Carrie Alexander

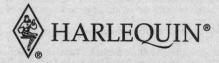

HARLEQUIN®

TORONTO • NEW YORK • LONDON
AMSTERDAM • PARIS • SYDNEY • HAMBURG
STOCKHOLM • ATHENS • TOKYO • MILAN • MADRID
PRAGUE • WARSAW • BUDAPEST • AUCKLAND

ISBN 0-373-71186-7

THREE LITTLE WORDS

This edition published by arrangement with Harlequin Books S.A.

® and TM are trademarks of the publisher. Trademarks indicated with ® are registered in the United States Patent and Trademark Office, the Canadian Trade Marks Office and in other countries.

Visit us at www.eHarlequin.com

Printed in U.S.A.

Books by Carrie Alexander

HARLEQUIN SUPERROMANCE
1042—THE MAVERICK
1102—NORTH COUNTRY MAN

Don't miss any of our special offers. Write to us at the following address for information on our newest releases.

Harlequin Reader Service
U.S.: 3010 Walden Ave., P.O. Box 1325, Buffalo, NY 14269
Canadian: P.O. Box 609, Fort Erie, Ont. L2A 5X3

CHAPTER ONE

THE MAN LOOKED like a smuggler.

In a *library?* Amused with the incongruity, Tess Bucek slid the card from the pocket of *Sis Boom Bah! A Survival Guide to Cheerleading Camp* and passed the book beneath the bar-code scanner. She was so accustomed to the task that it wasn't necessary to look away from the suspicious character loitering between the arts and history sections. As he moved to one of the study tables with a stack of books, she stamped a date on the card in red and returned it to the pocket.

"Due back in three weeks." Tess slid the book across the checkout desk to Sarah Johnson, who would have been her niece if she'd married into the family as planned. Instead, they were merely acquaintances, and lucky to be that since Tess wasn't on speaking terms with Sarah's father, Erik. "Have a nice time at camp."

"Oh, I will. Thanks, Miss Bucek," Sarah bubbled, thrilled about making the JV cheerleading squad before school had let out for the summer. "I can already do a super cartwheel, but my herkies…"

Tess smiled and nodded as Sarah went on about cheerleading stunts, surreptitiously rising off her heels and telescoping her neck to keep sight of the stranger seated beyond the girl's bobbing blond ponytail.

He was tall, dark and mysterious. Tess would have shivered if she was the shivering type.

A smuggler with a tortured conscience, she decided as Sarah finally said goodbye. There was an air about him—intense, conflicted, maybe even dangerous. Definitely shady.

Grosse Pointe Blank, Tony Soprano, *The Tulip Thief,* every detective novel she'd ever read…they all filtered through Tess's quick-firing synapses. After serving more than ten years as a librarian in a poky small town where ''danger'' meant icy roads or the fire index, pop culture was all she had for reference. She preferred fiction, anyway. Particularly when it came to the criminal element.

She'd honed a vivid imagination during the time when she'd been stuck in a one-bedroom cottage with her newly divorced and depressed mother, listening to a limited collection of Beatles, Bread and Simon and Garfunkel LPs. Ever since the bow tie that was really a spy camera in the song ''America,'' Tess had taken to making up little stories about everyone around her. Their next-door neighbor with the green thumb had become a poisoner burying bodies in the petunia patch. She imagined that her fourth-grade teacher, bland Mrs. Gorski, metamorphosed into a disco diva after the bell rang, complete with polyester wrap dress and sparkly blue eye shadow.

Even now, Tess continued to indulge her flights

of fancy. Cheap entertainment for the comfortably settled.

Impelled by an inward squiggly feeling—not a shiver—Tess stepped out from behind the desk and grabbed the half-filled return cart parked nearby. The wheels squeaked as she pushed it toward the 900s—the history section. The stranger looked up from his book, his gaze watchful. Perhaps leery.

She smiled her pleasant professional-librarian smile. "Did you find what you wanted, sir?"

The man had keen eyes, even though his lashes lowered and his gaze avoided hers. Oddly evasive, Tess thought with a genuine twinge of suspicion.

The stranger nodded and returned to the open book, ducking his head between hunched shoulders. The back of his collar gaped around locks of wavy black hair. The long hair and a chin shadowed with stubble gave him the intriguing devil-may-care air that had sparked her imagination, even though a similar look was affected by a good third of the local single-male population. On them it was scrubby and slapdash. On this guy—dashing.

Tess sneaked a peak at the heavily illustrated book he'd selected. *Lighthouses.* Just as he'd asked for. She'd volunteered to show him the way, but he'd wanted to browse.

He's the brains behind a Canadian smuggling operation, she decided. *A modern-day pirate.* Hence the lighthouse research. He'd come to Alouette scouting for a remote drop-off point. Guns or drugs, she imagined.

Or animal smuggling. Monkeys, marmosets or exotic birds—rare blue macaws. That's what Jack Colton had been doing in *Romancing the Stone* and she remembered an article in a back issue of *Smithsonian* about the trafficking of rare species. Except it didn't make a lot of sense, sneaking contraband across *two* borders....

Abandoning Dewey decimal, Tess blindly thrust a cookbook among the Egyptians. Black-bear organs—that was it! He was smuggling contraband *out* of the Upper Peninsula, not in.

Her imagination took full flight. A Chinese man with an eye patch was the contact. His name was Suk Yung Foo and he'd been sent by his gangster father to an American college to better himself. Instead, he'd met this guy, a former, um, *professor*...who'd been on the track to full tenure until the...*cheating scandal? Embezzlement of research grants?*

No. The man had too much sex appeal for his downfall to be anything but nubile young coeds.

Tess shook her head. "How predictable."

The stranger glanced back at her. "Predictable?"

"Oh." She blinked. "Why, uh, someone's misfiled a cookbook. *Dust Off Your Bread Machine* does not belong beside *Nubian Artifacts.*"

"You put it there."

"Did I?" The man must have eyes in the back of his head, but then she'd heard that of crooks.

He shrugged and returned to his reading. For a long moment Tess watched, frozen, as he flipped from illustration to illustration. Then she jammed the bread book onto her cart and wheeled it fast in the opposite direction, her heels clacking on the parquet floor. She slowed when she turned at the end of the row and peered back at him, catching glimpses of him along the aisles as she moved away at a more leisurely pace.

She was being ridiculous. He was a perfectly normal man reading about lighthouses. Alouette's Gull Rock Lighthouse, situated on the narrow, rocky peninsula that framed one side of the bay, was frequently photographed by tourists, and it had been featured in several travel books. Although the lighthouse was out of commission and not accessible to the public, it was too prominent and exposed to be the base of operations for a smuggling operation.

Even one that operated at night? Alouette rolled up the sidewalks by ten. A herd of zebras could stampede downtown and no one would know until they stepped in the evidence the next morning.

Tess shook her head. *Oh, stop it. Get back to your job.*

She slipped the cookbook into its proper place, made quick work of shelving the remaining books and returned to the front desk. The stranger was still seated at the study table. If he was doing any sort of serious research, he must have a photographic memory—he hadn't made a single note.

"Is he a tourist?" whispered Beth Trudell as she moved behind the desk, one hand splayed over her protruding midsection.

"Probably."

"He doesn't look like a tourist."

"No."

"You'd best stop staring at him and go take charge of the kids. They're waiting for their story. I can't promise how patiently."

With a small groan, Beth eased herself onto a stool. She was twenty-three, married for a year, and presently eight months, one week and three days pregnant, give or take a few hours. She had been Tess's assistant in one form or another ever since Tess had started working here. That first day, Beth had been a shy adolescent with spindly arms and thick glasses. She'd read Sweet Valley books until closing time and then helped Tess sweep, straighten chairs and water plants. The next day, Tess had introduced the girl to *Little Women, Anne of Green Gables* and Nancy Drew and asked if she wanted to help out with the new children's summer-reading program.

"You finished the craft project?" Tess asked idly. Delaying. She really wanted to know what the stranger was up to. Besides, the noise from the adjacent children's reading room hadn't escalated to the danger zone yet.

"Six Popsicle-stick planters, all set for repotting the nasturtiums."

"Only six?"

Beth settled herself more comfortably, wincing a little as she propped her feet on the rungs. "Grady Kujanen smashed his. He did it deliberately, so I didn't let him make another. We were out of sticks, anyway. Then he sat beneath the table and stared at my belly while he pouted." Beth chuckled. "Get this. He asked me when I was going to pop."

"Pop? Where in the world…?"

"I guess he heard it from his dad. Now the children think I'm a champagne bottle. Grady told them that when I go to the hospital the doctor pulls the cork, and *voilà*—a baby."

"If only it were that easy," Tess said.

Beth patted the baby in her belly. She called it Bump. "Yeah."

"Five more weeks, sweetie." Beth's due date had been circled in red on the library calendar ever since they'd administered a drugstore pregnancy test in the ladies' room one slow Thursday night. Neither having much experience with babies, they'd used every research tool at their disposal to compile a fact sheet for the next nine months. The first fact they'd learned was that "nine months" was a misnomer. Gestation was actually forty weeks. The extra days were making Beth a little crazy.

"Randy refuses to talk in term of weeks, ever since I had that meltdown at the thought of still being pregnant in July. From now on, he says, it's one day at a time." Beth wiped her forehead with the back of one wrist. "One hot, sweaty day at a time."

It was barely eighty outside, but Tess cranked up the fan that whirred from a shelf behind the checkout desk. They didn't have air-conditioning—no budget. "You look done in, Beth. Why don't you leave early?"

"Thanks. I'll take you up on that. But not till the

kids are gone. You know how hectic it gets when they're all checking out at once.'' Beth swiveled to face the library proper, which had been fashioned from the ground-floor rooms of a big Victorian house on Timber Avenue, one block from the elementary school and two blocks from downtown bayside Alouette. ''And we have our other patrons to keep an eye on,'' she added significantly. Her arched eyebrows disappeared behind curly, slightly damp bangs.

Tess shot Mr. Tall, Dark and Mysterious another glance. He was absorbed in his book, but she would have sworn his ears were pricked. Why a conversation about due dates and craft projects would concern a rogue pirate, she had no idea.

A shriek came from the children's area. Through the open doorway, Tess saw Grady Kujanen raising a picture book over his head. ''Take over for me,'' she told Beth before hurrying away.

Beth's eyes slitted as she whispered out of the side of her mouth, ''Synchronize your watch. We'll reconvene in fifteen minutes.''

Tess nodded, although Bump ruined the spy effect Beth was going for. Maybe if she'd been wearing a gabardine suit and a bow tie…

In the children's room, Tess stepped into the fray and snatched the book out of Grady's hands before he could bring it down on Sierra Caldwell's head. The children knew she demanded best behavior, so after she'd admonished Grady they settled down without much complaint, gathering on the bright pillows and beanbags strewn across the carpet of the story-telling nook.

Normally, Tess would have pulled the filmy blue star-sprinkled curtains she'd hung at this end of the room to give the nook a cozy feel, but today she wanted a clear view to the main room of the library. You never knew when a baby might decide to "pop" early, so it paid to be vigilant.

Of course, it didn't hurt that she could also see the study tables from her position on the storytelling throne, a tufted purple-velvet ottoman trimmed in bobbled fringe. The stranger had set aside the last of his picture books and was paging through a paperback by a local author, *Lighthouses of Upper Michigan.* Hmm...

Soon Tess had forgotten the suspicious unshaved ex-professor bear-organs smuggler and was absorbed by the story she read to the children, *The Princess Who Wished Tomorrow Would Never Come.* The group was a good one despite Grady's tendency to make himself the center of attention. When he'd first started in the reading program that Tess ran three times a week all summer long, his behavior had been much worse—loud, bratty and completely disinterested in books, despite a year of kindergarten. Tess had spoken with his teachers to determine the best course of action, and so far, her subtle efforts to engage the boy's imagination were working. He'd begun to understand the magic of reading, even though his mother considered the library little more than a convenient baby-sitting service and wasn't too happy about lugging Grady's books home with them.

Tess started each session with basic reading-comprehension work, then gave way to Beth for a fun arts and crafts project or mini-outdoor field trip—one day the children started nasturtium seeds, another day they chased butterflies in the library's flower garden. It gratified Tess that they considered the storybook she read to them at the end of the hour the best treat of all. There were so many good children's books to choose from, and she always got into the performance, using character voices and facial expressions with a theatrical flair that surprised even herself. Before she'd been dragged into performing with the local theater group a few years back, she hadn't thought she was the dramatic type.

Not that a little bit of small-town stage experience had changed anything. She was still only Tess Bucek, a librarian with a private life as unremarkable and familiar as a bowl of oatmeal.

"'The green-winged whippersnapper soared from the sky with a rose in its beak,'" Tess read. She turned the page. "'Princess Ella Umbrella Pumpkinella Fantabuzella—'" the children singsonged the name with her "'—took the rose and said...'" Tess pointed at Grady.

The chubby boy went on hands and knees to see the open book she held out. His lower lip stuck out with determination. After a few seconds, he read, "'Zip-per-zap.'"

"Zipperzap!" Tess agreed. She allowed Grady to

select a children's tattoo from a nearby basket. She always kept a stash of modest prizes like stickers and cartoon-character pencil erasers handy.

"Zipperzap," sighed Lucy Grant, a shy, delicate five-year-old with translucent skin. Her huge blue eyes shone with pleasure.

"'Once the magic word was spoken and the rose petals had been flung to the northerly wind,'" Tess went on, finishing up the story with a triumphant flourish, "'the sun came out from the dark clouds, the flowers blossomed and the creatures of the forest rose from their hundred-years' sleep.'" She looked up and saw the dark-haired stranger hovering in the doorway, listening to her with an intent expression. "'Princess Ella Umbrella Pumpkinella, uh, Fantas—'" No, not *fantasy*.

"Fan-ta-bu-zel-la," the children recited in unison.

Tess had lost track entirely.

The man saw that he'd disrupted her flow. "I'd like to speak with you after you're finished," he said in a low, serious voice that made her nape prickle. He walked away before she could respond.

Tess swallowed. What was that about? Why did she feel so remarkably different?

The kids were clamoring for the ending. Tess focused on the page, illustrated with a green-eyed, freckle-faced princess in a pair of bib overalls. "'And then the, um, princess said, *Even though today is beautiful, I know that tomorrow may be even better.*'"

HE COULD WAIT, Tess decided. Parents were arriving to pick up the children and there were gluey planters to be shown off and books to be checked out. When the library had cleared out finally, Lucy Grant was left behind. Her single dad, Evan Grant, was a gym teacher and basketball coach at the high school. Summers, he picked up an extra paycheck with a local builder and couldn't always get off work to deliver Lucy to her baby-sitter's house. Usually either Tess or Beth ducked out to take her there.

Not today. Tess put Lucy's stick planter on the windowsill to dry and settled the girl at one of the child-size tables with the second book in the Princess Ella series. Today, she'd call Evan at work. Beth would have volunteered, but her house was in the opposite direction—a long enough walk for a pregnant woman without adding a detour. And Tess couldn't leave the library unattended, whether or not there was a smuggler on the premises. Lucy would have to wait for her father.

Tess went back to the main desk to call Evan. The stranger loitered near the magazine rack, gazing out the window at the flower garden. Maybe he was conducting a surveillance of traffic patterns. Little did he know that on Timber Avenue, there was no traffic to surveil.

After hanging up, Tess turned to Beth. "Go on home. Evan can take a break, so he's coming for Lucy."

Beth smiled tiredly. "Good. I don't want to waddle any farther than I have to."

"You can take my car if the walk is too much for you today." Tess had been urging her assistant to quit her part-time position for the last few weeks of her pregnancy, but Beth said that waiting out the time at home alone in her tiny apartment, staring at her belly button and the movements of Bump beneath it, would drive her bananas.

"No, my doctor says I should keep walking." Beth groaned as she hoisted herself off the stool. "I'd like to strap a watermelon to his gut and send him around the block ten times. See what he thinks then."

Tess patted her consolingly. "Pour yourself a cold drink and put your feet up as soon as you get home."

"I'll have to pry my shoes off first. My feet and ankles have swollen like bread dough."

Tess offered her arm as they walked to the front door, a heavy slab of mahogany inset with leaded glass. She'd left it open to the June sunshine. "Randy's going to be home tonight, isn't he?" Beth's husband drove a bakery delivery truck and was sometimes away overnight because his route was so sizable. From one end of the Upper Peninsula to the other was more than three hundred miles, and he delivered to northern Wisconsin as well.

"He promised. His boss even promised that Randy wouldn't have to do any more overnighters, till Bump arrives, anyway."

"Good." Tess gave Beth a gentle squeeze. "You take care. Call me if anything happens. Or doesn't. Call me if you just want to talk."

Beth glanced into the main room of the library,

which opened off the small entry hall and had been formed by knocking out walls between the house's formal parlor and second sitting room. "*You* call me as soon as he leaves," Beth whispered. She jerked her head at the lingering stranger. "I want to find out what's up with him."

"He's probably going to ask me for directions to the lighthouse. Maybe he's a photographer."

Beth's nose crinkled. "Maybe, maybe not."

"Or a reincarnated lighthouse keeper bedeviled by nightmares he can't explain."

"Now you're talking. But I bet you could come up with an even better scenario if you tried."

Tess laughed. Her assistant knew her too well. "Go home, Beth."

Beth went, waddling with one hand pressed to the small of her back and the other making a phone shape at her ear. "Call me," she mouthed.

Tess waved Beth away, smiling to hide her unmollified worry over Randy's late hours. His boss wasn't as accommodating as he might have been, but there was no helping it. The Trudells were struggling to make ends meet. Beth's parents, an older couple who'd had their only daughter late in life, had recently retired in Florida. They planned to return soon for an extended stay, to help Beth out with the baby, but until then, Randy and Tess were the young mother-to-be's main support system. Aside from any number of do-gooders in the community who would be glad to pitch in and help in case of emergency.

Although the two women were primarily best

friends, there were times Tess felt like Beth's older sister, even her mother. If it was possible to be a mother when you'd never given birth yourself.

Tess frowned, spreading her hands over her flat tummy. Eleven years ago, she was on her way to a life just like Beth's when—

Tess brushed off the sad memory. Dismissing the tragedy that had shaped her life had become easier with practice. And distance.

She walked into the main room, checking first on Lucy. The girl, a dreamy, inward child, not unlike Tess at that age, was completely absorbed in the book.

Tess's second glance went to the make-believe pirate. "Sorry for the delay. How can I help you, Mr...?"

He came forward, not as tall as she'd assumed but still many inches past her five-two. Tall enough to make her tilt her chin up when she looked into his clear hazel-brown eyes.

"Connor Reed," he said, offering his hand.

"Tess Bucek." His hand was large and cool and dry. Hers was small and warm and moist. And they fit together just fine, for a brief moment that made her feel as if her cells were rushing like a warm river toward him. He let go then, and she blinked and said in a far too girlish voice, "Hi."

His eyebrows drew down. "Hi."

She said, "Connor Reed," mulling over the name. It was naggingly familiar. "Are you from around here?"

"Not really."

"I feel like I know you from somewhere...."

His features tightened. "I used to spend summers here, with my grandfather."

"Did you?" She tried to picture Connor Reed as a boy and no bells rang. Summer people. They came and went, very few of them leaving a mark except for the trash they threw off their boats, the cash in the tills of local businesses and the rising prices of shore-line property. Not many of them ventured into the library with the distraction of sun-soaked days at the beach beckoning so near. Lake Superior was practically lapping at her doorstep.

"I don't think we've ever met," she said doubt-fully, "so I can't imagine how I'd know—"

"You don't. You don't know me."

He was lying. She was certain. But why?

"Who's your grandfather?" she asked, letting her suspicion show. Close-knit families were important to local folks. Their ties were meaningful, binding, un-breakable. And closed to outsiders. She knew first-hand.

Connor hesitated. "Addison Mitchell."

She shook her head. Nothing.

"He moved away some time ago, but he's been back for about a year now."

"In Alouette?" The town was small enough that she knew just about everyone, at least by sight.

"Ishpeming. At a nursing home."

"I see."

Connor let out a soft breath. "He was once the Gull Rock lighthouse keeper."

The lightbulb went on. "*Oh.* Of course—Old Man Mitchell!" Tess's cheeks got warm when she realized how that sounded. "I mean, that's what we always called him. Kids, you know. He used to chase us away from the lighthouse grounds."

Connor said nothing in reply and her eyes narrowed. Sonny Mitchell had always lived alone, as far as she remembered, until the lighthouse had become automated and then decommissioned altogether a few years later. Gull Rock was quite isolated and austere. Sonny "Old Man" Mitchell had been a notorious crank.

She prodded for more information. "I still don't remember you, though, Mr. Reed."

"Connor," he said. He glanced over her, up and down, making her toes flex inside conservative Payless pumps. "I'm older than you—we wouldn't have connected when I was ten and you were…still in diapers?"

She doubted there was that much of an age difference, even though he had a sort of weary, haunted look about him that made him seem…well, not *old* exactly, but sort of cynical and worn out. "I'm thirty-two."

"Thirty-nine."

Okay, he had a point. She wasn't hanging out at the lighthouse when she was three. He might even be telling the truth about visiting his grandfather, except that she doubted he was telling *all* of it.

Unless her suspicion was only her vivid imagination run amok. Which, admittedly, wasn't all that infrequent an occurrence. It was fortunate she usually kept her fancies to herself. Outwardly, she was as regular as a metronome.

"Now that we've established my provenance," Connor said with a small twitch of one corner of his mouth. The hollows in his cheeks deepened. He was trying not to smile at her.

Not used to being found amusing, Tess elongated her neck, tilting her head back. She was short; imperious was a stretch, but she tried. "Yes?"

He sobered. "I have a favor to ask you. Or—well, not really a favor. It can be a job. I'd pay for your time."

She felt her eyes widen. He wanted her to help him load bear gallbladders off Gull Rock when she could barely stand to handle raw chicken giblets? Certainly not. She almost chuckled at the thought, before remembering that she was being ridiculous with her far-fetched imaginings and really must stop.

Right now.

"I saw you with the children, reading, teaching…so I wondered, if it's not an imposition—" Connor's gaze held steady even if his words were hesitant "—whether you might be willing to teach…"

Teach him how to read?

Tess tried not to look shocked. Suddenly all the little details made sense. The way he'd concentrated on the lighthouse illustrations and not the text. How he hadn't taken any notes. The intent look on his face when he'd watched her storytelling group. She'd taken it for his natural demeanor, but it might have been fierce concentration. Exactly the way Grady Kujanen concentrated on sounding out a new word.

Heavens. And here she'd pegged Connor Reed as a former professor gone bad. She couldn't have been more wrong!

"Of course I'll teach you how to read," she said, stepping in with a reassuring squeeze of his arm when he continued to hesitate over the request.

His eyes flashed. "Teach me?"

CHAPTER TWO

AT CONNOR'S OBVIOUS surprise, the librarian's chin came down and she leaned closer, exuding warmth and understanding. "Trust me, it's nothing to be embarrassed about. There are so many people like you, from all walks of life. I commend your courage in coming forward, really I do. This is your turning point. One day, you'll look back and—"

Suddenly she stopped the stream of platitudes, her mouth hanging open. Must have finally read his face.

"It's not me," he said.

She had clasped his hands with encouragement, but now she let go. "Would it be..." long pause "...a close friend?"

"My grandfather." There it was, baldly. Connor hoped Sonny wouldn't kill him for involving a third party. The librarian seemed kind, and possibly discreet. She'd certainly been surreptitious about checking *him* out. But not sneaky enough, because he'd noticed every one of her shy glances and speculative stares.

At first he'd noticed because she was an attractive woman, small and cute as a chipping sparrow, with bright eyes and darting hands and a shiny cap of copper hair. Then he'd realized that it was possible she'd recognized him as an infamous quasi celebrity.

He'd come to hate when that happened. Over and over again, he'd suffered the lingering stares, the double takes. Eyes widened with recognition, hands slapped over mouths. *That's Connor Reed. The man who set the killer free. I've seen him on the news. Despicable! He should be ashamed.*

He'd put up with it through the hearings and the aftermath, but now that it was over—or so he hoped—he'd known he had to get away. So he'd run. As far as he could.

Alouette, Michigan, a small outpost on the far northern border of the country, seemed to qualify as the ends of the earth. As he'd remembered from a few brief vacations at the lighthouse, people here were friendly but not intrusive. They'd gossip among themselves about Connor's culpability in the Strange case, but they wouldn't pillory him. Not in public, anyway. Even so, he planned to keep his head low.

The librarian was nodding. "Uh-huh. Your grandfather. Well. There are literacy programs that will help. I can put you in touch with a teacher who—"

"No. Sonny wouldn't want a program. Nothing official." As it was, Sonny would probably object to Tess Bucek, even on her own. He'd asked Connor to teach him to read—only Connor.

The librarian blinked. "Why me?"

Connor scrubbed a hand over his jaw. He was dead tired from a day and a half on the road—New York City to small-town Michigan in one shot—from one extreme to another in thirty-some hours. He'd gone first to visit Sonny at the nursing home, then drove into Alouette for a look at the old lighthouse, since that was all his grandfather had talked about.

Stopping at the library had been a sudden whim. A few books on lighthouses seemed like a good way to get his grandfather started. Connor had soon figured out that he didn't know the first thing about teaching a stubborn, crotchety old man to read. He'd been about to leave, when Tess's voice had drawn him over to the children's area.

Voices, rather. He'd watched long enough to see that while she had the verve to entrance the kids with her storytelling ability, she was also a patient and easy teacher. If anyone could charm Old Man Mitchell into proper reading lessons, it was Tess Bucek.

She was waiting for his answer.

"Why?" Connor shrugged. "I saw you with the kids. You seem to have a talent. And my grandfather's a special case…"

"A hard case, I expect." There was irony in her voice, but her gaze flickered uncertainly. Her eyes were green, not bright, but soft, like moss.

She'd do. "I can't deny it," Connor said.

"You need someone qualified to evaluate your grandfather's reading level, at the very least. I do have a little bit of experience and a minor in education, but I'm no expert."

"Exactly why I chose you." Connor didn't want to come right out and say that his grandfather wasn't expecting a teacher and wouldn't welcome one. If the first introduction was unofficial, a friendly how-d'ya-do, Tess could ease herself into the old man's graces—it would be a stretch calling them *good*—and begin to work her magic. For all his gruffness, Sonny Mitchell had a soft spot for any female with a soothing voice and nice legs. Tess's were…

Connor looked down. A canary-yellow skirt stopped an inch above her knees. Cute kneecaps. Curvy calves. Slim ankles. Tess Bucek's legs were more than acceptable.

Her head lowered, following the direction of his gaze. She tapped her toe. "You chose me for my shoes?"

"Uh, no." Connor looked up, his gaze colliding with hers. Her lashes were a pale reddish brown that gave her eyes a wide-awake, innocent-schoolgirl look. He had to remind himself that she was thirty-two. She seemed…untouched. Unmarred.

Especially by the likes of him.

He offered another useless shrug. "I'm going on instinct. You seem like the right person for the job. My grandfather can be difficult."

"I know. I remember, or at least I remember his reputation." Tess hesitated. "Maybe you should tell me more about him."

"Not a lot to tell. He's led a simple life. He was the oldest son of Cornish immigrants. Worked since he was eleven—any job he could get, but primarily in the iron mines. So his schooling took a back seat, I guess. Eventually he landed the job as lighthouse keeper and it stuck."

"You know, I never knew he was married. To me, he was always Old Man Mitchell, living alone at Gull Rock."

"Yup, he was married for more than thirty years. He and Grandma had one daughter—my mother. She was the one who sent me to live with Sonny for those first few summers after Grandma died. She hoped I'd keep the old man company."

"Did you?"

"Pretty much had to. There wasn't a lot to do at the lighthouse but talk. Or in Alouette, as I remember it."

"We manage to find ways to amuse ourselves." Tess blushed pink when Connor lifted his brows at that. She rushed on. "Where did your grandfather go when the state shut down the lighthouse?"

"My parents wanted him to live with them downstate. Sonny wasn't too happy about being away from the big lake, but he settled in eventually. He was satisfied until the past few years, when he started in about returning to his roots, before he..."

Connor winced at the surprising amount of regret he felt, thinking of the short time his grandfather had left. He should have made a stronger effort to visit instead of giving up so much of himself to his work. What had that got him except trouble?

Even the loss of his reputation and, it seemed, his will to write were put into perspective now that he was losing Sonny, too.

Connor took a breath. "Sonny's health isn't good. He's eighty-nine. He wanted to come home." To die.

Tess's expression was troubled. "He's eighty-nine and *now* he wants to learn how to read?"

"What can I say? This is his last chance to amend old regrets." Always a good idea, Connor told himself. And sooner was better than later, if only there was a way....

Tess's quiet voice filtered through his black thoughts, defusing the gloom. "This is your grandfather's dying wish, isn't it?" She had her soft hands on his again, pressing lightly, sweet with concern. "I'm so sorry."

Connor nodded.

Her lashes batted away a sheen of moisture. "Then I'll do what I can to help."

"Thank you," he said, his throat gone raw with the emotions he kept swallowing down. Struck by her empathy, he had an odd impulse to give her a hug, but it had been too long since he'd engaged in a normal relationship. He'd buried his emotions deep. Lost the ability to connect.

So he shook Tess's hand instead.

Sounds came from the foyer, breaking them apart. A man walked into the library, a tall guy with clipped brown hair and a healthy, vigorous air. He was dressed in a sweat-stained T-shirt, faded jeans and work boots. His handsome, all-American face lit up when he saw Tess. "Hey, Marian. Thanks for calling me."

"Evan. Hello. Lucy's waiting—"

The slight blond girl that Connor had forgotten about emerged from the children's reading room.

"Hi, Daddy. May I check out three books today, please?" Her voice was so soft it was barely audible.

The tall guy knelt to look at the storybooks she held out. "Jeez, Luce, I don't know. Are you going to make me read *all* of them to you tonight?"

The girl nodded, smiling hopefully.

Her father sighed. "Oh, all right. Give them to Miss Bucek so she can check them out for you." He rose, looking at Connor with open curiosity. Maybe because all strangers were suspect in a small town, maybe because Evan had seen him on TV or in print. Or it could have been because Connor's expression had changed when he heard that Tess was, beyond any doubt, a *miss*.

"Evan, this is Connor Reed. He's in town to visit his grandfather, Sonny Mitchell." Tess had moved behind the desk and was reaching over to take the books Lucy held up to her. "Sonny's before your time here, so you wouldn't know him, but he used to be the lighthouse keeper. Connor spent summers at Gull Rock."

The tall guy held out his hand. "Evan Grant. Sounds like you were a lucky kid."

"At the time, I didn't know how lucky." The men shook, matching strong grips. Connor's observational skills were sharp. Since so many people lied to him in the course of his work, he'd learned to recognize subtle signals and body language and make instant character assessments. Most of the time he was right in his judgment. He'd always known that Roderick

Strange was guilty, although that certainly hadn't taken any special skill.

In this instance, it was easy enough to calculate that Evan was a good, honorable, obviously hardworking man. Didn't mean Connor had to like the guy.

The familiarity between Evan and Tess was clear. Connor didn't know why that should unsettle him, when he wasn't even remotely in the market for a girlfriend. Yet the hair on the back of his hand had risen when he'd gripped Evan's hand, as if the shake had been about taking the measure of an adversary rather than a simple greeting.

Forget it. Tess Bucek seemed like a respectable person. He no longer was, according to his law-and-order critics. And Connor wasn't sure there was any good reason to refute that opinion.

"Staying in town long?" Evan asked, sliding his gaze from Connor to Tess.

Connor crossed his arms. "Indefinitely."

"Have you checked in to a hotel?" Tess flipped open a book. "There are only a couple options in Alouette, but if you're staying in one of the nearby towns—"

Connor cut her off. "I haven't decided."

She wasn't deterred by his shortness. "It's tourist season, but early yet, so something should be available. There you go, Lucy. All checked out." Tess handed over the books in a plastic "Great Summer Reading!" drawstring bag. "Will I see you on Monday, sweetie?"

Lucy nodded shyly.

"I've got to get back to work," Evan said. He aimed a casual grin at Tess. "Thanks, Marian." He nodded at Connor, fixing him with a serious stare, then walked out with his hand resting on his daughter's thin shoulders.

Connor took the look to mean: Don't mess with Tess or I'll cheerfully beat you into the ground like a fence post.

He waited until the pair had cleared the building, then said, "Marian the Librarian, huh?"

"The local theater group did *The Music Man* a while back. Evan's just teasing."

"You're dating him?"

She paused, wary. "Evan has a daughter. How do you know he's not married?"

"Hmm. I did notice that he wears a wedding ring."

Tess nodded, her forehead creasing a little. Concern or dismay? Connor couldn't be sure. "Ring or not, Evan's single," he went on. "Call me sexist, but he wouldn't be leaving work in the middle of the day to look after his daughter if there was a wife in the picture."

Tess said softly, "He's a widower."

"Tough break. But you didn't answer my question. Are you dating him?"

Her voice rose a notch to sharpness. "Why don't you tell me, Quizmaster?"

Connor weighed Evan's familiarity and protectiveness against the easy departure. "You might have dated at some point, but not currently. Your relationship is more the platonic kind—brother, sister, friends.'' A relationship compounded by a good dose of motherly longing, judging by Tess's gentle way with the girl, but he left that unsaid. It was too personal.

Yeah. Like her love life wasn't?

"You're right again." Tess stacked books briskly; he figured she didn't like being pigeonholed even though she was a walking endorsement of the friendly, intelligent, proper-librarian stereotype.

The thing was, he knew that everyone was unique beneath the surface. Each person has a story, and secret thoughts and dreams. Each person has justifications for who they are or what they've done with their lives. Part of his job as a true-crime writer was digging deeper to find what motives and meanings an ordinary appearance hid.

There was a lot more to Tess Bucek, even if it was tightly bound, but he had no intention of making the *what* and *why* of her his business. All he needed to know was that she had a skill for teaching. He'd buy her time, for his grandfather's sake. *But, for your own sake, stay away from the inner her. Don't delve deeper. Don't even make friends.*

Tess was talking. "…small, spartan stone cottages. Run-down and not very comfortable, I'm afraid. They're usually only booked by fishermen and hunters."

Connor nodded as if he'd followed. "Mmm."

"Maxine's Cottages," Tess explained to bring him back to speed. "The clientele is downscale, to be polite. You should try Bay House. It's a bed-and-breakfast inn up on the hill. It's undergoing renovation, but they're still taking guests. If you tell Claire, the manager, I sent you, she might be able to fit you in. Several of their rooms have a view of the lighthouse, although if a rock-bottom price is more important than quality—'' Tess's gaze touched on his unshaven, rumpled appearance ''—you might rather go to Maxine's.''

''Thanks,'' Connor said to dismiss talk of accommodations. He supposed he'd have to take a room somewhere. The lighthouse didn't appear to be habitable. He could camp on the grounds, maybe, if he wanted to spring for a tent and the accompanying gear. The isolation was appealing, but it was too long since he'd roughed it, Upper Peninsula style—which was only for the extremely hardy. At least for tonight, he wanted a real bed.

''I mean, you are interested in the Gull Rock lighthouse, right? Or were the books strictly for your grandfather's sake?''

''Both, I guess.'' Connor cleared his throat. ''Seeing as how I own it.''

A paperback mystery slid from Tess's fingers and dropped onto the desktop, pages splayed. ''Pardon me? You *own* the lighthouse?''

''There was a public auction a year ago…''

''Yes, I remember.''

''I put in the high bid.''

''But I heard—'' Tess gave her head a shake, making chunks of her short, thick hair bounce in the sunlight, shining like a handful of new pennies. ''The word around town was that a famous writer bought the place. Unfounded rumor, I suppose.'' She tilted her head, lifted a shoulder. ''That happens.''

But she was staring at him now. Any minute she'd make the connection. Connor kept his face blank. ''All I know is I'm the owner.''

Fortunately, she veered to another subject. ''Your grandfather must be pleased.''

''He says I'm crazy, but, yeah, he's damn pleased. I'm hoping to whip the lighthouse into acceptable shape and take him out there for a final visit.''

''Ohhh.'' Tess smiled fondly, looking at Connor as if he'd transformed from grungy stranger to Hallmark card.

''I'll sell it after he's gone,'' he said out of a certain perversity, denying the reasons he'd bought the lighthouse just to prove how cold he could be. He didn't need Tess to start thinking he was an okay guy when really he was a hard-hearted son of a bitch who'd barter grief for a good story. ''The thing's a white elephant. It was a crazy idea to bid on it in the first place.''

Although Tess's eyes had narrowed, she wasn't about to let him knock her down so easily. Instead, she smiled at his grouchiness, unimpressed and unintimidated. His estimation of her went up another notch.

''It's a local landmark,'' she said. ''You could donate it to the town. The historical society would be absolutely thrilled to take over management and develop the site as a museum.''

"Do I look like a philanthropist?"

Her gaze traced over him. Not with disinterest, if the glint in her eyes meant anything. Her lips pursed. "You don't want to know what I think you look like."

He shrugged. "That bad?"

"Nothing a shave and a change couldn't cure."

"I'll be more presentable next time you see me."

She blinked, catching herself staring. He smiled, liking—despite himself—the way she became ruffled, running a hand through her hair, stacking and restacking the books before her. Her fingers pattered nervously over the desktop.

"When can I take you to visit Sonny?" he asked. "He's at Three Pines."

"I, um, I'll have to—"

"The sooner the better."

She sighed. Squinted one eye at the clock near the desk. "This evening? I'm off work at six. Would seven-thirty be okay?"

"How about six-thirty? We'll have to drive to the nursing home in Ishpeming, and Sonny conks out pretty early. It'll be a very short visit."

"That barely gives me time to wash and change. I suppose I could grab a sandwich on the go."

"If your stomach can wait, I'll take you to dinner afterward." The words were out of Connor's mouth before he could censor them. *Damn.* "Nothing personal, of course. Just a business dinner. We'll discuss how to proceed with Sonny's lessons." *Make that how to persuade Sonny to accept lessons from her.*

Tess frowned. "If that's what you want."

She couldn't have been less enthusiastic.

"But I'm taking my own car," she added.

Yes, she could.

Connor uncrossed his arms and walked over to the study table where he'd left the lighthouse books. "Seems unnecessary, but whatever you want."

Tess defended herself, probably because she was too prim to be rude. "Suppose you choose to get a room outside of Alouette. This way, you won't have to drive me back."

He made up his mind. "It's more important that I be in town to work on the lighthouse. I'll try the B and B you mentioned. Bay House, was it?"

"Yes," she said faintly, looking worried, as if she suspected him of backing her into a corner.

Rightly. He was enjoying bantering with her a lot more than he should have. "Can I check these out?" he asked, sliding his books across her desk.

"You may, with a temporary guest card. You'll have to provide some personal information and pay ten dollars." She bent, rummaged through a drawer, then handed him a pale green card and a pen. The process seemed too trusting to Connor, but that must be how they did it in small towns.

He wrote down his New York address. Luckily, there was no line asking for his occupation.

Tess read over the card, then requested two forms of ID. Trust wasn't what it used to be. He gave her the money first, then added his driver's license, a credit card and threw his New York Public Library card in for fun.

She fingered it contemplatively. "Do you go to the branch with the stone lions?"

He said yes, on occasion, although usually he used the 115th Street branch closest to his apartment. "Have you been there?"

"Just once. On my senior-class trip. I was seventeen and already planning to be a librarian. The New York Public Library seemed so glamorous." She caught his skeptical eye. "Well, it was! For a library. I thought someday I'd be working there, if I didn't get in at the Smithsonian first." She gave a short laugh. "You know how it is when you're a kid. Anything seems possible. Even a sophisticated life in the city."

"What stopped you?"

"Nobody *stopped* me. I changed my mind."

Connor noted the switch of words. Tess seemed to have no ability to shield her inner thoughts. Already he knew that she'd once dreamed big, but had settled for small. Probably because of a guy. It was always a guy.

Briefly, Connor let himself envy Tess's guy, which was tolerable because the poor slob obviously wasn't hers any longer.

Tess had gone prickly. She straightened items on the checkout desk—the same ones she'd just pushed into disarray—with a brisk, thin-lipped efficiency. When there was nothing left to straighten, she stepped back, well away from him, folding her hands together in a gesture that could have been peaceful if she hadn't been gripping her fingers so tight. His questions had upset her more than innocent questions ought.

"We're settled, then?" She pressed her thumbs together, turning the nail beds white. "I'll bring my notebooks and a literacy test to the nursing home."

"No, don't do that. Not the first time. We can't rush Sonny."

"But I thought this was his request. Why shouldn't we begin tonight…if time is short?"

Connor answered easily enough since he was telling the truth. "Because he's crotchety Old Man Mitchell and his illiteracy has been a shameful secret up to now. We've got to take this slow."

"I see. Yes. I understand." Her words were clipped. She was waiting for him to go.

He took the books and started to the door. "I'll pick you up. What's your address?"

She closed her eyes for an instant and he thought she was giving in. Instead, her lashes lifted and she stared him down. "Did you forget? I'm taking my own car. After all, I barely know you."

"You've seen my ID."

"Which proves nothing."

"What kind of lawbreaker do you take me for?"

"That's yet to be determined."

He laughed. "Well, then, thanks for the free books."

"Don't be smart with me, Mr. Reed."

"Yes, Marian." He looked back once more from

the open doorway and saw that she was muttering to herself. He couldn't be sure, but he thought she said the word *smuggler*. He shrugged to himself. Smuggler was better than some of the names he'd been called lately.

TESS WAS GRATEFUL the library had emptied for the usual early-afternoon lull. She'd get a trickle of patrons wandering in and out the remainder of the afternoon and a final rush before closing time—which consisted of anywhere from two to five stragglers, most of whom would hurry in with a movie to return.

She wasn't sure why she'd let Connor Reed talk her into scooting off to meet his grandfather right after work, except that her heart twinged when she thought of the old man, alone for all those long, lonely winters in the lighthouse and not being able to read. She'd have gone crazy if she hadn't had books to keep her company all this time on her own, and she was nowhere near as isolated as a lighthouse keeper.

She went into her office, a small room on the other side of the entryway. It was a nook really, formed out of a coat closet and several borrowed feet from the dining-turned-periodical room. There was space for a desk and little else. Usually the office felt too tight, but for the moment it was a welcome haven.

With a few probing questions, Connor Reed had turned her inside out.

Suddenly she felt out of sorts with what had been a cozy, settled life. Was it because she found Connor disturbingly attractive, or that his questions had brought up old memories of the time before Jared?

Both, most likely. The attraction was interesting, even exciting. The other...

She thought of life now as A.J., After Jared, forgetting that she'd once been a different person. A girl. Silly, lighthearted and ambitious—even a little bit daring. Connor's curiosity had brought all that back to mind.

Tess's gaze went to the framed photo beside her computer. It was a classic pose—a proud young man in flannel and jeans holding up a gleaming rainbow trout, the lake behind him speckled with sunshine. Jared Johnson—her fiancé. Forever a fiancé, frozen in time because he'd been killed in a car accident the week before the wedding.

Tess stopped, making herself breathe, remembering when the thought of Jared had caused her actual physical pain. She was long past that now, but somehow she'd never quite moved on.

She'd been just twenty-one, Jared two years older. Young to marry, but the timing seemed right. She'd graduated from college that spring and Jared had immediately proposed. She knew he'd been pushing for marriage mostly because he didn't want her to accept a job out of the area, but she hadn't felt stifled. She was in love. An entry-level position at a large library system far from home wasn't as appealing as she'd once imagined it to be. Whereas the prospect of marrying her high-school sweetheart and officially joining the large, boisterous Johnson family had been irresistible.

Tess propped her chin on her hand. Eleven years had provided enough distance for her to see that marrying Jared had been the safe choice. A good choice, a happy and probably satisfying one—especially when she thought of the children they might have had—but mostly safe.

As the only child of divorced parents, security was important to Tess. Her father was long gone, barely a memory. Her mother had moved away more than a decade ago right after Tess's high-school graduation, satisfied that she'd finished raising her daughter and was therefore free to leave a town she despised. Tess had been okay with that—she was busy with college, and besides she'd had Jared's family, in many ways closer and more supportive than her own.

Then the accident had happened and the wedding was canceled, and she'd realized just how alone she really was. The Johnson family hadn't wanted anything to do with her because of her part in Jared's death. She might have been even more stricken by their abandonment if the mere sight of them—especially Jared's brothers, who looked so much like him—hadn't made her fall apart. The only way she'd survived was to cut herself off from contact with the life that had almost been hers.

Her new job as the one and only librarian of the Alouette Public Library had been a godsend. The structure and duties had helped her through the worst of her grief. Eventually, she'd found her place in the world again and had learned to be happy with all she had—friends, a home, her health, a steady job.

But she'd had eleven years of that now. Maybe she was a little bored. Her escalating fantasies could be a sign that she was ready to step out of her comfort zone.

Right off, it was apparent that nothing about Connor Reed would make her feel safe. Thrilled, fascinated, aroused, but certainly not safe.

Of course, he wasn't really a pirate or a smuggler, even though she couldn't help thinking that he'd look good in a pair of gold hoop earrings and breeches. But then, who *was* he?

A click of the mouse of her tangerine iMac brought it out of sleep mode. She had a suspicion. When she'd mentioned the rumor that the lighthouse had been purchased by a famous writer, Connor hadn't actually denied it. She couldn't place him, but hadn't he seemed familiar?

No, not familiar, really, except for a mental jog at his name. It was more that she'd been sharply, disturbingly aware of him. As a woman. But it was the librarian who'd solve the puzzle.

She logged on to a search engine and typed in Connor's name. In seconds, data flashed onto her screen. Success!

With dawning horror, she scanned the information. The hollow in her stomach deepened as she clicked on the first link, which led her into the archives of a popular weekly newsmagazine. Graphics popped up, followed by text, then pixel by pixel, Connor's photo, taken outside a courthouse. He was surrounded by reporters. His hair was shorter and he was dressed in a suit and tie, but the face was the same—drawn, serious, haunted.

She read the headline with a dry mouth. Crime Writer's Evidence Sets Murderer Free. Roderick Strange to be released from prison. Victim's family outraged.

My God! This wasn't fantasy—it was real-life drama.

Beyond her wildest dreams.

CHAPTER THREE

WHILE THE WOMEN who ran the B and B debated in loud whispers that carried from the next room, Connor stood in the middle of the Bay House foyer and looked around with dull disinterest. Under normal circumstances, he'd have paid more attention to the stately Victorian architecture and tasteful surroundings. But it was growing impossible to focus on details. His eyeballs were scratchy and his lids seemed to be lined with lead. If they didn't give him a room soon, he'd end up curled in a ball under the potted palm.

He took a few steps to the open doorway that led to a sunlit dining room, intending to hurry the process along. The hushed conversation stopped him.

"I won't let you do it, Claire." That was the older woman's voice. Connor had momentarily forgotten her name, but she was short and round with dumpling cheeks and a severe gray braid that pulled her forehead taut.

"We have no other space to offer. I hate to turn away a guest when we're struggling to turn a profit."

"What about the attic? Won't one of those rooms do?"

Claire Levander, who was the manager Tess had told him to seek out, made a discouraging sound. "Noah and Roxy are repairing the damage from last winter's frozen-pipe burst."

The innkeeper frowned at Claire. "I wish you'd stayed put. I didn't have to worry about the prophecy going into action when you were living at Bay House full-time."

Connor swayed on his feet. He was too tired to figure out riddles.

"Yeah, because Noah and I had sucked up all of Valentina's wedding karma." Claire gave a wry laugh. "Now that we're living together and practically engaged, your ancestor needs a new victim."

"Oh, you," the older woman fretted. "Hush. That's not the way to convince me to give Mr. Reed the bridal suite."

Connor stepped forward, putting a hand on the door trim and clearing his throat. Both women whipped around. "I need a room," he pleaded. "I'll pay whatever you like. I don't care if it's a bridal suite as long as it has a bed."

Claire, a thirtyish brunette who was very well put together, turned to the other woman. "Emmie—c'mon. What can it hurt if I give him Valentina's bedroom?"

Emmie's face puckered with indecision, but stubbornness won out. "No." When Claire opened her mouth to protest, she repeated, "No. You know why."

Connor's heavy head dropped forward. He didn't

need this hassle. "Does it matter if I tell you that Tess Bucek sent me?"

The two women looked at each other for one astounded, quizzical beat. Then they turned to Connor. "Tess?" they said in unison.

Emmie's manner did a sudden one-eighty. "Why didn't you say so?" she cried, coming toward Connor with her arms open. She gave him a welcoming squeeze. "If you're a friend of Tess's, you're a friend of mine. And you're in luck, because the best room in the house is available." That wasn't what she'd been whispering ten seconds ago, but Connor wasn't going to argue when Emmie was motioning the inn manager toward the foyer. "Claire will check you right in. Welcome to Bay House."

With an amused smile, Claire slipped behind a handsome polished desk and retrieved the registry book. She flipped it open, studying him closely. "Here you go, Mr. Reed. Are you a particular friend of Tess's?" Apparently satisfied with what she saw, she handed him a pen.

Connor took it and signed the book. He knew he looked disreputable at best, so why the sudden interest and approval? Was Tess's say-so that important? Or were they setting him up for…well, he couldn't imagine what.

"Nope," he said. "I met her for the first time about an hour ago. In the library."

Emmie looked less impressed, but Claire wasn't concerned. "All the same, we're very pleased that Tess sent you to Bay House." She glanced at the name he'd scrawled in the registry and gave a little start.

Connor grimaced. He'd told them only his last name when he'd arrived, but had forgotten and signed his name in the guest book in its notorious entirety.

Claire snapped the book shut before Emmie could lean in for a look. Very smooth. Her smile didn't even waver. Connor gave her full marks for discretion and for maintaining the warm reception, but he couldn't make himself care. He was accustomed to awkward reactions. All that he hoped was that when word spread, Tess wouldn't be besmirched by his unsavory reputation because she'd vouched for him.

A number of tagged room keys hung on a small Peg-Board on the pale gold wall. Instead of reaching for one of them, Claire took a small silver key from her pocket, opened a desk drawer and slowly withdrew a tasseled latchkey, almost as if she were a magician pulling silk scarves from a hat.

Connor was baffled by the significance. A key was a key and a room was a room. Wasn't it?

His sense of disquiet deepened. Both women were treating him oddly—for whatever reason—but that didn't seem to be why his scalp prickled. He glanced behind him, then up a staircase that was still grand despite its threadbare carpeting. A flash of movement on the second-floor landing was followed by a series of diminishing thumps.

"Who was that?" Connor asked.

Claire hadn't even looked. "Only the maid."

"Never mind her," Emmie said hastily.

"Shari won't bother you." Claire's voice had gone up two octaves.

Connor knew she was prevaricating and found it all very curious. "She's not related to Norman Bates, is she?"

Emmie reared back. "Good heavens, no!"

Claire produced a dutiful chuckle. "Mr. Reed was making a joke, Em."

Maybe not, Connor thought, although he was prone to finding sinister implications even where there were none. A hazard of his profession, where the boy next door was likely a freckle-faced killer.

"There is no crime at Bay House," the older woman scolded.

"Of course not." Claire avoided Connor's eyes so carefully he knew she was wondering if he was here to investigate a story.

"That's good to hear," Connor said. "Seeing as I'm on *vacation*—" he stressed the word for Claire's benefit "—I'd rather not be awakened by bumps in the night."

Claire scoffed as she came back around the desk and reached for his gym bag. "I'm afraid I can't guarantee that." Connor got the bag before she did. She straightened, giving him a genuine smile as she raised a hand to her mouth to whisper, "Shari has a heavy step."

He nodded, liking Claire. If she'd made an instant judgment on his name, she hadn't let it color her conduct.

"This way, Mr. Reed." He followed Claire up the

stairs as she rattled on about the history of Bay House and its owners, the Whitaker family. "I'm putting you in the bridal suite." She put the heavy latchkey into the keyhole and cranked. "The room is named after the family's infamous jilted bride, Valentina Whitaker. Don't be put off by any rumors you may hear. They have little basis in reality and are purely speculation." Claire's eyes danced. "Or so Emmie makes me say." She opened the door with a flourish.

"Sounds like a subject I'm not sure I want to explore." Connor dropped his gym bag to the floor as he moved into the room. It was bright and airy, decorated with a mix of homespun—rag rugs, a folded quilt, an old-fashioned washstand—and froufrou—a crystal chandelier and a lot of photos in fussy silver frames.

"This'll do," he said. The best thing about the room was the bed. A big and sturdy four-poster. He could peel back the pristine linens and delicate lacy stuff and collapse.

Claire gestured. "You have a small balcony and a private bath. And, of course, Valentina."

Connor looked at the wall she indicated. An oil-painting portrait was prominently featured above the fireplace. A serene blonde posed in her wedding gown, hands clutching a bouquet of white roses. "Uh-huh," he said. Claire was waiting for further reaction, so he added a salute. "Nice to meet you, Valentina."

"Nice?" Claire made a face. "That wasn't my reaction."

Connor turned away. "I get all kinds."

"Oh!" Claire looked mortified. She pushed a lock of hair behind one ear, making a dangling earring swing against her neck. "I didn't mean *you*. Valentina's the one I'm not comfortable wi—" She stopped, rolled her eyes, then started again. "What I meant was…"

Connor winced while she fumbled for words. For all that he told himself he didn't care, he remained hypersensitive about other people's reactions to him. Claire might be a rare open-minded individual, but few were immune to overwhelming public opinion. The gossip would start soon enough, and he didn't want to put these well-meaning people in the middle.

He shot a look over his shoulder, interrupting Claire. "Listen, don't worry. I'm not here to make trouble. I should be checking out in a couple of days."

Claire's face was pink and worried. She wasn't beautiful by any means, but there was a classic grace in her strong bones, tall form and abundant curves. Up to now, her manner had been assured, so he doubted that she was normally so easily flustered. It had to be him or Valentina. And who could be disturbed by a bride, even one who'd refused to smile?

"Please, Mr. Reed. You must stay as long as you'd like. We don't take reservations for this room, so it's yours for an extended stay if you wish."

"All right, thanks," he said, unsure of his plans but wanting to erase Claire's worried frown.

"Anything you need, please ask. Emmie and her brother, Toivo, the owners, are usually on the premises. I'm here almost every day. Breakfast is served in the dining room, or you can arrange for a tray...."

Connor nodded her out of the room, sensing that she was on the verge of asking him his business in the area if he gave her an opening. He didn't. His face was a mask.

Finally she said good-day. He closed the door and pressed a palm to one of the raised panels, leaning all his weight against it as his heavy eyelids closed.

Finally alone. Thank God.

The funny thing was that he used to be what was commonly called a people person. Go back to his college days, even a few years ago, and he was right there in the center of it all, ready to talk and argue and laugh with anyone who showed a glimmer of a fascinating mind.

Now he was so...exhausted.

Not only from defending himself. He was tired of talk, tired of words, tired of the way both could be twisted and distorted. As if it was all just a cruel game.

Be damn grateful you're no longer a player, he thought, but inside he knew that was a cop-out.

He'd played. And he'd lost more than he'd ever imagined.

A vital part of himself was missing.

TESS'S HEAD SWIRLED with horrific images and words as she drove to the Three Pines nursing home, twenty-five miles from Alouette on a twisty two-lane country road. The highway was a better route, but also longer and busier. She wanted time to think before seeing Connor again.

To think in peace. If she could get the awfulness out of her head.

She'd only scraped the surface of all the information available on the Internet on Connor Reed, though the majority of it—muck included—had centered on his most recent involvement with the overturning of the murder conviction against Roderick Strange. Several years ago, Strange had been arrested for the kidnapping and murder of a young woman in rural Kentucky. He'd also been suspected in several other disappearances, but there hadn't been enough proof. Finally, in the Elizabeth Marino case, he'd been convicted and sent to prison.

Until Connor's involvement.

Connor Reed was a very successful true-crime writer. The Alouette library had a couple of his books, including his blockbuster bestseller, *Blood Kin.* Even though she hadn't read any of them—being partial to cozy mysteries over the stark and often bloody reality of nonfiction—she was surprised she hadn't immediately recognized his name. Maybe making up her own stories about him had distracted her. Little had she known that by comparison with the truth, her imaginings were harmless.

About a year and a half ago, at the peak of the original trial, Connor had signed a ballyhooed, big-bucks contract with Scepter Publishing to write a book about Roderick Strange. According to the news reports, during the months after the man's guilty verdict Connor had uncovered vital evidence and given it over to the courts, which ultimately led to Strange's conviction being overturned. People had been in an uproar. There were protests, public debates, hate mail and death threats. Connor was roasted over the coals by many, defended by only a spare few.

Though he'd been invited to all the talk shows, he'd spurned the attention and made little public comment. Even that had been turned against him by those who said he was only looking to cash in by saving the inside story for his impending book.

So far, there was no book. Tess had perused the Scepter Publishing Web site, but found no firm publishing date for a work by Connor Reed. Which didn't mean he hadn't already written the manuscript....

She wrinkled her nose, slowing at the intersection where the country road crossed with the highway. The idea of such a book was distasteful. In good conscience, she couldn't argue too strenuously against Connor's turning over the evidence he'd found, as terrible as the result had been. She had more trouble with the idea of him profiting from the tragedy.

Perhaps he did, too?

The light turned green. She tapped on the gas and drove through the intersection. *Then what about his other books?* Those cases had also involved ugly crime, real people and grieving families.

On the other hand, who was she to be judgmental?

Tess skirted the town, finding Three Pines easily enough, as she'd visited before, delivering books to a longtime library patron who'd been in residence the previous winter. The nursing home was a horizontal structure, formed from a central hub with four wings that spoked out in a crooked H formation. She spotted Connor in the parking lot outside of Wing D, leaning against the bumper of a dusty Jeep.

Her heart gave a little jump as she pulled in beside him.

It was early evening yet, but the sun had lowered far enough to send slanting rays through the tall Norway pines that surrounded the facility. Sharp-edged shadows stretched across the paved lot, casting his brooding face in an appropriately murky light.

Tess got out of her car. "Hi!"

Connor nodded. "Thanks for coming."

"Beautiful evening," she said, compelled to combat her doubt with chirpiness. "You're looking well."

"I slept for a couple of hours."

"And shaved."

He touched his chin. "Just for you."

"Oh, I'm sure." She maintained a cheery smile while attempting an unobtrusive evaluation. He'd changed, too, into a fresh white T-shirt and belted khakis. But he still looked sad and withdrawn.

Her heart went out to him, even though her head kept asking questions. Was Connor Reed heartless? Greedy? Or merely an average guy stuck in a bad situation?

"So you found the place okay," he said.

"Yesiree. I've been here before."

He gave her a skeptical look. "You're Mary Sunshine."

"Is that wrong?"

"Just weird."

She cocked her head. "How so?"

He shrugged. "I guess it's the Midwestern in you."

"You say that like it's a bad thing."

"No, not bad. Not bad at all. Just makes me think I've been hanging out with the wrong people." He reached to take her arm. "Come on, let's go inside."

Without thinking, she withdrew, crossing her arms over her front.

Connor stopped. Looked at her for a long minute, his face darkening. Finally he shook his head.

"Suit yourself," he said shortly, and walked toward the paths that bordered the different wings in wide gray outlines. He took the one that led to Wing D, not even looking back to see if she'd followed as he made a sharp turn and was swallowed by the shadows beneath the wide eaves of the entrance.

Tess hesitated for another moment before hurrying after him. "Look," she said, trotting to catch up to his long strides. "I'm not—I didn't—"

He'd stopped at the door next to an outdoor aluminum ashtray overflowing with butts. "You know who I am," he said without looking at her.

She let out a soft sigh. "Yes."

"You can leave right now if you don't want to be associated with me. I understand."

"I wouldn't do that!"

He threw a glance over his shoulder. "How come? I'm generally acknowledged to be a pretty despicable guy."

She moved a little closer. "Maybe general knowledge isn't what it's cracked up to be?"

"Are you asking me a question?"

"I might be."

"Well, now's not the time." He opened the door and stood aside to allow her through. "Your choice."

She marched inside. She'd made a promise, after all.

They entered into a small reception area. An attempt had been made to improve on the sterile concrete-block look of the facility, with hunter-green paint, a couch, buffalo-plaid curtains and accessories that included duck decoys and wildlife prints. A predictable decor, but better than austerity.

A long hallway ran down the middle of the wing, with residents' rooms on either side. There was an unstaffed reception desk near the lounge, and an empty wheelchair and a gurney parked outside one of the rooms. The place seemed deserted, except for a uniformed attendant turning a corner at the other end of the hall.

"This way," Connor said. "Sonny's three doors down on the left."

An old woman with a walker poked her head into the hallway as they passed, looking both curious and eager for visitors. Tess would have stopped to chit-chat, but Connor was already disappearing into his grandfather's room. She smiled at the woman and said hello before hurrying to catch up again.

She arrived in time to see Connor giving his grandfather a careful hug. "So you came back, eh?" the old man said.

"Told you I would. And I brought a visitor."

A gnarled hand waved dismissal. "Bah. Visitors."

"You might like this one."

Tess stepped forward. "No, please, sit," she said, when Connor's grandfather saw her and started to rise from his chair by the window.

He didn't listen, and straightened slowly with one hand clenched on the head of a cane. His forehead pleated with a deep scowl.

Connor steadied his grandfather's stance. "Grandpa, this is Tess Bucek, from Alouette. Tess, my grandfather, Addison Mitchell."

"Mr. Mitchell." Tess offered her hand, hoping the lighthouse keeper wouldn't bite it off.

The old man clasped it briefly, but with a strong pressure. He peered at her with eyes that were sharply blue beneath eyebrows like fuzzy caterpillars. "Bucek? Don't recall any Buceks in Alouette."

"Right now, I'm the only one left. My parents were Tony and Annabel Bucek. I doubt you'd remember either of them, sir."

"Good people?"

She blinked. "Acceptable, sir."

"Sir?" He snorted. "I s'pose you can call me Sonny. Take a seat if it suits you, there." He lowered himself to the padded chair, letting out a rusty chuckle as Tess sat and crossed her legs. "Still a ladies' man, eh, Connor?"

"Tess is—" Connor shrugged, looking to her for help.

"Just a visitor," she said, smoothing her skirt. No need to embarrass the old man by baldly pointing out the reason for her visit. "I met Connor today in the library. I work there."

Sonny grunted.

Connor excused himself and went out to the hall to find another chair. His grandfather stared out the window, ignoring Tess. She looked around the room. Besides a hospital bed, there was a TV bolted near the ceiling and a small desk with a few framed pictures on it and nothing else. No reading material.

She cleared her throat.

Sonny's eyes swiveled to her.

"Connor asked me for help," she confided, leaning toward the old man. He was probably the prideful type who'd need reassurance that she could be discreet. "Just between us."

Sonny's speckled bald head wavered with a nod. "Fine by me. The boy's been on the rocks."

"Oh. Actually, I didn't mean his, um, dilemma."

"Dilemma?" Connor said, coming back in the room carrying another chair. He set it down beside his grandfather's.

"Nothing," Tess said brightly.

Connor glowered.

"You look just like your grandfather," she said, teasing him a bit. *In his heyday as cantankerous Old Man Mitchell,* she silently added, continuing to smile sweetly as Connor got settled.

"Thanks." He slumped back in his chair and his knee touched hers.

She sat up even straighter, edging away slightly. And got another black glower. There was no decent way to explain that she wasn't disgusted by him—she was magnetized. Disturbed, too, in every sense.

Sonny's lips had folded inward into a secretive sort of smile. For being nearly ninety and on death's door, he appeared to be in fairly good shape. A silvery fringe of white hair ran from ear to ear, his eyes were clear and active, and his posture was only slightly hunched even though he moved with the deliberation of old age and arthritis. He had a lean physique like his grandson, gone to scrawniness and skin and bone. Thin, age-spotted skin stretched taut over the knobs of his knuckles where he continued to grip the cane propped beside his chair.

Either he kept up with current events on his own via the television news or he'd been told about Connor's troubles. Tess thought it was cute how the old man had presumed she was "comforting" his grandson.

Wrong, but cute.

Although, if ever a man had looked in need of comforting...

She shifted around in her chair. Connor gave her a glance, but he kept talking with his grandfather, telling him about the trip back to Alouette and checking in to Bay House.

Sonny shook his head over the idea that the once

grand house had become a bed-and-breakfast inn. "Shame. The Whitakers still there?"

"Yes, they are," Tess said. "Emmie and Toivo. Sister and brother," she explained to Connor, in case he didn't realize. She'd been halfway positive he'd back out of the decision to stay at Bay House once he'd been introduced to its homey comforts and familiar hosts. He didn't seem like a homey and familiar guy.

"Bossy and goofy, them two," said Sonny with a scowl that was mostly for show.

Tess smiled. "You make them sound like the eighth and ninth dwarfs." She'd have called them energetic and endearing. But then she'd only had long-distance grandparents, so that was a soft spot for her. Soft, sore…same thing.

"What about the lighthouse?" Sonny asked.

Connor made an apologetic sound. "It's not looking so good, Grandpa. Really run-down."

Sonny huffed. "That's the government for you. I'da stayed if they'd have let me. Instead, I'm wasting away, good for goddamn nothing." He deliberately turned his head to stare out the window, exuding a deep dissatisfaction.

Tess was uneasy, even more so when suddenly the old man glared at her. "I ever run you off Gull Rock?" he accused.

She gritted her teeth. When she was a child, it had been a prank among the older kids to dare each other to sneak onto the lighthouse grounds. They would make bets of how far they'd get before the lighthouse keeper caught sight of them. One boy had been famous for getting swatted in the behind by the old man's broom.

"No, sir," she said.

Sonny squinted skeptically.

"When you were still the light keeper, I was only—" she calculated "—about six or seven." And frightened silly by the other kids' stories of the legendary lighthouse hermit. No one had ever mentioned that Old Man Mitchell's grandson had been visiting only several years back. It was probably more fun to scare each other.

"Buncha brats," Sonny said. "Always screaming like a pack of gulls."

"They were just being kids, Grandpa," Connor said. "I made friends with a few of them, my summers up here."

"Hooligans, the lot of you," the old man groused. "Came to no good, I betcha."

Conner smiled, though his expression remained somber. "Yeah." He sighed. "You could be right about that."

CHAPTER FOUR

"HE LIKED YOU," Connor said, glancing at Tess over the top of his menu.

"The whitefish is good—" She stopped and wrinkled her nose, giving a little laugh at Connor's faulty assessment. "Sonny liked me? How could you tell?"

They'd spent less than a half hour in the elderly man's room, with the conversation progressing in fits and starts. Sonny Mitchell had seemed bent on being disagreeable, although Tess had detected signs of grudging approval whenever she refused to be bullied by his gruff treatment.

He had a fighting spirit, she'd decided. Sonny sought out kindred souls, and very few passed muster. Tess wasn't sure she qualified, having grown up with the example of a mother who had no fight in her at all, and leading the uneventful life that she did.

Connor set aside the menu. "He let you stay, right?"

"Yes…"

"And he didn't object when you mentioned visiting again in a few days."

"No…"

"So you got further with him than anyone else has. Sonny's always been cantankerous. Even antisocial."

"I can't imagine what he's going to say when I announce that I'm there to teach him to read."

Connor made a face. "Uh, about that..."

"You've changed your mind?"

He grinned at her hopefulness. "Not so fast. It's just that I want you to go slowly with the reading lessons. Ease into it. Because I haven't exactly told him—"

"Terrific, Connor!" She tossed her menu on top of his. "I don't see how I'm supposed to teach him to read without his knowing that's what I'm there for."

A waitress arrived with their drinks. Tess took a sip of her white wine while Connor ordered the whitefish for both of them. When they'd emerged from Three Pines to a dusky sky, he'd told her to be the leader. In their separate vehicles, he'd followed her to a restaurant in downtown Marquette, a cozy place in one of the historic sandstone-and-brick buildings that overlooked the Lake Superior harbor. The view was of the marina, a redbrick bell tower and a slope of lawn that led to the harbor park, nearly empty at this hour. A rusty ore dock loomed to one side, long abandoned. They faced east, so the sky was leached of light, layered in cobalt and indigo over the lake.

"I realize the subject will have to come up." Connor's voice was deep and soft, but slightly rough. Mesmerizing, especially when she shut out the sounds around them and focused only on him. "Let's just take it slowly...."

Mmm, she thought, going soft herself before she realized what was happening. She sat up straighter, blinking her eyes back to alert.

He continued. "After Sonny has accepted you, I'll explain to him exactly why you're visiting."

"I think he already knows."

"Ah. Yes, perhaps. But he won't admit it out loud."

"Pride?"

"And independence. He doesn't like to ask for help, even now."

"Runs in the family," she said.

Connor was looking out the tall arched window to the lake. "Why would you say that? You don't know me—except what you've read in newspapers and magazines."

She chuckled. "I can draw my own conclusions, thank you."

He turned his intense gaze on her. It was a physical thing. She felt it on her skin, in her stomach, even deep in her bones.

Oh, but she was out of practice. There'd been no provocative strangers in her life for years, aside from the ones she invented. And it wasn't easy turning a middle-aged library guest wearing flip-flops into an international man of mystery. Most of the time, it wasn't even worth the attempt.

"Which conclusions?" Connor's gaze held steady and she couldn't tell if he was teasing. "That I'm a smuggler?"

Heat shot into her face. Her cheeks must be glowing like a neon bulb. "Pardon?" she croaked, not sure that she wanted the answer. There was no way Connor should know of her nutty mental meanderings. "How…?"

"I didn't read your mind," he said. "You muttered it as I was leaving."

"Ohhh."

He studied her face, awaiting an explanation. There was a glint in his eye. So he *was* teasing…but she was still on the spot.

"You have to admit you looked scruffy and suspect." She shrugged. "I didn't *really* believe you were a smuggler. That was just my…" She slid a finger along the stem of the wineglass. Might as well admit it. "My crazy imagination."

"I guess you weren't completely wrong. According to some, I am disreputable. But not a lawbreaker, I assure you."

"Don't mind me. I make up these stories in my head—" She tilted it. "Nothing to do with you."

His lips compressed on a smile. "Stories?"

"Fancies. Pure silliness. It's nothing."

"And I starred as a smuggler?"

"It was the lighthouse books," she explained, amazed she was doing so, but that was the effect he had on her. Her usual caution had come unhinged. "I made up a scenario where you were a bear-organ smuggler looking for a drop point." She skipped the part about him also being a libidinous ex-professor. "You were meeting a Chinese man at midnight to transfer the illegal cargo."

Connor laughed in disbelief. "Tess, you've been stuck in that library too long. The fiction has gone to your head."

"I know. But it's a chicken-or-the-egg question. I've been exercising a wild imagination for as long as I can remember. So did I immerse myself in books because they fed it or because they created it? You see?" She lifted a shoulder. "It's a small town. Books and fantasy were always my outlet."

He leaned forward. "An outlet would be having your own adventures, wouldn't it?"

She threw up a hand. "Oh, no. Don't give me that load of baloney. Just because I read doesn't mean I don't live. I have a full and satisfying life. I am not a pathetic weenie waiting for her real life to begin—"

"Okay, okay," Connor said, chuckling.

She took a breath. "Sorry. I got a little heated."

"I understand. I'm a writer—I've been treated to the same comments."

Then he knew that there was some truth to them, she thought. Not that she didn't live as thoroughly as the next person—which wasn't saying much, as the average Alouettian was as content as a cow—but occasionally there was a sense of being an observer more than a doer. She wasn't dissatisfied, exactly. Maybe expectant. And restless…especially today.

She looked at Connor as he lifted a pilsner glass of a golden brown ale that matched his eyes. Honestly, he was the most exciting person to walk into her life since the Alouette theater group had hired Geordie Graves to put on *The Music Man* and the ex-soap opera amnesiac had chosen her to play a lead role.

Oh, dear. She *was* a pathetic weenie.

Connor swallowed as he put down the glass. Around them, the crowded restaurant buzzed with conversation and laughter. To keep from staring at Connor, whose face fascinated her with its secrets and shadows, she let her gaze wander over other tables, the brick walls crowded with historic photos, a waitress passing by with an overflowing tray, hazel eyes with thick black lashes, the rows of liquor bottles behind the bar, a mouth that she wanted to kiss.

No, what she really wanted to do was ask Connor about his profession and how he had become involved in the Roderick Strange murder case. But he'd already exhibited reluctance, and she didn't want him to think she was judging him. Even though a part of her was, despite her best intentions.

She sighed, wishing to be a better person.

"We've established that imagination was my escape," she said. "What about you?"

He hesitated at the sound of silverware clinking and voices that rose and fell as if carried by waves. "Me? I was cursed with curiosity."

"Cursed?"

His eyebrows lifted. "Or blessed. At the moment, I'm feeling it was a curse." He brushed the comment away with a wry smile. "What were you escaping?"

She blinked. "There's that curiosity of yours."

"I can guess. Your parents."

"Sure you can guess. I already gave you a clue, back in Sonny's room."

"Most people don't call their parents 'acceptable.'"

"What can I say? They weren't ideal, but they weren't terrible. No abuse or blatant dysfunction." *Did it count as abandonment if you still had your mother?*

"But…?"

She gave in to his probing. The man was subtle and skilled; she *wanted* to talk. "Well, my dad was out of the picture." She flicked a hand as if to shoo her father away even though their contact had been sporadic at best through her growing-up years and practically nil since then. He'd never pushed for a rapprochement in all this time, and she wasn't willing to put herself forward for another rejection. As far as Tess knew, Tony Bucek had forgotten he even had a daughter.

"And my mother was barely functional, particularly when I was a child. She had frequent migraines—during her spells, she needed the house to be kept quiet and dark. We lived in the country, with only two neighbors. I was on my own a lot. So I developed an active imagination to keep myself amused."

Connor gazed at her for a long, quiet moment. Even the other tables had a lull.

She thought he might use a platitude. Instead, he asked, "Did you have an imaginary friend?"

She was so surprised at his whimsy, she blurted,

"Rosehip Fumblethumbs," as the waitress arrived at their table with a basket of bread and plates of salad.

Connor asked for another beer. "There must be a reason for a name like that."

Tess picked the onion out of her salad with the tines of her fork, moving it to the edge of her plate. "If there was, I can't remember. I was about four." Her father had left home; her mother was all doom and gloom. Tess had quickly learned to walk on eggshells.

Four years old and she'd begun to live small.

"Rosehip Fumblethumbs did everything I wasn't supposed to. She scratched my mother's records, she turned up the volume. She tore down the curtains and opened every window and door. She broke things. Bounced on the bed. Yelled out loud." Tess stopped and laughed at her own reverie.

Connor dragged a curl of escarole through blue-cheese dressing. "Sounds like a typical kid, if you ask me."

"I suppose so. But Rosey did have green hair, orange freckles and fairy wings. She slept outdoors, in a bed of roses. We had tea parties under the porch."

"Vivid imaginings for a four year old."

Tess tried to remember. "Rosey developed over the years."

"Years?"

"She stayed around until I was at least ten."

"That's a long time. Most imaginary friends have shorter life spans."

"You're an authority, are you?"

Connor grinned. "You caught me. I'm talking out my ear."

"No imaginary friends of your own?"

"Not that I recall."

"Even at the lighthouse? It must have been lonely there."

"Yeah, at times. But I considered it an adventure, even when the road was washed out and we had no electricity. My grandfather was a widower by then, so life at the lighthouse had become rather rough and undomesticated. Perfect for a ten-year-old boy."

Growing up, Tess had longed for a normal life with fancy guest soaps, home-baked chocolate-chip cookies, seasonal holiday decorations and waxed floors scattered with rag rugs. The sort of domestication she observed at friends' houses, when her own mother could barely summon the strength to climb out of bed and go to work. When she'd discovered the boisterous closeness and comfort at the Johnsons', she'd believed that she had finally come home.

"Why did you stop coming?" she asked Connor, forcing her mind back to the lighthouse. It didn't do her any good to regret her losses, after so long.

He chewed, swallowed. "I guess because I became a teenager and developed other interests. But that was also around the time that the lighthouse was automated."

"And you never returned to Alouette until now?"

"No reason. Sonny had been persuaded to move downstate to be closer to family." Connor winked.

"And I can run my smuggling operation just about anywhere."

She gave him the same stern look Grady Kujanen got when he'd been shouting in the library. "Did no one in your family realize that Sonny was illiterate?"

"There were hints. First my grandma, then my mother probably had some idea, because they always took care of his paperwork—insurance, taxes, that sort of thing. He'd grumble about hating red tape and jumping through government hoops. Otherwise, he'd somehow always managed. He seems able to read at a rudimentary level, at least enough to understand road signs and basic necessities."

"Perhaps, but people learn amazing ways to handle the problem, from what I understand. It's not usually a case of being incapable—illiterates use more brainpower to work out their coping mechanisms than they'd need to learn how to read."

Connor nodded. "I thought he was just a rotten cook, mistaking ingredients and burning things when I first came to stay with him at the lighthouse keeper's cottage. Now I see that he must have gone to the grocery store and bought unfamiliar packaged meals so I'd have the balanced diet my mom harped on. But Sonny couldn't read the directions. After a few disasters, we ended up subsisting on sandwiches and SpaghettiOs, and a few basic meals that didn't require recipes."

"Of course," Tess said. "Bachelor food."

Connor speared a cucumber slice. He seemed dismayed by the memories being brought up. "It's true about hindsight being twenty-twenty. Now that I'm looking back, it's obvious that Sonny also practiced avoidance, even deception. He used to sit with a newspaper in the evenings. Other than that, he claimed to have no use for books."

"What a shame. How did he ever last so many winters out at Gull Rock with nothing to do?"

"He filled time with chores around the lighthouse. Shoveling snow in winter, gardening in summer. He had a radio—we used to listen to a lot of baseball games during the summer. And there was a small black-and-white TV, but it didn't have good reception."

"The simple life," Tess mused.

"Yes. It has its appeals. After the first shock of rusticity, I grew to enjoy my summers here."

"Your grandfather must have been glad to have you for company."

"We got along, in our fashion. Sonny's not what you'd call demonstrative, but he's a good man beneath the rough exterior."

"What are your parents like?"

"The best. I have an older sister and younger brother who came to the lighthouse for shorter stays. We're all reasonably close. Mom and Dad still live downstate in the big family house, so that's been our gathering point over the years." Connor looked at Tess and she schooled her expression to friendly interest instead of longing. "What about yours?"

"My mother's in a Minneapolis suburb. Remarried, to an older man who's very authoritarian. She likes that—being taken care of, having no decisions to make. I can't blame her, after being sickly and on her own for so long, but I don't feel very comfortable at their house, either. We see each other once a year at most, if I invite myself and make the trip.''

She summoned up a bright smile. ''But I don't mean to paint myself as the poor little match girl. Between my job and social activities, I have more going on here than I can handle.''

She paused, casting about for proof. ''In fact, you've arrived just in time for our annual community Scrabble tournament. I'm the director this year. We can always use another player, although I must warn you that the competition gets cutthroat in the later rounds. IQs have been questioned. Dictionaries have been called out.''

She laughed awkwardly, aware that she was trying to distract him from the realization that she'd given too much of herself away to a stranger. ''Gus Johnson and Alice Sjoholm are still arguing over a game-winning word from five years ago. I've been boning up on the rule book in preparation.''

Connor's gaze was on her face again, looking at her in a way that made her believe he was seeing past her cheerful facade into the workings of her mind. Not what she wanted him to see, even though she'd already let him in with her blatherings. Suddenly she understood why he'd chosen to be a true-crime writer—his insight was sharpened like a pencil point.

''Hmm, maybe I'll look into playing,'' he said. ''I know at least five q-without-u words.''

"Wow. An aficionado."

"You forget. I'm a professional wordsmith." A quick frown. "At least, I have been."

"Are you changing careers?" she asked, surprised.

Connor brushed off the question with a shrug. "I wonder..." His head tilted toward hers, as if they were telling secrets. "Do you still talk to Rosehip Fumblethumbs?"

Tess blinked, having expected something...else. "Of course not! I'm far too normal."

"Outwardly, perhaps." Connor's eyes had darkened. "Except I've already figured you out. You're a happy, singsong Marian the Librarian to all appearances, but inside, beneath the cocoon of small-town life, is another person waiting to burst free. Like a butterfly."

The muscles in Tess's stomach clutched, even though he was getting carried away. She really was the nice, normal person she claimed. She didn't need to be set free.

From what? she silently scoffed. Her life was her own. Entirely her own.

"Well, Connor, that sounds nice, it really does. But on the other hand I'm pretty certain that you just called me a caterpillar."

He smiled, but his gaze was even deeper and softer than before. It enfolded her. "By any other name..."

THE EVENING WAS so balmy they agreed to take a short after-dinner walk on the paved path that encircled the harbor park. The streetlights of downtown

Marquette were behind them, and no one else was around except for the cars that followed the lakeshore boulevard, their headlights pinpricking the darkness like fireflies. Stately homes perched atop the steep hill that overlooked the park and marina, screened from below by rampant vegetation.

Returning had been the right decision. Already Connor felt easier inside his skin. Part of him even wanted to take Tess's hand as they strolled, but her arms were crossed over her chest again. She was keeping to herself.

After he'd gone all flowery on her with the butterfly analogy—which she'd sensibly knocked down— they'd kept their dinner conversation light and innocuous. She'd filled him in on small-town life and local events. Apparently he'd missed the past weekend's Lilac Festival, but the Scrabble Scramble and the Lions Club's pancake breakfast were coming up.

In turn, he'd told her about life in New York and making his living as a writer, skimming only the surface of his actual genre, even though he was wagering she'd made herself acquainted with plenty of the details. They'd talked books for a long while, comparing favorites. Where he had a fondness for historical biographies, she was all about mysteries—the kind where sweet old ladies with knitting needles prodded criminals into confessing. Luckily, she kept to fiction, although he could see the stirrings of curiosity over his books in her expression and had managed to steer the conversation in another direction.

Tess finally spoke. "So you did get a room at Bay House?"

"I did."

"And you met Claire Levander?"

He nodded. "Also the other woman, the owner…?"

"Emmie Whitaker."

"She didn't want to give me a room, until I mentioned your name. Then—" he snapped his fingers "—she couldn't welcome me fast enough."

"That's odd."

"Why? You seem like a respectable woman."

"Of course I am," Tess said, not realizing he was teasing her, "but that's not what I meant. It's odd that Emmie would hesitate. She's usually very welcoming."

"Maybe she thought I was a smuggler."

Tess groaned. "I'm already sorry I told you that."

They had circled past the playground and into a parking area, empty except for a few vehicles pulled up near the water's edge. Tess led him back onto the path, where they stopped to look out over the lake. Small waves glistened in the distance past a bobbing buoy, but inside the enclosure of the breakwater the obsidian surface was barely ruffled.

"The inn was booked," Connor said. Tess's profile was outlined in moonlight.

He cleared his throat. "But I ended up getting the best room in the place, after Emmie's sudden turn-around."

Tess turned to him with wide eyes. "Not the bridal suite!"

"I guess that's what they called it. I was so sleepy, I wasn't paying much attention."

"You have Valentina's room? The white bedroom with the bride's portrait over the fireplace?"

"That's the one."

"Oh, no." Tess gave a funny laugh that sounded less than amused. "I can't believe Emmie would do that. And Claire! What was *she* thinking?"

Connor remembered the way the women had whispered about prophecies and wedding karma. "There was some discussion…"

Tess turned on her heel and walked away, along the path that ran beside the harbor inlet. Connor hurried after her, bypassing benches and large round planters filled with petunias. Old-fashioned globe street lamps illuminated the way. "Want to explain?" he said when he'd caught up.

She continued at a fast clip, looking agitated. "It's nothing. It's silly." She gritted her teeth. "I'm going to strangle them."

"I'd rather you didn't. I'm on vacation from crime."

That made her smile, at least. She shook her head. "Please don't ask. I'm too mortified to tell."

"Then I'll have to investigate."

"Just don't drag me into it. I don't want to be involved."

He had no idea what she meant, but he knew that she was wrong. She was already involved. And so was he. Which was the last thing he'd expected when he'd arrived feeling half-dead and completely empty.

"I can make no promises when I don't even know what 'it' is."

Tess still wouldn't tell him. He followed her up the slope to the short side street where they'd parked. "Thank you for a lovely dinner," she said, puffing slightly from the quickened pace. "And for the chance to meet your grandfather."

"We didn't really talk much about Sonny and the reading lessons."

"I need to get in touch with a woman I know, who runs a literacy program I've volunteered for in the past. She'll be able to tell me the best way to proceed. Shall I call you, to set up my next visit with Sonny? Do you have a cell phone?"

Connor had trashed his cell months ago, when the number had gotten out to too many reporters. Their harassing calls were interspersed by pleas from his agent and editor, to turn in his manuscript of the *Strange Mind* project. Little did they know that not only had he not written one word after Strange's release, he'd also burned every page of the previous work. Being less available by phone had worked for a while. Then they'd started showing up at his door.

"If you need to see me, you can leave a message at Bay House. All right?"

"Sure." Tess fiddled with her key chain, unlocking a small, tidy, bright yellow Toyota.

"There's not much time to spare."

She lifted her gaze. "I'm aware of that. Except…"

"Except?"

She made a reassuring sound. "I get the feeling that Sonny will hang on as long as he needs to. Have you told him about fixing up the lighthouse?"

"Not yet."

"Maybe you should. Give him something to look forward to."

"Aside from your visits?"

She was pretty when she blushed. She ducked her head again, smoothing a hand over her reddish brown hair. "You've already persuaded me to do your bidding. No need to spread the blarney now." She rushed on. "So I'll try you at Bay House. Or you can get in touch with me. I'm always at the library."

He opened her car door. "Have I said how much I appreciate this?"

"I believe so." She paused, glancing up at him while she ran nervous fingertips over the edge of the window glass.

"Thank you again, then."

Her head bobbed. "You are welcome, sir."

"Drive carefully. I'll follow you back to Alouette. It's a lonely country road between here and there." Twenty or so miles of nothing but trees and wild creatures—he'd forgotten how small the population was in the U.P. until his marathon trip back to Alouette.

"Don't worry," Tess said. "I've been driving it since I was sixteen."

He gripped the edge of the window, leaning his chin on his hand. Reluctant to let her go. "Then maybe you should follow *me*."

"I'm sure you've faced more dangerous situations." As soon as the words were out, she started backpedaling. "That is, I mean—uh, we're relatively crime free. No killers lurking in the bushes—" She winced.

"Tess," he said, drawing up again. "You don't have to avoid the subject. I'm a true-crime writer. Author of multiple articles and five books. I became infamous through no fault of my own—at least, from my perspective. Others have differing opinions."

She looked at him, her teeth biting into her bottom lip. "You were touchier on the subject before we visited your grandfather."

"Yeah, well, I'm sorry for snapping at you. It's no justification, but I've been vilified so often over the Strange case that I've come to expect negative reactions. So I get defensive."

"I understand."

Tess nodded, but she didn't go on to offer him any bright—and false—reassurances about his ill treatment or her own open-mindedness, either. Honesty he respected. Even when he wanted more from her.

More? Ever since Strange had been set free thanks to Connor's investigation into the case, he'd wanted *less.*

Less notoriety, less guilt, less human contact.

Tess drew her finger along the curve of the car window, not stopping until she'd reached his hand. For a few seconds she hesitated, and he was amazed that out of all the strife in his world, what mattered most in that moment was that she would touch him.

Her index finger lifted, hovered for another world-spinning fraction of time, then lightly stroked across his knuckle. The hair on his hand prickled. And then she smiled, exuding a warmth that entered him at their point of contact. A trickle at first, then a stream, gathering strength and loosening every taut muscle in his body.

"You shouldn't be so hard on yourself," she said.

She covered his hand, squeezed it, then slid into her car. He let go of the window and pushed her door shut. Stepped back. Waved. Every action mechanical because his head was still reeling.

She knew it wasn't the public condemnation that had disabled him.

It was his own.

CHAPTER FIVE

Two days later, Tess gave herself the afternoon off and drove up to Bay House, leaving Beth in charge of the library for the remainder of the afternoon hours. Although she hadn't spoken with either Sonny or Connor, they were never far from her mind. She'd made progress with the former, having met with a teacher who was experienced with illiteracy, gleaning her advice and gathering materials and a better sense of how to proceed. As for Connor...

She didn't know what to do with her feelings for Connor.

Beth was urging Tess to explore the possibilities. She'd practically pushed her co-worker out of the library, showing an astonishing strength. Tess blamed it on pregnancy hormones.

However, Beth knew her well. Tess was humming with anticipation as she drove through the Neptune gateposts of Bay House. The large red sandstone inn was a local landmark, built in the early 1900s. Over the years, it had fallen into disrepair when the Whitaker family's fortune dwindled in the absence of their lumber-baron patriarch, Ogden Whitaker. Emmie and Toivo were the children of Ogden's grandson, who'd scandalized proper Alouette society by marrying a Finnish parlor maid named Mae Koski.

Tess veered off the circular driveway to the parking area on one side of the property. She scanned the vehicles for Connor's banged-up Jeep, but it wasn't there. No matter. Emmie kept tabs on her guests, as well as on every person in town. She would even know where the mysterious Connor Reed had gone.

Skipping the formal front entrance, Tess went around to the back door that opened onto the kitchen. Cassia Keegan, a Bay House boarder, had parked her wheelchair in the backyard. She was bent over an item in her lap. When she raised her head, the sunshine lit up her red hair like a bonfire.

"Hiya, Tess!" She lifted the thick paperback book she'd been studying. "Look what I've got."

"Hi, Cassia." Tess squinted, leaning over the railing of the short ramp that led from the door to the newly laid brick paths of the unkempt, patchwork garden. The sweet scent of the lilac hedge hung heavily in the air. "What is it?"

Cassia smiled, doing a devious twitchy thing with her eyebrows. "An up-to-date edition of the official Scrabble dictionary." She made an evil chuckle.

"Not you, too."

"Yep. I'm determined to win the tournament this year. I've been practicing with Emmie and Claire."

"Good luck. In the later rounds the competition's especially tough," Tess warned.

"Sure. But I'm now a girl who knows how to spell *xebec*."

Tess laughed. "Then I'll leave you to it." She gave a quick knock on the screen door as she pushed it open. Bay House was a casual drop-in, yell *yoo-hoo* kind of place. "Hello? Emmie? Claire?"

Emmie called a greeting from the depths of the kitchen. "Come in, come in. I've been expecting you."

Tess entered. The recent renovations hadn't reached the kitchen. The large, homey room was the same as ever—ugly linoleum with worn spots in front of the stove and sink, fruit-patterned curtains faded by the sun, banks of country cabinets painted cream. "You've been expecting me? How come?"

Emmie turned back to the pie she was brushing with raw egg. "Our new guest has mentioned you several times. I saw the books he carried home from the library." Reaching for the sugar bowl, she glanced at Tess. "Mr. Reed's an enigma. I knew you'd come around sooner or later, wanting to figure him out."

Tess squirmed inside. "I'm helping Connor with a project."

"The lighthouse?"

"Um…"

"He's already had Noah out there, looking the place over." Emmie made a *tsk-tsk* sound. "That young man had better plan carefully. The lighthouse will be an even bigger money pit than Bay House."

"I think it would be wonderful if the lighthouse was fixed up. It's a tourist draw even in its tumbledown state. Imagine how many visitors would come if there was an historic Gull Rock tour available.''

Emmie sprinkled the piecrust with sugar. '''Spose so.''

''You'd get more guests.''

''We've got enough as it is, since Claire took over. She advertised us on some Web sites, and we're nearly booked up for the rest of the summer. Except for the rooms that aren't fit for occupancy…'' Emmie trailed off, looking exasperated.

''And the bridal suite,'' Claire said, entering from the dining room through a swinging door. ''Hi, Tess. Emmie won't let me book Valentina's room. I keep telling her it's one of our best selling points. What woman wouldn't want to stay in a room with such a tragically romantic history?''

Tess made a *whoa* gesture. ''Don't try to sell *me*. I'm with Emmie.''

The innkeeper dusted off her hands. ''See?''

Claire just shook her head. ''Tess, I'm surprised at you. Are you superstitious?''

''I'm…cautious. I've heard the stories.''

''I've heard them, too,'' Claire said with a smile. ''Some people even think I've lived one of them. But business is business. We have no concrete proof that there's any substance to Valentina's wedding prophecy—''

Emmie snorted. ''Ha! You just wait, missy. You'll be married before the year is finished.''

''Only because you keep nagging me!''

"'Spend the night in the bridal room,'" Emmie quoted, her tone brisk.

"'Turn of year, thee shall have a groom,'" Tess finished. She knew the words well. She and her girl-friends used to sing the couplet while skipping rope in the schoolyard. The girls had lingered over the romantic aspects of the legend, repeating the tales of how many times Valentina's prophecy had come true for Whitaker family members and various guests. Whereas the boys had relished another slant on the story—the tragic suicide and reputed wedding "curse."

As a jilted bride, Valentina Whitaker had sworn—mere minutes before she took a fatal swan dive off the cliffs—that any guest who stayed in the so-called bridal suite of Bay House would be married before the year was out. Conversely, the marriage of any couple who slept there would end in sorrow.

Or so it was claimed.

Tess wasn't sure she believed any of it, but in her imagination...

"It was coincidence that I met Noah after sleeping in Valentina's room," Claire said with a sportive tone that told Tess the argument was familiar and ongoing. Claire Levander had come to Alouette on business two months ago. Via Toivo Whitaker's mischievous machinations, she'd ended up in the Bay House bridal suite.

"How *is* Noah?" Tess asked.

"He's good." The words were simple, but Claire radiated bliss.

"Engaged yet?"

"Hey. It's only been—"

Emmie interrupted. "Time has nothing to do with it, under certain circumstances." She scowled, pinching her lips into a pucker.

Claire shrugged. "Em disapproves of me living at Noah's cabin for the summer," she confided to Tess while the innkeeper turned her back to put the pie in the oven. Emmie closed the door emphatically.

"I didn't realize," Tess said. She knew the couple were a hot item, the frequent topic of conversation among the local wags. But last she'd heard, Claire was still living at Bay House while she managed the business.

Claire chuckled. "Then you must be the only one who missed the gossip."

While Alouette was something of an old-fashioned town, it wasn't entirely immune from modern ways. The townspeople had experienced a share of petty crime, progress and scandal, including out-of-wedlock shenanigans. It was just that they were extremely interested in keeping up with each other's private lives. In her day, even Tess had been the subject of speculation. Those with long memories were still apt to bring up her history with the Johnsons. Around town, she was defined as the nice spinster librarian with the tragically perished fiancé. That was the way of small towns—people didn't forget.

"If you and Noah were engaged, at least," Emmie was saying.

"Don't rush us." Claire had become close to Emmie in her short time at Bay House. Their mutual fondness was evident, even when they squabbled. "It'll happen."

Watching the mother-daughter closeness between the two women gave Tess a pang. She resolved to call her own mother that evening. And to be only sweet and supportive during the long recitation of the woman's woes.

"But don't expect me to deliver a prophecy-fulfilling wedding," Claire finished with a bashful laugh that told another tale.

Emmie didn't protest, but Tess saw her clamping her lips together against further comment as she collected her baking utensils in the sink and wiped down the countertops.

"Which brings us to Connor." *Might as well throw myself into the fray.* "You put him in Valentina's room," Tess scolded. She crossed her arms, looking from one woman to the other. "Shocking. Just shocking."

"I didn't want to do it," Emmie said.

Claire chimed in. "But the poor guy looked so exhausted."

"And then he mentioned your name."

"Uh-huh," Tess said.

Claire shrugged. "We certainly couldn't turn down a guest you'd recommended."

"Against my better judgment, we put him in the bridal suite," Emmie admitted. The expression on her round face was too innocent and kindly to be genuine.

Emmie was kind, but usually in a bossy, tart-tongued way.

Tess wasn't taken in. If Emmie had given Connor the bridal suite, it was for a reason. "Please tell me you weren't plotting against me."

Emmie blinked. "What in the world do you mean?"

Tess looked at Claire, who was acting equally innocent. She tucked a hank of her hair behind one ear then idly tapped her cheek with an index finger. "Gosh. Does the prophecy work if a *man* checks in? I hadn't thought of that."

Another voice joined the discussion. "D'ya think Connor's going to get stuck with a groom of his own?" A giggling Cassia nudged the screen door open with the wheels of her chair. The motor whirred as she traveled over the threshold and into the kitchen. "Poor guy. I'm pretty sure he doesn't swing that way!"

They all laughed, even Tess, whose stomach was hollow and tingling. Of course, Valentina's wedding prophecy was a bunch of colorful, entertaining, far-fetched hooey.

But in Tess's *wildest* imagination…

Emmie clucked at the frivolity. "We haven't had many men check into the suite, as far as I remember, but another version says—Sleep all night in the bridal room, turn of year, thee shall be a groom."

"There you have it," said Claire.

Cassia pointed. "You'd better watch out, Tess!"

"Oh, come on," Tess wailed. "Why not *you*, Cassia? Or Em, for that matter. You're both closer to the—the—'' Tess waved a hand. There were no words for the absurdity of the wedding prophecy. Other than pure fancy.

She'd enjoyed far too many flights of fancy for that to be any reassurance.

"Maybe it'll be Shari." Cassia tittered. "She's been loitering outside Mr. Reed's door every chance she gets. This morning, she waited for an hour with a breakfast tray. Probably hoping to crawl into bed and serve him right there."

Emmie didn't care for that. "Claire, have a word with Shari. We can't have her annoying Mr. Reed."

Good, Tess thought before she could stop herself. Oh, she was far gone if a desperately single middle-aged housemaid was getting her jealous!

"I can try," Claire said, dubious at best. Shari Shirley was obstinate. The entire town was betting on when she'd worm past Emmie's guardianship of the bridal suite and snag herself a husband. Several of the single men in town had plans to make themselves scarce, should Emmie slip up.

"Shari never did get to see him," Cassia said.

Emmie looked interested. "No?"

"He went out early this morning. I was up, I heard him leave." Cassia tilted her head. "I don't think he sleeps much. My room's right beneath his. The floor creaks when he paces in the middle of the night."

"If he didn't get the breakfast tray, he didn't eat," Emmie said. "My goodness. That man is already too skinny. I can't have a guest of Bay House going around starving. What will people think?''

Claire, who was dressed in a smart pantsuit, slid her hands over the curves of her ample hips and thighs. She rolled her eyes at Cassia and Tess. ''Trust me, Em, everyone already knows that your cooking would turn even Kate Moss into a plus-size.''

''Pshaw. The food won't do Mr. Reed any good if he's not eating it.'' Emmie opened the refrigerator and began piling one arm with sandwich fixings. ''I'm going to make him a picnic lunch.''

Claire threw up her hands. ''She does this all the time! We'll never turn a profit.''

Emmie went to a door that opened into a well-stocked pantry. She lifted down a wicker picnic hamper. ''Will you bring it to him, Tess, dear?''

After a moment of silence, Cassia chuckled knowingly. She arched her brows at Tess, waiting for her answer.

Tess tried not to blush. She couldn't think of a word to say, because of course she was eager to see Connor, no matter what room he'd checked into.

''I wouldn't be putting you out of your way, would I?'' Emmie advanced toward Tess, round and rosy in one of her tracksuits, a pink cotton version, overlaid with a linen apron. There was a steely, you-can't-say-no glint in her blue eyes. ''You did come here to speak to Mr. Reed, didn't you, so surely sharing lunch wouldn't be an imposition?''

''Leading questions,'' Cassia muttered, backing her chair up a few feet. ''Watch out.''

Tess pressed against one of the chairs pushed up to a kitchen table covered in a practical vinyl tablecloth. "I...guess not. I mean, that would be fine. I do have to, uh, confer with Con—Mr. Reed."

Emmie stopped and clasped her hands beneath her chin, all smiles, now that she'd gotten her way. "Wonderful."

Cassia flipped her curls from her face and laughingly drew a fingertip over her exposed throat. "You're cursed."

Claire said nothing, merely patted a hand over her heart. Tap-tap, tap-tap.

Tess closed her eyes, just for a second, shutting out their hopeful, helpful faces. She often imagined, but never believed, that one day a tall, dark and handsome stranger would walk into her life. But here he was, and she...well, she...

Tess looked at Claire. Tap-tap, tap-tap.

Be still my beating heart.

IT HAD BEEN about a year since Connor bought the lighthouse, sight unseen. His friends, even his parents, had thought he was crazy. At the time, he'd been riding a wave of good fortune. His fourth book, *Savage Bounty,* had been on the bestseller lists for weeks, and the early word on *Blood Kin* was so favorable it had been optioned for a movie even before its impending publication. He was flush.

Instead of investing or buying an apartment, he'd put in an outrageous bid on the lighthouse, completed the paperwork to transfer ownership from the state, and then forgot about it as *Blood Kin* was released amid much hoopla and the attendant author tour. The book had debuted at number one on the nonfiction bestseller lists. And as his grandfather had been in relatively fine health at the time, Connor had brushed off nagging concerns. He'd allowed himself to believe there was plenty of time to return to Michigan, visit the folks, finally do something with the Gull Rock property…

Standing at the foot of the cream brick tower, every muscle aching and his shirt drenched in sweat, he wondered if he'd been out of his head all along. First, to buy the lighthouse. Then, to leave it to rot even further. Now, to think he could make enough headway on his own to give Sonny his nostalgic goodbye to the historic structure that had been his cherished home.

"Hopeless," Connor said. But his flagging spirits lifted when the wind rose off the rocks, carrying the scent of sunbaked stone and fresh lake water, cooling his hot face as he lifted it, letting his gaze reach higher, searching the railing of the observation deck, imagining Sonny standing there once more.

Forty-six steps.

Connor had remembered counting them as a kid, his shoes ringing on the metal treads of the spiral staircase inside the tower. He'd counted them again this morning, to be sure.

Forty-six steps. How the hell was he going to get Sonny up them?

He ripped off his T-shirt and flung it over a bramble bush at the base of the tower to dry out. Heaps of trash dotted the small square of yard around the keeper's cottage, just about the only flat land available on the small humpbacked peninsula.

It had been a full morning's job just to empty the structure. Hauling the junk to a dump would be another enormous undertaking. He'd either have to get the causeway repaired and then hire a vehicle that could make the rugged trip to the lighthouse, or carry everything out by hand.

Several of the small wrens and chipping sparrows that had been hopping and fluttering about the edges of the yard suddenly rose into the air. Connor's attention was drawn to a flicker of movement and bright color in the border of trees that had become tangled and dense in his long absence. Someone was coming.

Tess appeared around the bend in the steep, rocky path that led away from the lighthouse to the mainland. She was dressed in jeans and a raspberry-red shirt with short sleeves, carrying a picnic basket. Her hair flashed and her face was lit with a smile.

Connor felt good just looking at her. As he waved, his grandfather's voice came to him over thirty years' time: *Bright as the sky, she was, and sweet and warm as jam on toast.* Sonny had been talking about his wife, but Tess was that kind of woman as well.

"Hello, Connor," she called. "I hope you don't mind…"

"Not at all." He hurried to take the heavy basket from her, recognizing without much surprise that he didn't mind her interrupting his solitude. Not at all.

The privacy and seclusion he'd sought didn't seem as important now that he was in a smaller world. And now that he'd met Tess.

"Compliments of Emmie," she said, motioning to the picnic hamper. "I stopped by Bay House hoping to find you, and one thing led to another, which led to food, as it usually does with Emmie—" Tess broke off with a laugh, not quite looking at him, although the air between them hummed.

"I *was* getting hungry." He hadn't been, for quite a while now. Maybe the physical exertion was working up his appetite. "I'll thank Emmie tonight and have her add the lunch to my bill. You'll join me, won't you?" Tess nodded and he shifted the basket to one hand and took her elbow, helping her over a spot in the path where rocks had heaved during the winter.

She hesitated, then scrambled nimbly across them, slightly out of breath. "I've forgotten how steep and rocky the path is on this side of the causeway. Easy to break an ankle."

"It's been neglected, but that's probably a fortunate thing. Not many vandals made the crossing."

The lighthouse perched on top of a hillside. The grounds were made up of no more than five acres, a handful of rocks and soil that poked up from the water—the curled tip of the finger peninsula. During storms, waves crashed over the rocks, submerging the bent knuckle of land that connected Gull Rock to the jagged shoreline. A causeway road had been built up from hard-packed rock and gravel, but it had eroded over the years. Presently, visitors had to park on the mainland and cross to Gull Rock on foot or bike, or come across the bay by boat.

"Vandals?" Tess raised a hand, making a visor as she scanned the lighthouse. Aside from the normal weather damage that was to be expected, windows were broken and the front door bashed in. Spray-paint graffiti had been scrawled across the brick in several places. "Oh," she said, soft-voiced. "How sad it looks. I haven't been here in years. From a distance, across the bay, the lighthouse seems so invulnerable."

"It's going to take some clearing and cleaning to bring it up to snuff for Sonny's visit."

"*Some,*" Tess said, looking over the piles of trash as they reached the yard. Her gaze darted to him, then quickly away.

The way she did that made him feel weirdly naked, so he retrieved his T-shirt and pulled it over his head. "I guess a few parties have taken place out here over the years."

Tess was squinting hard, her attention fixed on the top of the tower. "After the lighthouse was abandoned, I'm afraid it became a tradition for the senior class of the local high school to come out here around graduation time. There's usually a bonfire, a keg or two, lots of horseplay." She shrugged. "You know."

"That explains the graffiti. The graduating class has left their mark—still fresh."

Tess motioned at the scribbled loops of blue and black spray paint. "Those are waves, in the school colors. The local high school's sports teams are called the Alouette Galestorm.'' She sighed over the damage. "Sorry."

"Not your fault. Unless…"

She owned up. "I was here. Fifteen years ago. Wow—has it been that long?"

"And what happened?" Connor asked, picturing Tess as a high-school senior. She probably wore her hair in a ponytail and got straight A's. Played clarinet in the band. Or she might have been a cheerleader— the pure-of-heart kind. For sure she was full of school and community spirit. There would be a high-school sweetheart, of course. Someone she was devoted to.

"What happened?" Tess mused. "Not much. Beer and chips, a little marijuana, then lots of loudmouth bragging about how we were going to conquer the world. Or buy Corvettes. Whichever came first." She chuckled. "A new sports car—the height of teenage aspirations."

Her head angled back, looking up the tower again. "Some of the kids climbed into the cottage through a broken window. I left after two of the football players dangled a girl named Gloria over the railing of the lighthouse tower. She was screaming, but she liked it. Tipsy *and* stupid."

Connor had followed the story, but even more, he'd read her face. She was holding back. "Who was your date?"

Tess met his eyes. "Jared Johnson."

"A good guy?"

"Yeah."

"Does he still live around here?" Maybe she'd

never gotten over her thing for him and that was what subdued her.

"No, he's dead."

"Oh. I'm sorry to hear that."

Connor continued to watch Tess's face, fascinated. She was being very careful about staying on an even keel. Too careful.

"It happened a long time ago." She took a deep breath. "He was my fiancé."

"I see."

"No, you don't see," she said with a sudden vehemence. "Your eyes are like razor blades, but you're jumping to conclusions all over the place. I am not still grieving for Jared. I'm not this tragic, gothic heroine who is all…all…" She flapped her arms, sputtering with irritation. "What's the Faulkner story they teach in high school?"

"'A Rose for Emily.'"

She glared. "You know all the answers. Or you think you do."

Connor felt his eyebrows creeping higher and his throat getting tighter even though he was trying not to get involved in whatever psychodrama she had going on in her head about her dead fiancé. Jared Johnson. Without a doubt, a big, healthy, all-American good guy. A fair version of Evan Grant. *Not right for Tess.*

But now she'd never know it.

She'd stalked off in the direction of the tower, saying over her shoulder, "I am not an Emily, or a Miss Havisham, so you can quit looking at me like that!"

After a minute, Connor followed with the picnic basket. Tess was sitting cross-legged amid the long grass, looking out over the sparkling lake. The expanse of water was endless—nothing on the horizon except more of the deep cold blue.

"Trying to see Canada?" he said.

She rested her elbows on her knees. "I used to do that."

"Me, too." He put the hamper down, lowering himself beside it, willing to go along with her wishes even though something dormant in him had been awakened. He wanted to collect all the pieces and put the Tess Bucek puzzle together so that she made sense to him. And that feeling, the familiar curiosity, was exciting. He'd thought he'd never know it again.

"I also used to look for Alcatraz, China, sharks named Jaws and—" the corners of her lips tilted up "—pirate ships."

He smiled back. "My grandfather would tell me stories about famous shipwrecks. I used to sneak up to the tower, sure that the ghost of the *Edmund Fitzgerald* would sail by, if I could only stay out late enough."

"Then I'm not the only one with a vivid imagination."

"I don't know if mine's imagination as much as it's plain old-fashioned, stick-your-nose-in-everyone's-business curiosity."

"You don't have to apologize, Connor. I'm the one who flew off the handle."

"I wasn't apologizing."

"Oh, well, then, I guess I should..."

"Naw. Don't bother. I like a good heated discussion."

"No, that was the second time I've been shrieky with you. I don't know why, but I'm sorry. I just feel—" She gave a shiver, rubbing her arms.

"Like an exposed nerve."

She looked sideways at him, the wind off the lake ruffling her hair across her face. "Like an exposed nerve who keeps finding herself on a psychiatrist's couch."

"That's my fault. I have a habit of asking a lot of questions. Yell at me to quit when it gets annoying— that's what my friends do."

"I believe that's what I just did, more or less." She flipped open the lid of the hamper and burrowed inside, pulling out sandwich packets, plastic containers of macaroni salad and raw vegetables, a water bottle and a thermos.

"Gotcha," he said, vowing not to treat her like a subject. If only he could remember how to approach a normal human being....

She glanced up. "No, it's my problem."

"You don't have problems. You're the most stable, levelheaded, pulled-together person I ever met."

She made a face. "Don't give me that baloney, either."

He stretched out sidelong on the grass, crushing it flat. Now he could see nothing but blue sky and the lichen-covered rocks that crowded the hillside. And Tess. "In fact, you're practically boring."

"Almost everyone in Alouette would agree."

"Then they're blind."

She wrinkled her nose, then folded back waxed paper and lifted a corner of bread. "Maybe it's that I'm so settled here. I haven't had to explain myself in a long time, and when a person gets that comfortable, it's a shock to the system to be jarred out of it." She handed him the rejected sandwich. "Meat loaf, ketchup and onion."

He found another one and checked its contents before offering it to her. "Do you like egg salad?"

She accepted the sandwich. Deliberately, he grazed his hand over hers, slowly sliding his palm along her arm before letting go. His body stirred. *Signs of life.*

"Some shocks are good," he said, taking a big bite. "Like the taste of a raw, sharp onion."

"I hate onion."

"I know."

"There's onion in this egg salad," she said, chewing.

"Small chunks. You'll hardly notice them."

"I notice them. They crunch."

"Eat up anyway and you can have a cookie for dessert."

"I always do," she said, and he tried to figure out if she meant the duty or the reward.

Gulls were swooping out of the sky, hopping across the rocks, pecking and cawing at each other as they jostled for position. Tess lowered her sandwich and drew in a deep breath, eyes closed, face lifted to the sun.

Connor stopped chewing. For once, it was better to lay off the probing and analyzing and just look at her. She was a simple pleasure. Raindrops on a windowpane. The salt and crumbs at the bottom of the potato-chip bag. Stretching after a nap on the sofa.

He moaned softly, pointing his toes and flexing his sore muscles. Took another bite of the sandwich with its thick slab of meat.

Tess's eyes opened, going sharp when she looked down at him. "Let's talk about you for a change," she said.

He stared at his half-eaten lunch. For sure, an eye-watering onion sandwich would be more palatable than talking about himself.

CHAPTER SIX

HE DIDN'T LIKE THAT, she saw straight away, but this time she was going to push it. "You're this famous author," she began.

He groaned again, and sat up.

"Pickle chip?" she asked, tossing him a snack-size bag. They were having fun, right? A picnic by the lake—who could ask for more?

Not me. She hadn't been able to look squarely at Connor since she'd seen him with his shirt off. A little delving into her past was worth putting up with for *that* treat.

"Celery stick? Radish rose?"

"You're kidding me—Emmie did not send radish roses," he said, like he cared.

"Yes, she did. Emmie's like that." *The mother I never had.*

The thought made Tess shake her head. What was wrong with her? Connor and his subtle—and not-so-subtle—questions had her all whipped up inside.

She shoved the container of veggies toward him. "What's it like—being on the bestseller lists and getting interviewed on TV?"

"Surreal."

"I'd like more than a one-word answer, please."

"Okay." Connor wolfed down the rest of his sandwich, crunching the raw onions like a dog with a steak bone. He licked two of his fingers, disregarding the napkins Emmie had supplied. "It was amazing, seeing my name on the *New York Times* list for the first time, especially after my first few books were only modest successes. I bought ten papers and opened every one of them to the book page. Kept them on my table for a week.

"And then my agent sold the movie rights to *Blood Kin*. That book had a massive first printing. And it still sold out. The publisher did a second printing, and a third, and a fourth." Connor scratched the back of his neck, where his damp hair was plastered in upside-down question marks against his skin. "What was even stranger was that suddenly I was someone. A name. Not exactly a celebrity. Authors aren't that notable—" He broke off with a frown. "For the most part."

"We have several of your books in the library," Tess said. "I, at least, should have recognized you."

A ghost of a grin passed over his face. "It was nice, being anonymous."

"It's the notoriety you dislike, though—not the fame. Is that right?"

"Not really. Sure, I enjoyed the attention at first. I was getting these invitations to glitzy parties, like fashion shows and art openings and elegant après-theater soirees. But then there were the interviews and author tours—that wasn't so great. I'm not comfortable going under the spotlight myself. I had to do photo shoots, for God's sake.''

Tess was enthralled by a life so different from her own.

"So," Connor said. He clasped his hands around one knee, staring off at the lake. "It didn't take me too long to figure out that the glamorous stuff wasn't for me. I've always been the kind of guy who likes stopping by for drinks and darts at a grubby Irish pub. I own two suits—one for business, one for weddings and funerals—and I don't wear them more than a handful of times a year. My idea of a good vacation is spending a week in a surfside bungalow on Cape Cod.''

"Not at a run-down lighthouse on Lake Superior?"

"This isn't a vacation. It's an extreme getaway."

Tess let that percolate, waiting to see if he'd get into his reasons for escape.

The silence between them expanded, filled only with the rush of waves and the squawks of gulls. Several of the birds hopped closer, beady eyes on the picnic lunch, until one ran at another with an open beak and suddenly smooth white feathers exploded in a fury as the gulls scattered across the rocks.

Connor didn't flinch.

Tess quit trying to catch hold and let him soar away. She ate potato salad instead, straight out of the container with a plastic fork. After a while, she rolled her jeans up to her knees and settled back to bask in the sun. It was a beautiful day, warm as proper summer except that, thrust out into the lake as they were, the wind was cool.

She'd closed her eyes, but she could still feel when Connor looked at her. Lights and colors danced on her inner eyelids. "Can I see inside the lighthouse?" she said.

"Anytime."

"How about now?" She popped back up, almost bopping him in the nose. He'd been leaning over her. A shiver washed through her at the idea that he might have wanted to kiss her. She rubbed her arms, blaming the lake breeze.

"Sure, let's go," Connor said.

"We have to put the picnic stuff away, or the gulls will be at it." She set aside a few crusts and packed the rest up.

Connor stood and drank half the water in one long slug. "It's dirty inside, full of cobwebs and dust. There are a few broken boards." His gaze lowered to her legs, exposed beneath the rolled-up jeans. "You might want to protect yourself."

Rising swiftly, she let out a discreet cough. "Don't be fooled. I've spent too many years wrestling heavy tomes in the dusty corrals of the library to consider myself fragile."

He plucked a piece of grass off the front of her shirt, holding it up for the wind to take. "We're all fragile. One thing I've learned from my work is that our lives hang on tenuous threads that can be snapped at any moment."

She licked her dry lips. "Is that a blessing or a curse, being so aware of that?"

He shrugged. "Both."

"I'm familiar with the concept," she said, thinking of Jared. For several long weeks, her brain had been incapable of accepting the fact that he really was gone, that she would never see him again. All in the blink of an eye. The screech of tires on rain-swept pavement.

"But time has a way of dulling even the sharpest edges," she added. She laid a hand on Connor's shoulder, patting him soothingly. "Eventually, you'll feel less...jagged."

He studied her face. "I'm terrible company. I can even ruin a picnic in the most beautiful spot in the world."

"Am I complaining?"

"You're too polite to complain. I bet you never complain."

"Clearly, you don't know me. Ask my assistant, Beth, what I do when our absolute *favorite* patron, Mrs. Ethel Lindstrom, calls with a page-long list of questions and requests. Someone told her that librarians will answer any question, so now she believes I live to serve only her. Last week, she wanted to know if the chloride in a swimming pool will affect the color of her nail polish."

Connor cocked his head. "And?"

"I told her only if she forgot to wear a swimming cap. What she really wanted to know was if the chemicals would alter the coloring in her hair. Only her hairdresser is supposed to know she's gone gray.''

"Uh-huh, and how old is she?''

"About eighty.''

Connor laughed as he picked up the hamper. "I'm glad I don't live in a small town.''

"Oh, I think you've been treated to some idea of what it's like, having everyone know your business.'' Tess tossed her crusts to the birds, creating a brief fracas. "What you don't know is that there's also a plus-side to our coziness. People really care about each other here. And we protect our own. No one gets fed to the sharks, even the people who might deserve it.''

When she heard how that sounded, she wanted to take it back. She had doubts about Connor, but with every minute they spent together she became more positive that his motivations were not as self-serving as everyone assumed.

They walked to the lighthouse. Connor was frowning in contemplation, but there was something in his eyes, a light…

"Do you think I deserve it, or is the jury still out on that one?''

Her smile was tentative. "I need to see the evidence before I can decide.''

"Well…'' He let out a short *huh* of a laugh. "That puts you one up on the pundits who crucified me for setting a murderer free and creating scandal and upheaval among the state police association.''

"I never listen to anyone who calls themself a pundit."

"Excellent policy." He set the picnic basket on the concrete doorstep of the light keeper's cottage and wrenched open the door, which had a gaping hole and was hanging half off its hinges. "Shall we?"

Tess hesitated for a moment, taking in the cottage. It was a medium-size, four-square brick building, two stories tall with pairs of narrow windows on each side, a few touches of decorative brickwork and small octagonal windows in the peaks. Plain, but charming. The attached tower had four sides that narrowed toward the red-capped lantern room at the top.

"How many bedrooms?" she asked, stepping up to join Connor.

"Three, but they're small."

"The wind must be fierce in the winter."

"My mother was raised here—she tells some hairy tales of whiteout blizzards. When she got older, she was sent to stay with friends in town during the worst months so she wouldn't miss school. But she still hates winter, and isolation. Give her a group of friends and a warm, crowded shopping mall and she's happy." Connor was waiting for Tess to enter, but the interior was musty and dark and she just wanted to stand beside him on the sun-splashed doorstep, listening to the deep tenor of his voice, so tactile it felt like suede on her skin.

He went on. "Sonny never complained, except to brag about how tough he is. Mom swears the worse the weather got, the more he liked it." Connor motioned with his head. "Go ahead, go inside. I've kicked out *most* of the four-legged occupants."

"Oh, thanks." She stepped onto creaky floor-boards, walking past the entry with a steep staircase that led up into gloom. The narrow windows in the first room gave little light, even though the planks that had been nailed across them had mostly been torn away. There was extensive water damage where one of the windows had been smashed.

"Four rooms downstairs," Connor said, escorting her through them. "This is the office—" a small cubby with a second door but no windows "—and the dining room, and the kitchen. Watch your step here, the floor's soggy."

It gave a little as she crossed into the kitchen, an unsettling feeling. The room was drab, even the faded print wallpaper stripped almost bare, but she could see that it once might have been cheerful. For cooking and heat, the kitchen had an old-fashioned woodstove with a small oven and a warming shelf that only needed cleaning. She lifted the round lid of the fire-box and peered inside, imagining being the light keeper's wife, feeding wood into the stove while the gale winds whistled and the waves crashed against the rocks. She shuddered.

"There are no ghosts here," Connor said.

"Are you sure? Every lighthouse should have a ghost."

"Maybe it'll be me."

"Why not Sonny?"

"I think you have to be tortured to be a ghost."

"Now you're laying it on too thick." She shook her head at Connor and moved to the window, where an oil lamp with a glass hurricane chimney still sat. Amazing that none of the vandals had broken it. She held it up at shoulder height and gave an eerie "Woo-ooooh."

"What's that?"

She set the lamp on a warped countertop. "My ghost impression."

"Uh-huh. Scary." Connor turned away and touched the distressed table that was the only piece of furniture left in the room. It looked handmade. "This is where we sat." He hunched, peering through the window. "You can see the sandstone cliffs on the other side of the bay."

"Yes, there's Bride's Leap. Speaking of ghosts…" Tess rubbed at the dirty windowpane. "You know the story of Valentina Whitaker, don't you?" She hoped he didn't. Already she was getting warm at the thought of Emmie and Claire trying to hook her and Connor up, and if she had to spell out the details of the wedding prophecy…

He was a quick guy. He'd put one and one together.

"Vaguely. Sonny was more into maritime history. I remember a couple of the local boys mentioning it once, a long time ago. She was a spinster who lived at Bay House?"

Tess tapped a finger on the window that faced the cliffs. The trees were too thick to point it out, but Bay House was up there among them. "Not exactly a spinster, although she was older. Valentina Whitaker was a jilted bride. She jumped from the cliff and washed up on the rocks below. I've looked through the old newspaper records. There were doubts about what really happened, but no proof.'' Good, stick to the basic elements of the story, not the fancy.

''The police always have questions with suicide,'' Connor said.

''This is right up your alley, hmm? Maybe your next book should be an historical true-crime mystery. You could settle the case of Valentina Whitaker once and for all.''

Connor's expression flattened. ''I'm out of that racket.''

She caught her breath. ''You are?''

''After the Strange debacle, I decided I'd had enough of it.''

''But aren't you supposed to be writing a book about the case? I read—um, it's highly anticipated, isn't it? The insider's view and all.''

''You've been reading my press clippings.''

''What can I say? I'm a librarian. I have a question, I research it, especially when I'm not getting answers from my source.'' She stepped toward him, hands on hips. ''That would be you.''

''Then *you* write a book. I'd rather be a source than the author.''

''You're serious? Don't you have a contract?'' And an immense advance, according to publishing insiders.

''Contracts can be broken.''

There'd been no public report of that yet, so she

wondered if he'd announced his plans to his publisher. Or had he simply taken off, without word, to
hide out here in the U.P. where no one would ever
find him?

Ah, she thought, remembering how he'd said he
wasn't having a vacation but a getaway. If you
wanted to get away, this was the spot. Alouette's unofficial town motto was "Not the end of the earth,
but we can see it from here."

"Then a different type of book would be just the
thing to dive into," she said, trailing Connor as he
left the kitchen. They crossed back through the small
square cube of the living room, furnished only with
a potbellied woodstove, and into the office again.

"No," he said, opening another door. "I'm not
writing. Do you want to go up to the lantern room?"

"Yes, of course. But—" She scurried after him
through the passageway between the cottage and the
lighthouse tower. "You're not writing *at all?*"

He started climbing the spiral staircase, raising a
clatter on the metal steps as he moved swiftly upward
without pause. Sounding like the surly man she'd met
that first day in the library, he said, "Do you have a
problem with that?"

Tess didn't answer. She was already panting, trying
to keep up. The pitch was steep, and there were a lot
of steps. They wound higher and higher.

She glanced down to the cement floor and gulped,
reminding herself that she was not afraid of heights.
She gripped the handrail more tightly. Rusty and
wobbly, not a good combination. The property needed

a lot of work, but the possibilities were exciting. If Connor wasn't such a sourpuss, he could live in the lighthouse and write gothic thrillers, full of crashing waves and ghosts who carried lanterns up to the tower at midnight.

And smugglers, she thought. Dark and mysterious smugglers who appeared to be dastardly villains, but in the end proved to have hearts of gold when they saved their heroines' lives and swept them up into their manly embraces....

Now, *that* was going too far.

"Careful on this last step up to the platform," Connor said, softening. "Give me your hand."

Said the smuggler to the damsel in distress. Except they weren't. Not a bit.

She gave him her hand anyway, taking a big step up through the hatch and into a vista of endless blue.

"Ohh." The lantern room was glass all around, with the platform for the light at the center. Crates filled much of the floor space, so she didn't try to circle the enclosure. Staring out at the greatest lake in the world was enough. "Oh, Connor. This is where I say *magnificent* or *gorgeous,* one of those words that aren't nearly enough."

"I'm partial to *breathtaking.*" His eyes were on the horizon, where one of the gigantic Great Lakes ore boats inched toward the harbor in Marquette. "When was the last time you were up here? Not high school, I hope."

"No, but it was years and years ago. Three of us from the historical society came out to evaluate the property for rehab. I wanted us to buy it—in fact, I tried again when the lighthouse went up for auction. The others weren't as enthusiastic. It was just too big a project for our small group. The town board was encouraging, but little help. They're always strapped for funds.'' She reached for the door. ''Can we go outside?''

''Wait a minute. I want to show you something first. As a member of the historical society, you should be interested.''

She scrunched her nose. ''It's really just me and a half-dozen nice, older ladies who are more interested in gabbing about old times than—what is that?''

Connor had lifted the top off one of the crates. Inside, padded by straw-type batting, was a large piece of what she took to be the light. ''A Fresnel lens,'' he said, kneeling to reach into the crate and shift the lens. ''One section of it.''

''A Fresnel lens…?''

''It's a lucky break for me,'' he said. Almost enthusiastically. ''The largest crates had been left up here. I found the rest of them in the old root cellar. Still nailed shut from the day the lighthouse was decommissioned. No one had touched them since.''

When she moved closer, a beam of light bounced off the glass, reflecting in colors. ''It gives off rainbows—like a prism.''

''Exactly.'' He dusted a hand over the circular, ridged piece. ''Do you know how it works?''

She shook her head.

''Fresnel lenses were made in France and shipped

over in sections to be assembled on the spot. Once the prism pieces are fitted together inside a metal frame, they work by gathering light and focusing it into a single, concentrated beam. It's something to see up close, turning and flashing.''

"Can you put it together again?''

"I'm not sure if it's worth the bother. Even if I get Sonny out to the lighthouse, he won't be able to make it up this high. He's the only reason I'd consider it.''

"But...'' She liked hearing the zeal in Connor's voice and wanted it to continue. His eyes had lightened when he talked about the lens. There'd been an electricity in him, a fire, that was most intriguing.

"You should do it,'' she urged. Connor needed this as much as his grandfather. "Who knows, maybe it will make all the difference.'' To one of them.

"I don't know about that.'' He was standing and replacing the lid on the crate. "It's a big production, lighting the lamp the old-fashioned way. Aside from reconstructing the lens, there are weighted pulleys, like a clock—''

"Oh, but it would be a thrill for the town to see the lighthouse working again.''

"That can't happen. It would throw the ships off, to see a light where there shouldn't be.''

"So you tell them.''

"Doesn't work that way.''

She wasn't going to give up on the idea that easily. "I'll look into it. I know someone in the Coast Guard.''

Connor squinted an eye at her, a grin flickering on his lips. "Another old boyfriend?"

"Sure," she said, though it wasn't precisely true. She'd struck up a conversation with a Coast Guard officer at a maritime exhibit and had recruited him to do a presentation at the library. They *had* gone out for coffee afterward.

"Maybe you can get a special dispensation then— if he wants to get back in with you."

She was getting that fluttery feeling again. "How do you know he didn't break up with me?"

"They don't let crazy men into the Coast Guard."

Her eyes widened. All she could say was "Um…"

Connor took her hand. "Let's get a better view." He opened the door to the narrow catwalk that encircled the lantern room, offering a full 360-degree view. The wind lashed them, but not with an unpleasant force.

The distance and space were dizzying. Tess pulled free from Connor so she could keep a two-fisted hold on the railing. Gulls wheeled in the sky, and when she leaned into the wind she felt as though she could, too.

"Look," she said, pressing closer to the railing. "We can see most of the town. How pretty." She frowned. "But it seems so small." Boats dotted the marina, rocking in the water. Blocky brick buildings and slant-roofed houses speckled the center of town, scattering up the hillside like pieces of an upset Monopoly game, interspersed by evergreen spires and the green umbrellas of maples and oaks. "It *is* so small."

"You sound sad."

"I just..." Tess's buoyancy was sinking like an anchor. "Seeing Alouette this way reminds me of what an insignificant life I've led."

"What about your friends and family? All your community projects? You're the one who was telling me about how much people care here. I thought that meant something to you."

"Yes, but..." She laughed. *"But."*

"But nothing."

"Your opinion doesn't count. You've done things. All the people that you've met and the places you've gone—important people, exotic places. I'm nobody, in comparison." She laughed again, even though it felt like she was sandpapering her throat. "In Alouette, we know each other's choice of breakfast cereal. There isn't a person I don't recognize by face, if not first name. We get excited about a new item on the menu at the diner, for Pete's sake. By the way, stay away from the Cajun rainbow trout. Not one of the cook's more successful additions."

"You don't have to stay in this town if you don't want to."

"But I like it. I do. How could I ever leave this?" She swept her hand over the scene—pure, sparkling water, puffs of clouds in the bright sky, the streaked red-and-white rocks, the picturesque, dollhouse-size town. "And, anyway, where would I go?"

"New York, like you wanted to. The lions are still there."

Pleasure spread through Tess. He remembered.

"I can't imagine that," she whispered.

Connor put his arms around her, giving her a squeeze. "C'mon. *You* can't imagine that?"

"Okay, maybe I could." Suddenly, she was absurdly happy. What had happened to Even-Keel Tess?

Connor's face was near hers. He was looking toward the town, but when she continued to gaze at him, quietly smiling, his eyes swerved. An intimate recognition flickered between them. She moved a hairbreadth closer.

He touched her lips with his mouth. Not a peck, but not quite a kiss. An experimental foray.

"Was that okay?" he said, close to her ear.

Okay, but not enough. She was shimmering inside. "Yes."

"May I…"

He kissed her again, softly, quickly, lips barely open.

"…do it again?"

"Yesss."

Another kiss. And another. Slightly moist, but not lingering. His breath was warm. She leaned into him. His palms skimmed her shoulders, then cradled her face, fingers laced through her hair.

"Is this…"

Kiss.

"…what you…"

Kiss.

"…came here for?"

Kiss. Velvet and honey. Pure sensation.

Her intentions about Sonny, so noble and altruistic,

were forgotten. Her desire—ah, that was another matter altogether.

"If I say yes, will you kiss me again?"

Connor's eyes crinkled.

Her fingers folded around handfuls of his shirt. She nodded beneath his palms. "Yes."

Kiss.

CHAPTER SEVEN

"I KNOW FULL WELL what you're up to, girl." Sonny slapped away the workbook and shoved the swivel table toward Tess. The thin paperback slipped off the tray top and splayed on the hard linoleum floor.

Tess sighed. Of course he knew. She'd tried to be subtle about easing into the reading-assessment exercises, as Connor had suggested, but Sonny was partially illiterate, not completely dense. And now he was glaring at her, as if he was more than ready to throw her out.

Even though the man liked a good fight, butting heads with him wouldn't help. Keeping her response calm and reasonable, she set aside her tablet and leaned down to pick up the adult-literacy workbook. "Then why not cooperate? Connor said this is what you want."

"Ask me straight," Sonny huffed. "Then *maybe* I'll consider it."

"I would have done that, but Connor said—"

"Eh, Connor talks too much. But he never offered a pretty girl."

Tess lifted a finger. "Mr. Mitchell…are you flirting with me?"

"You look like a schoolteacher I once knew."

"But I'm a librarian. You see—" she waggled her finger "—I have the raised finger and the 'shh' down pat."

Sonny pulled his overgrown eyebrows into a deep frown. His lips folded inward, covering his teeth. She'd begun to recognize that was his way of smiling.

"All right, Mr. Mitchell, I will ask." She cleared her throat. "Sir, will you allow me the pleasure of teaching you how to read?"

Sonny's face darkened, the way that Connor's did when she brought up his recent trouble. She forged on anyway. "I realize that you want to keep this private—"

The old man snorted.

"I know. Privacy is a rare commodity in Alouette. But since we're meeting clandestinely, out of town, there's no reason for anyone to guess where I am or what I'm doing." Tess smiled with encouragement, hoping the *clandestine* would appeal to him.

"Won't work," he said. "That woman across the hall, the old biddy Sjoholm, will see you here. She's always lurking. Pokes her head in the door ev'ry time I belch or roll over in bed."

Tess nodded. "And she'll tell her sister, Alice, who will tell her daughter who works in the café, where the Alouette grapevine really heats up...."

Sonny was also nodding. "That's right, that's right. My girl, Dorothy, never understood why I kept to the lighthouse, but you know even better'n Connor."

"I understand." Tess was gregarious for the most

part, but there were times she very much appreciated that her house was far out of town, without nosy neighbors. "We can figure out a way around that. For instance, I can give an excuse for my visits." She chewed her lip in thought. "I know! How about if I say that I'm visiting you for a research project—recording your memories as the Gull Rock lighthouse keeper."

Sonny didn't respond. Tess didn't let that stop her. After only a half hour of working with him, she already knew that anything less than a bullish snort or a blustery "No!" should be taken as a positive sign.

She warmed up to the idea. "We should do that for real, in fact, don't you think? Now that Connor owns the lighthouse, there may even come a day when it's reopened. Maybe as a museum. And you're practically synonymous with Gull Rock. I mean, you were the keeper for so many years—"

"Yup—1939 to 1978," Sonny said with pride.

"Thirty-nine years! Why, you're a living treasure, Mr. Mitchell."

"Bah," he scoffed, though he looked flattered.

"I'll get Connor to help," she mused aloud, her mind whirring. That was brilliant! Two birds with one stone. Ever since yesterday at the lighthouse, it had been nagging at her that Connor had said he was no longer writing. The statement had been so blunt and hard, as if he'd dropped off the edge of the earth into the troughs of despair and there was no going back.

She'd dipped into one of his books at the library, and it had been so absorbing she'd had to force herself to put it down when patrons arrived. Connor was a talented writer who shouldn't quit altogether. Roping him into a research project with his grandfather would get him back on track. Her idea of a historical true-crime book wasn't bad, either. No one could get hurt in a decades-old investigation.

Satisfied that she'd tidied another corner of the world, Tess returned her focus to Sonny. She'd started out by chatting about local events, using a newspaper she'd ''happened'' to bring along. Through subtle comments about the headlines, she'd discerned that Sonny could recognize a limited number of common words, which was a relief. They wouldn't have to start from scratch. Next, she'd opened an adult-literacy text that her friend had supplied and tried interesting the old man in the first of the diagnostic tests. Clumsily, judging by his reaction.

If Sonny would agree to the reading lessons, she could begin again properly.

She cleared her throat. With a casual air, she straightened the newspaper, books and notebook spread on the tray table. ''Well, what do you say, Mr. Mitchell?'' She looked up at him, a pen in hand. ''I'm willing to lie for you, if you're willing to cooperate in the lessons. We'll record your Gull Rock memories at the same time, with Connor's help.'' She clicked the pen. ''Does that sound like a plan to you?''

After a moment, Sonny leaned forward, resting his elbows on the cane set crosswise over the arms of his chair. ''I might do it. For my grandson. If you're game. The boy needs an interest.''

The old man's insight disarmed Tess. "He has the lighthouse...."

Sonny nodded. "Yah, that's good, that's good. But it's not what he needs."

The room had become tight and still. Tess swore she heard her heartbeat. And her lips—they were twice their normal size. She licked them and said carefully, "What does he need?"

Me, she was thinking.

"Company," Sonny said.

"Company? Social interaction, that sort of thing?"

"Kinda. See, the boy's like me, in some of his ways. Dorothy used ta complain about him holing up. With all the reading and writing he does, Connor can stand to be alone for a long time. But that's not good for him just now."

"*Now,*" Tess repeated. Was Sonny referring to the Strange case? She still wasn't sure that he knew all the details.

"People been harping on him. He needs to meet some friendly types for a change." For a couple of seconds, Sonny's eyes sharpened to starbursts, reminding Tess of Connor. "Maybe a pretty girl like you."

"Stop with the flattery already, or I'll start to think you like me." She clenched her fingers around the pen and touched her knuckles to her lips, smiling behind them.

"Eh, you're not bad. Don't know what Connor thinks."

"He likes me well enough—considering what an antisocial grouch he is."

"He changed," Sonny said with a shake of his head. "Used to be a real outgoing kid. Made friends ev'rywhere he went. Now he says he's going to bunk in at the lighthouse, away from folks. That's not right for Connor."

"Ah, but you know how friendly Alouette is. People will accept Connor with open arms and hot casserole dishes, if he appears the least bit willing." Tess moved her fist under her chin. "I was trying to get him to enter the Scrabble tournament, but it's starting this afternoon and I doubt he'll show up."

"Huh. Too busy at the lighthouse."

"He's determined to make it livable." Though perhaps a tad obsessive about it, she thought, remembering the ton of trash he'd single-handedly hauled from the neglected structure. True, he had reason to press. Time was short. And Connor was a man with a mission to do right by his grandfather.

Sonny's eyes had misted over, focused beyond the window again.

Tess's heart squeezed. "What do you think he'll do with the lighthouse, in the…end?" She winced at the indelicate choice of words. "I—uh, I had thought he might donate it to the town, but I couldn't blame you for wanting it to be kept in your family."

Sonny blinked, turning his mouth down. "Won't matter none to me when I'm pushing up daisies. He can do what he likes."

"I wonder if he'd consider living there."

"It's not a place to raise a family. Kids are spoiled these days—they gotta have all the fancy electronics. None of them appreciates simple pleasures like clean air and fresh water. Gull Rock is better'n any of the rich houses on Bayside Road."

"I think so, too." The amount of longing in her voice was surprising.

Sonny noticed. When he gave her a sly look, she hurried to add, "Connor might choose to live alone."

"He needs a woman. Even I had a woman."

Tess held her pen ready and clicked the tip in and out several times. The idea of being Connor's woman was thrilling—and alarming. "Yes, Connor said you were married. I didn't remember that." She slid the notebook from the pile and flipped it open. "What was your wife's name?"

"Mary Angela Charboneau. She taught school."

"Ah. The schoolteacher you mentioned?"

"Yup. She was the prettiest red-haired schoolteacher I ever saw. Gentle ways, my Mary Angela had. Bright as the sun and sweet as jam on toast." Sonny looked at Tess, making a bashful *harrumph*. "I wasn't near good enough for her, but she liked me anyway."

Tess swallowed, moved by his plainspoken but poetic testimonial. "When were you married?"

It took a while for Sonny to answer—confusion showed on his face. "The war years," he finally said. "Pearl Harbor had already happened."

Tess realized his memory had fogged. She put down *m. 1942?* after Mary Angela's name. She would look up the records. "And then Mary Angela moved into the keeper's cottage with you. Did you live there all of your married lives?"

"We did."

Tess was calculating dates. Connor had said that his grandpa was newly widowed when he was sent to visit as a boy, around thirty years ago. So Sonny had lost his wife sometime in the 1970s. Thirty-odd years they'd had together in splendid isolation at Gull Rock. The marriage and the lighthouse would be inexorably intertwined in Sonny's mind. She'd thought of Old Man Mitchell solely as a grouchy old hermit, but her memories actually encompassed only his last few years of lighthouse duty.

Funny how for all this time she'd been making up little absurdist fantasies in her head without opening her eyes to really and truly look around her. There were probably others whose true stories were just as fascinating as anything she concocted. And even better for being real.

With a self-effacing smile, Tess went back to notating Sonny's facts. "You moved out of town after the lighthouse was decommissioned?"

"A while after. Mary Angela was gone. The lighthouse was gone. No reason to stay."

"Connor said you lived with your daughter down-state."

Sonny's head lifted, wobbling slightly. He set his cane on the floor. "Dorothy's big old house needed looking after. She married a businessman." *Snort.* "Not a bad type, just too much money and not enough know-how. I never did see the sense in hiring a man for work I can do myself.''

"So you were also close to Connor while he was a teenager? That was lucky for both of you.''

"He was a good boy,'' Sonny said. "Never disrespectful, like some of the young punks you see.''

Tess flushed. During her early teen years, there were times she'd been disrespectful, even filled with anger and hatred. Mainly out of frustration that her father had split and her mother was always too sick and depressed to make an effort. Fortunately, she hadn't been the type to run wild. She'd been more or less adopted by the Johnsons when she and Jared had started going out in her sophomore year of high school, and by then her adolescent rage had abated.

Such a long time ago.

Sometimes she felt as though she hadn't progressed at all beyond the night she'd lost Jared. She had a sort of life, filled to the brim with activity, but it wasn't enough.

She wondered how much Connor had changed since his teen years. With all that he'd seen of the worst side of human nature, it was no wonder he'd lost the optimism that she still clung to.

Tess glanced at her watch. "Oh, the time. I have to go, Mr. Mitchell. There's the tournament to prepare for. Opening day is the busiest, until eliminations cut the field.'' She gathered her things. "May I return tomorrow? I'll bring along a Scrabble game and we can make up words.'' Perhaps he wouldn't feel self-conscious when engaged by a game.

Sonny didn't react. For a moment, she thought that he'd fallen asleep. Then she saw that he was tensed and watchful, staring into the trees outside his window with complete concentration, knees akimbo, one knobby hand resting on the curved head of his cane.

She looked. "What is it?"

"Doe."

"I don't see…"

"There, among the poplars. Standing still."

She searched the trees. Was he delusional? Then, faster than a blink, there was a flash of movement and a flick of a white tail as the deer bounded away. "Your eyes must be better than mine."

"Eighty-nine and never wore glasses." Slowly Sonny got to his feet, intent on seeing her to the door. He was most gentlemanly after he'd been rude. "Don't know if it counts for much, but my mind's sharpest in the morning."

"In the—oh, for the lessons." She smiled, relieved that he'd finally agreed. "I can do mornings. The library opens at ten, but I can be a little late." The library was even more quiet than usual in the morning, and Beth wouldn't mind coming in early for a while—she complained of being sick and tired of sleeping on her back and having Bump kick her awake at 5:00 a.m.

"Is tomorrow morning too soon?" Tess asked as she and Sonny inched toward the door.

The man's mind was drifting. "Mary Angela knew. She hinted. But she never spoke it outright. My pride.

Stubborn man, she said. Like a mule. She would have taught me…but I…''

Tess patted Sonny's hunched shoulder. "It's all right. You'll learn. It's not too late, I promise."

Sonny muttered. She hesitated at the open doorway, not sure about leaving him alone. But he turned and tottered toward his bed, stabbing the cane at the floor with each step. She waited for a few seconds, then softly said goodbye.

Sonny had dismissed her from his mind. As she left, though, she could hear him muttering about red-haired schoolteachers and picking blackberries for jam.

CONNOR WAS TRAPPED between two men on a stiff, high-backed sofa in the Bay House front parlor. He wasn't sure how that had come about.

He'd been up since daybreak. After six hours of hard physical labor out at Gull Rock, which included numerous trips back and forth across the causeway and to the town dump in the truck he'd hired at a local garage, he'd finally packed it in for the day. He'd returned to his room to shower and change. On his way back out again, Toivo Whitaker had suddenly appeared to lure Connor into the parlor with a plate of cookies, fresh from the oven.

Then Toivo, a goofball male version of his sister, Emmie, had started talking. And he hadn't stopped. He was a garrulous sort, even though half of what he said was hard to follow, mangled by frequent chortles, Finnish phrases and malapropisms.

No wonder the fellow on Connor's right, Bill Maki, was so silent. He'd said three words since sitting down: "Meetcha," "Sugar" and "Aye-yup."

While Toivo rattled on about fishing for steelheads and Bill watched the Cubs play on a thirteen-inch TV set atop a doily on a fine English antique, Connor finished off the cookies. They were plain vanilla cookies with currants, substantial, but still not enough to take the edge off Connor's appetite. He hadn't eaten yet. There was no fast food to be had in Alouette, so he was planning on grabbing the biggest burger he could find when he drove over to visit his grandfather.

If he ever got out of here.

He put the empty plate down, waiting for Toivo to take a breath.

"Me 'n Bill got us a sweet fishing hole on the Blackbear. You're welcome to come along. I don't tell hardly none of the guests about it, least not after the doofus from Minny-soda went and threw beer cans in the river, but, dad-gum, you're a grandson of old Sonny Mitchell, and me 'n him go way back to the days when I used ta haul groceries by boat to his wife. Then the *Kalevala* bashed on the rocks and I never did get the hole patched right—"

"Fished ankle deep that year," Bill said, rousing himself. He looked at the empty cookie plate and frowned.

Connor grabbed his chance. "Speaking of Sonny, I have to go—don't want to miss visiting hours."

He stood to make his escape, but could hear someone approaching from the direction of the dining room and kitchen. The old wood floors creaked badly. With little hope, he eyed the door to the foyer. No way to make it out before he was intercepted by Emmie or Claire.

Toivo's sister poked her head into the parlor. "My, how lucky. I've caught all three of you. We girls are on our way to the Scrabble tournament. Who wants to come along?"

Cassia rolled up in her wheelchair, saying, "Don't bother unless you're wearing your good undershorts, boys! I'm planning to beat the pants off all opponents." Belatedly, she saw Connor and snapped her mouth shut, blushing furiously.

He chuckled at the comment, hoping to put her at ease. She was usually wide-eyed and silent when he was around. He'd assumed she disapproved of him.

Roxy Whitaker arrived next. She was the niece who worked around the place as a handywoman. Connor had come across her once or twice, dressed in baggy T-shirts, jeans shorts and work boots, with her hair in a messy bun and a tool belt slung around her hips. She'd dressed up for the community event by taking off the tool belt and putting on a pair of sandals.

Roxy made a face. "Lucky thing I put on a new thong, special for the occasion."

Clearly sarcasm, but Connor thought Bill's eyes were going to pop out of his head. With his long scrawny neck and beaky nose, the man resembled an ostrich as he goggled at Roxy's long bare legs.

Emmie pushed forward in a neon yellow top and shin-length green stretch pants. She jiggled like a lemon-lime Jell-O mold, with waving arms and clapping hands. "Snap to! Which of you has a brain?" She seized on Connor. "You. Come with us. There's no sense in wasting your day watching baseball with these clowns."

"I'm going to see my grandfather."

"It's Sunday afternoon—he'll be napping. You can go a little later, after you lose to one of us in the early rounds."

Toivo was chuckling as Emmie pulled Connor from the room. "Word to the wise, Connor. Don't let her con you into leaving an opening to a triple space. Em hoards her good letters for the big strike."

Emmie pursed her lips. "You be quiet, Mr. Pank-is-so-a-word."

"Pank?" Connor echoed, reluctantly letting them take him even though they seemed to have a language he knew nothing about. He had no objections to seeing Tess again. It was facing a roomful of strangers who would all be clued in to his past that put lead in his heels. Especially when it wasn't only himself who would be affected. Working on the lighthouse and spending time with Sonny again had given him the notion that he should be upholding the family reputation.

"Yooper idiom," Cassia said as they reached the front porch. She glanced shyly at Connor. "It means to press or pat firmly. As in, to pank snow."

He laughed. "I remember when I didn't know what

a Yooper was, either.'' The word was a popular nickname for citizens of the U.P. or Upper Peninsula of
Michigan.

Outside the air was warm and moist, with dull gray
clouds massing overhead. Emmie sent Roxy back inside for umbrellas. ''We'll have to take two cars. Cassia's chair can go into the back of Connor's Jeep.''

And that was that, there being no arguing with Emmie. Connor drove alone, but he couldn't take off
with the redhead's transport.

He followed Emmie's ten-year-old station wagon
down the hill into the center of town, trying to think
of a way out. By the time they'd parked outside a
three-story redbrick building and got Cassia settled in
her chair again, his growling stomach had given him
an excuse. ''Listen, ladies. I'll have to take a rain
check. I haven't eaten, so I really need to go and find
lunch—''

''You work too hard and eat too little,'' Emmie
scolded. She clamped him by the elbow with fingers
like pincers. ''I should have sent you off this morning
with another picnic basket. But lucky for us, there's
always a potluck spread at the Scrabble Scramble.
Most of the dishes aren't up to my Mama Mae's standards, but we'll get your belly filled.''

Emmie looked over her shoulder. ''You did remember to bring my casserole, Roxy?''

The handywoman juggled the umbrellas and a chaf-
ing dish with a glass cover beaded with steam. ''I
have it.''

''And I have the lumberjack cookies,'' Cassia said,

peeping beneath the foil cover of the plate in her lap. "But there aren't as many as there were before...."

"Toivo," Emmie clucked as Connor licked a piece of currant off his back molar.

They had reached the front doors, along with a trickle of other arrivals. Several ogled Connor. He started to wish for a Harry Potter invisibility cloak, but Emmie, bless her assertive heart, plowed right in and began introducing him around as her guest, a famous writer from New York City. They made their way inside the building, which appeared to be an old school converted into a community building. Rows of lockers still lined the halls.

By the time they reached the noisy, bustling hall that would once have been the school's lunchroom, Connor had given up on remembering names. He nodded and shook hands. Reactions to him varied from hearty good cheer to quiet suspicion. While there were several quick whispered explanations passed along from person to person, the public introduction wasn't nearly as awkward as he'd imagined.

The assembled group was composed of a lot of middle-aged women carrying hot dishes, with a smaller number of men of varied ages hovering at the edges of the room. One of them, a chubby nerd in glasses, was furtively paging through a Scrabble dictionary until a blond athletic type walked up and punched him on the arm, knocking the book out of his hands. Young mothers were trying to corral their hyper children, and a few teenagers had gathered in a knot by a card table filled with soft drinks, juice pitchers, water bottles and the largest coffee urn Connor had ever seen. Beside that was a long table filled with the growing accumulation of potluck dishes.

Connor grinned. Apparently the townspeople of Alouette played Scrabble so seriously they became dehydrated and ravenous.

He was still hoping to duck out before the tournament began, but Emmie hauled him over to the sign-up table near a white ceramic water fountain. And there was Tess, armed with a clipboard, looking very authoritarian to anyone who didn't know how her lips softened when they were kissed.

"Connor!" She beamed. "You came. Are you going to play?"

"No, I—"

Emmie thrust a pen into his hand.

"Not for long," he amended. "This looks like serious business." If you didn't count the plethora of bundt cakes and macaroni-and-hot-dog casseroles.

"You'll see," Tess said, smiling at him with pink in her cheeks. "First round is random draw, beginning in ten minutes. Take a number and you'll be assigned a seat." Arranged throughout the room were card tables with numbered folding chairs.

"Are you playing?"

She shook her head. "That would be a conflict of interest, don't you think?"

"I'd trust you." He touched her hand over the sign-up sheet. "But then, my interest isn't conflicted at all."

Her fingers curled up into his for one brief moment before she pulled them away. Her voice lowered. "Stop it, Connor. I'll be accused of playing favorites."

"Not a chance. Our Marian is above reproach," said a male voice over Connor's shoulder. He glanced back at Evan Grant, with his daughter, Lucy, at his side.

"Hi, Evan. Hi, Lucy." Tess's hands fluttered over the sign-up sheets. "Here we go—the children's game. You did want to play, yes, Lucy?"

Lucy pressed into her father's leg, shaking her head.

"Why, Luce, at home you said you did...." Evan crouched to offer the shy child encouraging words.

Tess explained to Connor. "We run a very simple child's version, to keep the kids occupied during the first elimination." She bent forward, leaning low with her elbows on the table so she was closer to the girl's level. "Lucy is a good speller, so I know she'd have no problem."

Connor gave Tess a nod and moved on, letting them sort it out. He wandered through the crowd, avoiding eye contact with anyone who seemed ready to talk, and ended up at the food table. The plates of sandwiches were covered with plastic wrap, so he assumed it was too early to eat. *Damn.* The smell of lasagna was making him salivate.

"Here you go," Cassia said, pulling up beside him in her chair. She offered him a large wedge of cake on a napkin. "I snuck you a piece of coffee cake.

Teri Sjoholm saw me nabbing it, but she's the kind who thinks I'll crumple up and die if she looks cross-eyed at me, so she didn't say a word. Probably thought I needed sustenance to keep up my strength.''

"Thanks." Connor consumed the cake in four bites.

Cassia was looking over the competition, ticking them off on her fingers. She seemed to have overcome her shyness. "Myron Mykkanen—not a bad player, but if you get him talking he's easily distracted. The brunette with the glasses—super uptight, a stickler for the rules. Apply some heat and she folds like an iron-ing board. But look out for that one, the chubby woman in the blue Galestorm T-shirt. She has six cats and plays champion-level computer Scrabble. Name's Jessie Smith and she won the tournament two years ago by making a one-in-a-million Bingo triple with the word *zygotes*."

"What about that guy, Evan Grant?" Connor mo-tioned with his chin. Captain America was still hang-ing around Tess.

Cassia gripped the sides of her chair and lifted her-self up a few inches. "Tess only dated him because of Lucy. And, well, he is fine to look at."

"I meant what kind of player—"

"Eh, he's not a player. Just a good guy, all the way. Too bad for me, huh. I like them dark and mys-terious." Cassia glanced up, turning bright red. "Sort of like you," she mumbled.

"Uh," Connor said. "Thanks?" She was more predictable when she'd been shy.

Cassia wagged her head back and forth. "Well, jeez, don't worry that I'm going to jump you. I know you and Tess have a thing going on."

"Uh," Connor said again. "Wait a minute. I was trying to ask what kind of Scrabble player Evan is, not—" He thrust his hands into his pants pockets. "You know."

"Sure you were." Cassia studied the ceiling, letting him squirm. And he'd thought getting into a conversation about his controversial past would have been awkward.

"Why Lucy?" he asked.

"Some women are like that about kids—they have to mother them." Cassia shook her head, apparently mystified by that phenomenon. "Not me, though. No way."

"So Tess wasn't interested in Evan at all?"

Cassia shrugged her thin shoulders. "It's not like I'm her confidante. But that's what we all decided."

Connor laughed. "Okay, as long as you all decided."

"That's the way it is here. People are watching. Don't do Tess wrong."

"I don't plan to." He had no plans whatsoever, aside from the immediate. If he couldn't write, he'd eventually need a job, but that could be put off a while. Maybe he'd stay in Alouette after all, live at the lighthouse until he became known as Old Man Reed.

The idea wasn't appealing, but he had the uncomfortable feeling that was the direction he was heading if he didn't learn to live with the choices he'd made. Guilt was like acid, eating him up inside.

"That guy looks like a contender," Connor said, to change the subject. "The one with the Clark Kent glasses and the dictionary tucked in his armpit."

"Johnathon Kevanen, aka the Scrabblenator." Cassia groaned. "According to himself."

"I've fallen down a rabbit hole," Connor mused.

Cassia had tensed. "What's *he* doing here?"

Connor followed her stare. The Scrabblenator had stepped back, revealing a fair-haired young man standing with his arms crossed over his chest, surveying the room like a lion on the veldt. He saw Cassia watching and aimed a pistol finger at her, laughing when she quickly turned her head away.

"Pete Lindstrom," she said, glowering. "I'd rather play the Scrabblenator."

"He's good?"

"I doubt it, even though he loves to remind everyone how he went to Yale. He's not as smart as he thinks." Cassia hit the toggle of her chair's controls and whizzed away into the stirring crowd.

At the other end of the room, Tess had climbed atop a chair. She clapped, calling for attention. "Welcome to the Sixth Annual Alouette Scrabble Scramble." The contestants cheered.

"We have a record number of participants this year," she continued. "Sixty-three adults and twelve children!" More cheering.

"Because we have an uneven number of entrants, last year's champ will have a bye in the first round, as stated in the official rules.'' Tess cleared her throat and threw a quick glance toward one side of the crowd. Her head bobbed. She seemed so wooden that Connor's curiosity was raised. ''Gus Johnson, take a bow.''

Johnson, he thought. Aha.

Tess waited until the applause for Gus had faded, then held up a sheet of paper. ''The official rules are at the sign-up desk, if you haven't already seen them. Or in case any controversies should arise. Alice and Gus, that means you.'' Mutterings and laughter rose from the crowd.

''For new players—'' Tess scanned the group until she found Connor. Her smile made a number of the contestants turn and look at him with doting approval. He'd have almost preferred to be vilified.

''For new players, I'll give a quick rundown of the rules. We've randomly chosen opponents for the first round. Find the chair with your number. Please remember to use the chess clocks on your table, tapping the bell to signify the end of your turn. Each player has a cumulative forty-five-minute time limit per game. Each minute over costs you ten points.''

There was some grumbling at that announcement. Most of the players were used to leisurely living-room games. ''Sorry,'' Tess said cheerfully, ''but with sixty-three players we need quick games in the early rounds.'' She put on her stern-librarian face. ''As always, all word challenges will be settled with the official Scrabble dictionary.''

More joshing from the crowd. Connor wondered

how quickly he could throw a game and get out of here. Except that would disappoint Tess, which he really didn't want to do.

She was concluding. "So without further ado, let the games begin. Be careful out there, people. Play fair, play hard and play smart!"

CHAPTER EIGHT

ONCE THE PLAYERS had settled down to their matches, Tess wasn't needed, except for the occasional question. The children's game was being run by a couple of volunteers in another room. For the most part, silence prevailed, accompanied by the gentle clicking of letter tiles. Now and then moans erupted when a player pulled bad letters, or hushed conversations grew around a table with spectators.

Tess kept to the sign-in table, her ears tuned for potential quarrels. Fortunately, the first round was less intense than the later ones, when the best players went head to head.

After a while, there was no more paperwork to fiddle with and she got up to stroll around the room and check on progress. Myron was being whipped by Johnathon, the Scrabblenator. Cassia, looking worried, was playing Jessie Smith of *zygotes* fame. Tough draw.

Tess surveyed their board. Cassia was trailing by forty points, with mostly low-scoring letters on her rack. But as Tess watched, she put down *houri* in an excellent position and collected points by making multiple two- and three-letter words in the other direction.

"Twenty-seven," the redhead said triumphantly.

Jessie frowned and pulled out a pair of glasses. Getting down to business. Tess gave Cassia a discreet thumbs-up and moved on.

Emmie Whitaker had drawn Alice Sjoholm in a battle of the buxom gray-haired domestic goddesses. Claire Levander had entered with her guy, the shaggy-haired former hermit Noah Saari. They sat at adjacent tables, each of them playing a member of the Johnson clan. Tess waved hello as she quickly skirted past, pretending an interest in a discussion between Roxy and her opponent across the room.

Tess settled the point of contention—*Ka* was not allowable, much to Roxy's chagrin—then made another scan of the room. Beth had promised to stop by with Randy. There was no sign of them. That was worrisome, but Tess knew they'd call if the baby was arriving early.

She continued searching. Ah, yes, there was Connor, playing Kitty Bailey, teenage daughter of the town's sheriff.

Tess watched from a distance. The girl was obviously dazzled by her dashing partner. Never the sharpest crayon in the box, she was gazing dopily at Connor and barely glancing at the board.

Poor Connor. He looked uncomfortable. Kitty wore a tank top that showed a good four inches of plump cleavage. Every time she leaned closer to giggle and toss down a word, he had to look away.

Tess walked up behind Kitty and gave the straps of the tank a tug. "No fair distracting your opponent, Kitty."

Kitty looked down at the dolphin tattoo that plunged toward her cleavage and giggled. "Yes, Miss Bucek."

Connor raised his eyebrows at Tess. "I'm not distracted." He laid down tiles that spelled *nevus,* pluralizing Kitty's *jet.* "Double-double word score," he said. "Thirty-eight points."

Kitty's mouth hung open. "Holy wah." She recovered and tried simpering at Connor. "I don't even know what that word means. You're so smart."

Tess lifted the S to display the pink square beneath it. "That was bad placement of your word, Kitty. Never leave a double-score square open like that, particularly in such an advantageous position for your opponent." She sounded spinster librarianish even to her own ears.

"But I wanted to use my J!"

"Strategy is just as important."

Kitty rolled her eyes. "Yes, Miss Bucek."

Tess moved away from their table. "I'll let you two keep playing."

Connor grinned after her. "Yes, Miss Bucek."

Before long, a few of the games began to finish up. Tess got her clipboard and circled the room, recording winners for the next round. Emmie had eked out a victory over Alice. They hurried off to tend to the potluck.

One by one, other players dropped by the wayside.

Claire and Noah both won, but then the Johnson family was more into outdoor sports than board games. Gus Johnson, the patriarch who'd once asked Tess to call him grandpa, would have to carry the family mantle once again. He was a sharp old gentleman, a railway worker by trade, and a frequent visitor to the library. Also the only one of the Johnsons who spoke to Tess without awkwardness. He was even willing to bring up Jared's name and the fond memories they shared.

A grumbling Roxy Whitaker reported in with a loss. Connor's game ended with Kitty hanging off his arm, trying to get him to join her at the refreshment table. He broke away and came over to give the score to Tess, whispering in her ear, "I'm never going to forgive you for this," while Kitty snapped gum and made googly eyes at him.

Eventually, only one game was still in progress. Cassia Keegan versus Jessie Smith, and it was close. Both were checking the clock to be sure they didn't go over the time limit, intense with concentration as they scoured the board.

Jessie made the word *envoy,* putting her twelve points ahead.

The onlookers stirred. Unless Cassia could use all three of her letters, she was sunk.

The redhead fiddled with her tiles. She had only a few seconds to spare before she went into a time penalty. Suddenly her eyes flashed. She flung down her tiles and said, *"Kayo,"* with a punch of her fist.

"That's not a word." Jessie wilted as she added

up the points. She fingered her smudged glasses, checking and rechecking the board. "It's an abbreviation. Right, Tess?"

John Kevanen paged through his dictionary. "It's a word!" He handed the book to Tess.

"Legal," she agreed. "Eleven points—score's tied."

With a deep sigh, Jessie tossed her last tile onto the board. She had to deduct one point from her score.

Cassia clapped. "Woo-hoo, whaddaya know? I won!"

After the applause and chatter over the close game had died down, the contestants descended on the buffet. The second round would be played after the dinner break.

"You look hungry," Tess said to Connor, catching up to him in the buffet line.

He dug into a tuna casserole with potato chips and cheese on top. "Dodging giggly come-ons from a six-teen-year-old with a tongue stud and a dolphin tattoo is hard work."

Tess gave him the eye. "I never thought of the Scramble as a pick-up joint."

"Depends who's trying to pick up whom."

"I noticed you beat Kitty by only seventy or so points. You should have tripled her score. Distracted much?"

"Only by the food." Holding an already heaped plate, he surveyed the table, which was packed pot holder to pot holder with hot dishes and cold salads.

"I'm famished." He scooped up a cheese-oozing square of lasagna. "Want some?"

She passed, so he squeezed the lasagna onto his plate. "Did Emmie forget to give you lunch?"

"I was at the lighthouse."

"Of course. How's that coming? By the way, I saw your grandfather this morning and we came to an agreement." Tess noticed Alice hovering over her glorified rice, ears open. The woman plopped a healthy spoonful onto Tess's plate. "I'm going to record his memories of Gull Rock."

Connor lifted his head. "Really?"

"Let's find a seat so we can discuss it." Out of Alice's earshot.

He took Tess's plate while she went to get them drinks. The boards had been cleared off the game tables to make way for dinner. Refreshments were always a large part of any gathering in the town, and the number of attendees seemed to have swelled since the sign-in. Toivo and his friend, silent Bill Maki, arrived and immediately headed for the buffet. Tess merely nodded and smiled at the latecomers. In Alouette, the saying went, "Give them food, and they will come."

Connor stood like a gentleman when she arrived at the table in the corner he'd chosen. She got a little shiver. He was clean-shaved, dressed in a taupe Polo shirt tucked into black jeans. The exhausted, drawn look he'd had when they'd met wasn't as apparent. But even though grins were more frequent, somberness still clung to him.

"I didn't intend to win," he confessed as he held out her chair.

Tess twisted to look up at him. "You were going to throw your game? I'm shocked."

"If I'd had a halfway decent opponent..."

"It's not so bad being among us, is it? Has anyone called you names or beat you up for your lunch money?"

That drew a smile. "It's not so bad," he agreed.

"Then you'll stay for the second round?"

"Guess so. How long will this tournament take? I was going to visit Sonny."

They munched through their loaded plates while she explained that there was one more round of eliminations that day. The next two rounds took place on alternate weekends, with the championship match scheduled for a feature event of the August Blueberry Festival. "It draws a crowd," she said. "I know what you're thinking. We must be starved for entertainment."

"But little else." Connor surveyed his plate. "I can't identify some of this food, but every time I reached for a serving spoon there was another woman urging me to try this and try that. If I didn't take a helping, they'd pile it on themselves."

Tess chuckled. "In Alouette society, it can be considered a faux pas to pass up a particular woman's casserole in the buffet line."

"Uh-huh. But you didn't take the lasagna."

"Ah, but I have in the past, so I'm allowed some leeway. Whereas you're a newcomer. You have to prove that you'll eat everything or someone might be insulted." She waved at his gloppy plate. "Certain ladies get overenthusiastic about seeing that doesn't happen."

"I will do my best." He took up his fork again and picked at the kidney beans in a taco salad. "Tell me about your visit with Sonny."

"It went pretty well." She lowered her voice, aware of being watched by curious neighbors. "We agreed to reading lessons. My cover story is the history of Gull Rock project. Which is real, by the way. I hope you'll help me with it."

"That's a good idea," Connor conceded. "What do you want me to do?"

"Talk to Sonny. You're most likely to get him to open up. You can record the conversations, but I'd also like you to take notes of your impressions. So much is lost from a transcription of a simple recording."

Connor considered that, chewing slowly. "Hmm."

Tess kept a sunny expression. "Is that a problem?"

"Would this have anything to do with—" He stopped.

"Yes?"

"Never mind."

"I think it will be an ideal opportunity for you to get close to your grandfather."

"We are close." Connor frowned. "Or we were, before I moved away."

"Well, then, it's been a lot of years. This is your

last chance." Tess smiled encouragement. "Think it over. I know you'll want to do it."

"All right, we'll see." He shrugged. "How do you expect the reading lessons to go? I'm sure you've noticed that Sonny's mind gets fuzzy at times."

"Well, I want to give him a proper reading-comprehension test to determine his level, but in general he seems to understand the basics. It's only a matter of putting together letter combinations and phonics. I thought of bringing along a Scrabble game next time. We can work on forming simple words and see how he does."

Connor reached across the table and took her hand. "You're a gem for doing this, Tess."

She felt the calluses of his fingertips. "Thank you. I may even enjoy it, when Sonny's not grumbling at me."

"If he gets too grumpy, rap his knuckles or twist his ear."

"Does that work with you, too?"

Connor laughed. "I'll try to be good so you don't have to abuse me."

She lowered her lashes. *When he was good, he was very, very good. And when he was bad, he was…beguiling.*

CONNOR AND EVAN GRANT faced off in the second round, as the group of thirty-two winners was whittled down to sixteen. Connor went in thinking that this time he could manage to lose gracefully and discreetly, but his competitive nature was aroused. Especially when Evan wanted to talk about Tess.

"She's the best," he said. "Lucy loves her."

Connor grunted. *What about you?*

He had crappy letters. He switched a couple of them around and put down *duel*.

"You're probably wondering..." Evan let his voice trail off as he studied the board. "Duel, huh?"

"Wondering what?"

"What happened between me and Tess." Evan smiled, showing too many white teeth, and made a fair score by putting *plow* alongside Connor's *u-e-l*.

Connor decided he'd better concentrate if he didn't want to lose for real. "Nothing serious happened, according to Tess." He nodded at the other players in general. "And everyone else."

"Who's been gossiping?"

"Don't you mean, who *hasn't?*"

They exchanged wry looks and settled into the game.

"Tess needs a family," Evan said after several turns had gone by in silence. "She hides it well, but I think she's lonely."

"She's been telling me that the community is her family...."

"You don't believe that, do you?"

"Nope."

"Lucy wanted me to marry Tess," Evan mused, gazing across the room at the lady in question as she bent over a couple of battling gamers. John the Nerd was getting red in the face and stabbing at the board, rattling tiles. "Sometimes I think I should have."

"What stopped you?" Fool, Connor wanted to add.

"No chemistry."

Connor's eyes narrowed. "Even after experimentation?"

Evan smirked. "So you're not so sure that *nothing* happened." He played his tiles, tapped the clock and drew his replacement letters, taking his time about all three before continuing. "Don't worry. Nothing happened. Tess doesn't experiment with just anybody."

"You're not that. She likes you."

"As a friend."

"Good," Connor said. He couldn't help himself.

They played a few more rounds. Outside, distant thunder rumbled in the darkening sky. The murmuring in the room grew when several flashes of lightning lit up the high, schoolhouse windows. Raindrops spattered the glass.

"Tess *deserves* a family," Evan said.

Connor set his Z back on the rack. "What are you trying to tell me?"

"Don't toy with her affections. You don't exactly look like a family man, so be aware that you'll have just about a thousand angry people on your back if you do anything to hurt Tess. If you're not going to stick, don't even start with her. She's had enough of being left behind."

"You think I'd intentionally hurt Tess?" Connor cocked his head. "Does this have something to do with my reputation?"

"I don't give a damn about what went on with that murder case. This is personal. It's about Tess, lunkhead."

Connor sat back. "Lunkhead." He let out a short hah. "I've been called a lot of names, but that's a new one."

Evan laughed, but he also offered a grudging, "Sorry."

"Yeah, well, I don't intend to hurt Tess." Connor looked over at her. The thunder clapped and she jumped, then moved hurriedly away from the windows. "But I'm not interested in signing some kind of ironclad agreement after a week in town and one dinner and picnic, either." He glanced back at Evan. "You won't find many who would. Or is that the grand master plan? Scare off all potential suitors so you have Tess in reserve for yourself."

Evan flushed.

They didn't get to finish the discussion. Evan's daughter, Lucy, bolted into the room and ran to his side. He put his arms around her. She pressed her face against his neck, whispering to him in squeaks and whimpers.

Tess hurried over. "Is everything okay here?"

Evan shrugged an apology. "Lucy wants to go home."

Tess hunkered down beside the girl. "But we haven't put out the desserts yet. I brought your favorite, Luce. Homemade lemon meringue pie."

Lucy shook her head, still hiding her face. The

lightning flashed and she pressed in even closer, letting out a tiny shriek. Evan stroked her back.

"Does the storm scare you, honey?" Tess patted the child's head. "Me, too. But we both know that it can't hurt us, isn't that right?"

"Sorry," Evan said as he stood, awkwardly lifting Lucy in his arms. She wouldn't let go of his neck. "I'll have to forfeit the game and take her home. Talking doesn't help much when she gets like this."

Tess nodded. "How about if I walk you out? I'll wait with Lucy by the door. That way you can drive right up and Lucy won't have to get too wet." She gave the girl a pat. "She's made of sugar and spice, you know. She melts in the rain."

Lucy snuffled and loosened her hold a little. She sent Tess a watery smile.

"I have an idea. Why don't you slide down and we can go and get you a slice of pie to take home."

"And one for my daddy," Lucy whispered as Evan set her down.

"Of course." Tess took Lucy's hand and led the girl away.

Connor looked at the concerned expression on Evan's face and felt ridiculous for clashing with him over Tess. Like a couple of mountain goats, beating their brains in. "Listen," he said.

"I was out of line," Evan said distractedly. "It's not up to me to give orders about Tess's love life."

"That's true." Connor shook the man's hand. "Thanks anyway. For the…advice. I'll proceed carefully."

"But you will proceed?"

Connor shrugged. "Can't say for sure."

Loud thunder shook the sky.

"However you handle it, be sure," Evan said. "At least do Tess that favor. She gets this look when she's near you...."

Lightning flashed. "Like there's electricity in the air," Evan continued. "She's plugged in. She never had that feeling with me." With a shrug, he walked away, joining Lucy and Tess at the exit.

Connor slumped into his chair. The letters on his rack spelled out *pots*. He switched them around and came up with *stop* instead. A solution for his indecision?

Great. Now he was reading deep meaning into board games.

With a snort of disgust, he dumped the tiles into the bag.

CONNOR LEFT on Evan's heels, still planning to make a fast visit to his grandpa. He came across Tess standing near the doors and exchanged a few words with her, but she was distracted, glancing worriedly up at the sky as the rain lashed the building. He reassured her that Lucy and Evan would get home fine, and she smiled, murmuring, "Of course they will, of course they will," as she walked alone down the hall to resume her Scrabble Scramble duties.

Her wary behavior was still lingering on Connor's mind when he returned to town nearly two hours later.

He'd tried to put it down to concern for Lucy, but wasn't convinced.

On impulse, even though he guessed the tournament would be over, he drove to the old school building instead of taking the road up to Bay House. The thunderstorm had abated while he'd been visiting Sonny, but now the rain was starting up again, turning the parking lot into a sheet of shiny obsidian. It was empty, except for one car.

A little yellow Toyota, bright as a beacon in the rain-soaked darkness.

He parked beside it, making out Tess's shape behind the wheel. Unsuccessfully dodging raindrops, he got out of his Jeep and loped through a puddle to tap on her window. She reached across for the door latch, yelling for him to get in. He flung the door open and jumped into her car.

"What are you doing here?" they said in unison.

"I was on my way to the inn," he said.

She shivered at the cold air he'd brought inside. "I was on my way home."

"The car won't go until you turn the engine on." He raked his fingers through his hair, shedding rain like a wet dog.

"Right." She laughed uncomfortably, leaning over the wheel to look at the rain as it splashed across the windshield. "I was, um, thinking."

Thinking? They'd both been doing too much thinking, in his opinion. "How did the tournament go?"

"No problems. Cassia and Noah upheld Bay House tradition and made it to the next round. Claire lost to

John Kevanen. He's good, the favorite to win, now that Jessie was ousted by Cassia's upset. That is, unless you do something spectacular, since you're also in the final sixteen. The other players were buzzing about you. You've got them worried.''

Connor was puzzled. Tess's voice was pitched higher than normal, and she was chattering. Nervous, he thought, except there seemed to be no reason for it.

She was gripping the steering wheel, staring out at the rain. ''You're the dark horse of the tournament.''

''What about Gus Johnson, last year's champion?''

''Yeah, there's Gus. He's always a contender.''

''Would he be related to Jared, your—you know.'' *Dead fiancé* didn't sound polite.

''Gus was Jared's grandfather.''

''So you must know him—Gus—pretty well.''

''I did. I was close to the entire family.''

''What happened to change that?''

Her voice went flat. ''That's obvious.''

''No, not necessarily. Some families grow closer after a tragedy.'' But he also knew that many of them broke apart. He'd interviewed his share of miserable parents who'd added a divorce to their problems.

Tess raised her eyebrows. ''Why are you asking this?''

''I noticed that things are strained between you and the Johnsons.''

She drew in a breath. ''I wasn't rude, was I? I would *never* want to be rude to them.''

''No, that wasn't it.'' He patted her leg. ''It wasn't

so obvious that anyone else would even notice. I'm just good at picking up on the little signs. There was an awkwardness, that's all. I sensed your discomfort, and maybe even theirs. I was surprised. You said it's been a long time since Jared died. Ten years?''

"Yeah, eleven, but..." Tess's head tilted, as if it was so heavy she had to lean it against the window. Her eyes closed briefly, the lids trembling. "They haven't forgiven me. I *know* they haven't forgiven me. And after eleven years, it doesn't look like they ever will."

Connor waited. He wanted to hold her and soothe her until the pain in her heart had faded, but he was accustomed to being the patient observer, not a participant. And at the back of his mind was Evan's warning about making promises—even unspoken— that he might not keep.

"How do you know this?" Connor asked quietly.

"Because, after the funeral, I went to the wake at the Johnsons' house and—" Tess stopped and gulped air, making a small, sad sound in her throat "—and Jared's parents said they couldn't stand to have me around. Because I was to blame."

She squeezed her eyes shut again. "I was driving the night that Jared died." She took another shuddery breath, but her voice was twisted too tight to unwind. "It's not a big secret. And I'm not still blaming myself. It was just an accident. But ever since, Jared's family can't bear the sight of me, so I try to keep away from them as much as I can."

Tess straightened and looked at Connor almost defiantly, her eyes red and narrowed, but dry. "This hasn't ruined my life. Don't feel sorry for me. It is what it is…that's all." She squirmed in the car seat. "So much time has passed, I don't usually think about it. At least, I don't *dwell*."

"Then why were you sitting out here after everyone else has left?"

Her lips compressed. "I don't like driving in a rainstorm. I was waiting for it to taper off."

It didn't take him long to put two and two together. "Oh. The accident?"

"Yeah," she breathed.

"I'll drive you home."

She was surprised. "You're not going to ask me what happened? You mean I don't have to relate my sorry story and be consoled?"

Connor slid his arm around her shoulders, pulling her toward him until her head rested on his chest. She went willingly enough, in spite of her caustic words. "Only if you want to," he said, grazing her hair with his lips. Her usual subtle powdery sweetness was washed by the scent of rain. "Only if you need new ears and a fresh shoulder."

"To cry on." She sighed. "No, I don't cry about Jared anymore. That's done."

Rain beat against the windows in sheets, making the inside of the car seem like a glistening cocoon. Connor could barely discern the shapes of the buildings around them. Tess was warm and round in his arms, stirring both tenderness and arousal inside him.

"All right. I'll tell you." One of her hands reached

up to his chest, resting there without moving. Although a molten sensation flowed through him, outwardly he remained motionless. "It's simple enough."

He made an instinctive sound of encouragement, then wanted to take it back. He'd always been a good listener. It didn't take much except a willingness to let a person speak. But there were subtle techniques to promote the aura of trust, techniques he'd refined by questioning untruthful witnesses, half-crazy criminals and resentful victims. He didn't want to use any of that on Tess.

"We were a week away from getting married. Jared was only twenty-three, young and rowdy yet. He'd been with friends at a bar that night, while I hung out with my girlfriends. We came together at some point in the evening, the way we usually did. By the time it was dark, the sky was thundering. When it started to rain, we called an early night. It was just an ordinary thunderstorm. The roads weren't especially treacherous. There was no...portent of doom, or whatever you want to call it."

Tess's voice had remained low and even, but he felt the fine shivering of her shoulders beneath his hands. "Jared didn't want to give up the keys, but I insisted. I *thought* I was being sensibly cautious." Her head gave a quick shake and she amended that. "No, I really was. It was the right thing to do."

"Yes."

"I tell myself that. Truth is—maybe, maybe not. It

was raining hard and it was dark...." She lifted her head, looking out the front window. "Like tonight."

Connor gave her a squeeze.

She went on in a mesmerized voice. "I was driving *below* the speed limit. We should have been fine. But...the car hydroplaned on the wet road and I don't know, I must have hit the brakes when I shouldn't have, or I turned the wheel too sharply, because I lost control and the car slammed into a bridge piling and rolled, and even then it would have been okay, except that Jared—Jared was thrown from the car and he..." She thrust herself from Connor's arms and sat up, covering her face with her hands. "He suffered massive internal injuries and he died."

"Oh, Tess, I'm sorry." *Damn inadequate words.* He'd used them more times than he could count, and never had they felt so totally useless.

She didn't seem to have heard. "I was still strapped in the car. I heard him, you know. Calling in pain. I tried to get out to go to him, but I had a broken ankle, and when I finally got my seat belt loose, I fell against it and passed out from the pain. At least that's what they tell me—they found me halfway out of the car. The next thing I remember was being rushed into the hospital."

"And what happened with Jared?" Connor asked. Not because he wanted to know. For once the details weren't important to him, but it was important for Tess to tell it all. She wasn't as distanced as she claimed. With every word, he recognized the painful mix of emotions that had shredded her soul. A mentally healthy person could knit themselves back together, but would never feel the same.

"He was still alive, but critical. Rushed into surgery. The family gathered. I'd had my ankle set and I made a nurse wheel me out to be with them while we waited. Some of the family started asking me about the accident." She shuddered. "What could I say? I'd insisted on driving."

"They must have understood that was the right thing to do. There's no way to predict what might have happened. The accident could have been even worse if Jared had been driving impaired."

Tess glanced at Connor, a strange, mirthless smile on her lips even though tears had streaked down her face. "Well, that's the thing. Jared's brother Erik had been out with him that night and he saw it differently. Right there at the hospital, he said that Jared hadn't drunk that much, only a few beers, and he could have driven perfectly fine. That maybe it was *me* who shouldn't have gotten behind the wheel."

She nodded at Connor's look of surprise. "The family believed Erik. They saw to it that I was given a blood test for alcohol content. I was clean—I hadn't touched a drop, but by then the doctors had come out to say that Jared hadn't made it and, well, those were the worst moments of my life. Deb, Jared's mother, broke down. I was numb, from shock and pain medication, but I remember Erik turning on me, and some of the others, asking me how it happened, how I could have let it happen...."

She stopped and took a deep breath. "There was

no answer.'' Slowly, she stretched out an arm until her palm was pressed to the window. On the other side of the glass, the rain continued unabated. She spread her fingers, flexing them as if she caressed her own wet cheek.

''Tess,'' Connor said, ''you have to know that grief can make people say cruel and unthinking things.''

She flinched and pulled her hand off the glass. Wiped her eyes. ''That's what I clung to. For the longest time, I hoped that they'd forgive me. After I'd put my own guilt behind me as much as I could, I tried again with the Johnsons, thinking that Jared's mom and dad would have—'' She sighed. ''I was going to say *recovered,* but that's not accurate. Parents don't recover from the loss of a child. Never.''

''But they must have realized that you were grieving, too.''

''Yes, I suppose they did. But they weren't in any shape to think of me. The rumors in town that I'd been the one who was drinking didn't help the situation. Even though the Johnsons knew that wasn't true, somehow that didn't matter. I was still guilty.''

Indignation gripped Connor. ''Did they let others believe the rumors?''

''Oh, no. They were fair. Even Erik admitted he'd been wrong to throw doubt on me—for *that* part of it. But it didn't really matter. I was the one driving. Nothing can change that.''

She looked at Connor over a lifted shoulder. ''I told you. The accident happened. After dealing with all the guilt and blame and regret, I learned to live with it. These days, I can even think about Jared without the pain. Perspective, you know. Maturity.''

''Yet his parents continue to shun you.''

''It's not that harsh. I talk to Gus. I can say hello to Deb and get a cordial response. We've even talked about the weather, or the library. But we don't socialize. And it's better that way, truly.''

''I don't think so.''

''You don't know beans.''

''You're forgetting my profession.''

Tess had found her purse where it had fallen to the floor and had removed her car keys. Grimly, she pushed her hair back from her face before sticking the key in the ignition. ''Writing about traumatic events is a lot different than living them.''

''Maybe so, but isn't it possible I can see the situation more clearly than you?''

She grimaced, staring straight ahead, right hand poised to turn the key. ''It's possible.''

''Trust me. I know about being dispassionate.''

''Is that…how you did what you did? Disconnecting your emotions?''

He paused. ''Yeah.''

''Uh-uh. I can't do that.''

''You shouldn't,'' he said. *I shouldn't have, either.* That's what haunted him.

She looked at him from the corners of her eyes. ''Then what *do* you suggest?''

''Talk to the Johnsons. Forgive them, and I think you'll find that they've forgiven you.''

''How neat and tidy that would be.''

Connor offered a tentative smile. "Isn't that how you like things?" he said, when what he really wanted to ask was how long she intended to live in limbo.

Until he remembered that he already knew.

CHAPTER NINE

THE KEY WAS PINCHED between her fingers. All she had to do was turn it.

Rain drummed on the roof. No thunder or lightning, but that was little reassurance. It wasn't that she let rainstorms disable her—she'd driven in them plenty. Maybe not plenty, but some. She avoided it when she could. And having to start up the car and calmly drive away right after Connor had wormed the entire story out of her was—

No big deal. Right? No. Big. Deal.

"What I've had enough of is sitting in this car, talking," Tess said, feeling testy. "Now I know why you're so successful. You got me to spill my guts once again and I know no more about you."

Connor shrugged. "I'll tell you anything."

She glanced at him, her body turning, leaning, before she put the brakes on. If she listened solely to her body, she'd be snuggling up in his lap like an affectionate cat. "Would you really?"

He smiled, so damn attractive and compelling, the sight of him opened a hollow inside her, even after the potluck supper and all the desserts a woman could eat.

"*If* you let me drive you home," he said.

He was so casual about it, it was easy for her to concede. "Okay, but I don't want to go out in the rain. You'll have to slide over. And what about your Jeep? If we leave it here, everyone will know."

"Are you asking me to sleep over?"

"What? I—uh—uh—" Her tongue was hopelessly tangled. The wicked glint in his eyes flustered her, so she couldn't think fast enough to untangle it.

He laughed. "Never mind. If the gossip really matters to you, I'll drive your car back here to pick up mine."

"Then they'll notice that my car was left here overnight. Even in a raging flood or a biblical pestilence, someone would notice and ask me why."

"Say it broke down. Or smile mysteriously. Nothing wrong with giving your reputation a twist, is there?"

Put that way, she liked the idea. Why not turn people's expectations upside down? "All right," she said, then looked at him and down at herself. "But how are we going to do this?"

"You lift up and I'll slide over."

She shimmied out from behind the wheel. "I don't want to end up in your lap."

There was amusement in his voice. "Should that happen, I'll maintain my gentlemanly demeanor."

She stopped with her hips up in the air, thinking too bad.

"Let me just—" Her rump hit his knee and she flinched, levering herself off him and turning at the same time, grabbing on to the seat behind his right shoulder. For a few seconds, they were snarled, face-to-face, and the car filled with his panting breath and her loud heartbeat. Again she was drawn to him, the familiar desire lighting up inside her, so she felt it beaming from her lips and her eyes, practically begging him for a kiss.

She thought he was going to do it, but then his knee came up and he was sliding out from beneath her and all she had was the brush of his chest against hers, a warm puff of breath on the side of her neck. She fell into the seat, slumping with disappointment. Why hadn't *she* kissed him?

Next time, next chance, she would.

"That wasn't *too* awkward," Connor said.

"Oh, no, not at all!" she chirped, before she saw the mischief in his grin.

"I haven't grappled in a car since I took Melissa Stroudt parking at Lookout Point."

"High school," Tess scoffed. "We all did that."

Connor started the car. "Who said I meant high school? That was only last year."

Tess chuckled, strapping herself in. "I don't believe you for a second."

"The local area must be make-out heaven—plenty of private parking opportunities on the backwoods roads."

"I'll say. There are out-of-the-way spots tucked down every road. And the kids know them all. What they don't realize is that so do their parents. Even I— well, *ahem,* you get the idea."

Connor chuckled. "I don't suppose it's only teen-agers who sneak off for some privacy."

"There have been a few incidents of adults who should know better getting caught with their pants down, so to speak."

"Not you, I'm sure. Not with your spotless reputation as The Good Librarian."

She sighed. "Sadly, you're right."

"I suppose you've even forgotten where to go...."

"Oh, no. There's High Rock Road and Boswell Lake and the logging road out past the Buck Stop—" She caught his eye and stopped suddenly. "You tricked me! I'm not saying I've been to all those places, I only *heard* about them—" She broke off again, laughing. "Guess I should shut up now, while I'm behind."

Connor was keeping his eyes on the road, but the way he was smiling made her feel all warm and melty. What a goose she was. She looked out the window and realized that he'd been driving throughout the conversation and she hadn't been worried at all.

"You could give me a tour," he said. "Which way am I going?"

"Keep heading north out of town on Blackbear Road, past Maxine's Cottages." A puddle splashed high as the car made the wide turn onto the road to her house. Tess gripped the strap of the seat belt angled across her chest. She wasn't nervous, just a little edgy. Logically, she could see that Connor was a competent driver. The roads weren't treacherous.

"What about it?" he said.

She closed her eyes, letting the swish of the windshield wipers steady her. "What? A tour?"

"Of your favorite make-out spots."

She smiled faintly. "It's been so long..."

"Uh-huh."

They drove in silence along the empty country road. Eventually they passed the rustic stone cottages on the Blackbear River that Maxine Robbin rented to hunters and fishermen. "Another mile," Tess said, watching the road again as it twisted and turned through the woods. The headlights lit the slackening rain into silver threads. "Look out for deer. They shouldn't be moving in the rain, but you never know."

"I'll be careful."

She breathed, but softly so he wouldn't notice she'd forgotten to. "I know."

"You remember," he said, coaxing her to talk. It took her a few beats to figure out he was referring to the make-out spots again. "Did you go parking with Jared?".

She liked that Connor was willing to bring up Jared's name. Many years ago, she'd had enough of being the delicate flower struck by tragedy. By now it was frustrating to be treated that way. Yet some of the locals still seemed to expect her to break out into tears at Jared's mention.

True, there were times she was sad to think of how relentlessly life had gone on without him, even when she'd been sure hers had ended, too. But there was also something comforting about that—holding on to the knowledge that there was more to the world than any one person, or any one town. The earth was not as fragile as its human occupants.

"Now that I recall," Tess said teasingly, quite ready to set aside somber discussion, "the road out to the lighthouse was another favorite. And the grounds, too, when we could still cross the causeway. In fact, I let Jared get to second base, parked beneath the tall pine near the rocks."

Connor shook his head. "And I only got a single."

"But that was on your first at bat," she said. "Jared's average wasn't as high in his first few attempts."

They exchanged a look. Tess's heart beat a little faster, wondering what he expected. She'd never jumped into bed with a man who could qualify as a stranger in many aspects. All of her sexual relationships had come about after due deliberation. Despite her flights of fantasy, it was her nature to take lovemaking as a serious act of intimacy. She really shouldn't be contemplating otherwise....

Except that she was. Connor made her think—and feel—in all sorts of unexpected ways.

Through the drizzle, the Coopers' old, abandoned farmhouse and barn loomed on the left. She cleared her throat. "My house is over this hill and around the bend."

"Over the hill and around the bend, to Tess's house we go," Connor sang, a little off-key and lighthearted in a way that wasn't characteristic of the man she knew. But it looked good on him.

"You don't have to try so hard," she said. "I'm not a basket case. You've already distracted me enough. *And* we're home. Turn right, here at the willow—this is my driveway."

Connor turned the car beneath the graceful branches, tires squelching. The short dirt driveway was all mud. "Home safe," he said, braking the car at the very end of the driveway, as close to the house as possible. He peered at her home through the windshield as the wipers stopped and the raindrops collected in fat splats. "Why do you live so far out of town?"

"Because one day I was biking out here and I came across this house and fell in love with it. I could afford it because it was a fixer-upper. I've been fixing for nearly five years now, and there's always more to do, but I've enjoyed every minute of it."

She was extremely house-proud. Not because her bungalow was grand or showy—it wasn't. The modest two-bedroom house was vintage 1920s. But she'd worked hard on the place, completing many of the repairs herself with the help of every fix-it book available in the library. There was comfort in knowing that not only had she recovered from the blow of Jared's death, but she'd thrived. She was self-sufficient. And she believed that a strong woman was a woman less easily hurt.

Independence could be lonely. But Tess would rather that than her mother's alternative.

"I guess it doesn't look like much to you," she said to Connor over the sound of raindrops plonking on the hood and roof of the car. The bungalow was small and cozy, comfortably old-fashioned.

"You forget, I live in New York, where apartments are known to be cramped, or on the road in a series of look-alike hotel rooms. Your place is a palace."

"It's not up to Bay House standards. No stately grandeur or sweeping views."

"No gnomish hosts holding you captive. No lurking maids rattling the doorknob."

Tess thought *she* might rattle his doorknob, given the chance. "Speaking of Bay House, do you intend to stay until the lighthouse is habitable?"

"I don't know about habitable. I hired Noah Saari to do some of the basic carpentry repairs. He recommended an electrician and plumber who are willing to take a look and give me estimates. Other than that, I may strip the wallpaper and paint some of the rooms so the place is presentable. After my grandfather visits…we'll see."

"You could live there. It's perfect for a writer." She chuckled, realizing her assumption. "Or maybe not. I'm buying into the stereotype of the lonely, tortured writer wrangling with the demons in his head in splendid isolation. What writers probably need is reliable electricity, Internet access, friendly companions to bounce ideas off and cups of hot cocoa on demand." With another light laugh, she reached across and pulled the keys. "Forget the lighthouse. You should stay at Bay House permanently."

Connor did not follow her lead. "You're overlooking one thing. I'm no longer writing."

"Oh, but you will. I'm sure of it."

His head cocked. "How come?"

"I've started reading your books, Connor. You have such skill. You can't abandon it."

"There are some who would applaud exactly that."

"Because of the Strange case? Pah."

"How can you dismiss it? Before, when you first found out, you looked at me like I was a monster."

"I didn't know you then. I jumped to conclusions."

"Knowing me doesn't change the facts. I let a murderer out of jail and chances are he's going to attempt another abduction. When he does, it won't be only a matter of guilt on my conscience. I'll have blood on my hands."

Connor thrust the door open and stepped out of the car into the rain. He raced around and opened her door. Cool, fresh air washed across Tess's heated cheeks as they hurried along the cobblestone walkway to her sheltered front door.

"I'll leave you here," he said, dodging away.

"Wait. You don't have the keys." She selected the house key and turned the lock. In Alouette, most citizens didn't bother locking their doors, but she was safety conscious, living alone out in the country. After swinging the door open, she fumbled with the key ring, taking her time to remove the car key for Connor. "You should come inside and dry off," she said, sounding like she'd swallowed a cup of gravel. She kept her head down. "The rain is stopping."

He'd stopped under the overhang of the peaked entry roof, apparently not noticing that the runoff was dripping down the side of his head and splashing his shoulder. "Tess," he said, almost a groan.

"I'll give you a cup of hot cocoa."

"You're too good."

"I'm not Emmie. It's only instant."

"Not the cocoa. You as a person. You're too generous in your outlook. You see the best, where others see—" Suddenly he shuddered, plucking at his shirt and wiping the side of his neck. The cold rain had trickled inside his collar.

"Come inside," Tess said, tugging him closer to the door. And to her. "I'll get you a towel."

"This might not be the best thing for you, but for me…" He let her pull him inside. "I couldn't dream up a better scenario."

Scenario? What the hell did that mean? It sounded so…false. Like a fantasy.

Right. Her bailiwick.

She said, "I can make my own decisions about what's good for me, thank you."

"You were right, you know. I may not be a smuggler, but I'm still not someone you should be involved with."

"Too bad. I'm strangely attracted to tortured artists," she whispered, setting aside her questions to stroke his wet cheek. "Wait here."

"What kind of guy was Jared?" Connor called, standing obediently on the needlepoint rug in her small foyer.

This time, she felt a spurt of annoyance at his use

of Jared's name. It was as if Connor was purposely trying to put a damper on the evening.

She came from the bathroom with a hand towel. "Jared was about your height, muscular and stocky. Dark blond hair, blue eyes. He was the opposite of a tortured artist. Very open, to the point of bluntness. A simple guy, I guess you'd say. He liked sports and the outdoors and he liked me. Sometimes I think he liked me so much because I wasn't as clingy as other girls. He could take me fishing and I'd be happy sitting silently in the boat for hours, sipping my lemonade and reading a book."

Connor wiped his face and neck, then scrubbed the towel over his hair. There was a big wet patch on the shoulder of his Polo shirt. "You two were together for more reason than that."

She lifted her hands in a shrug. "It's been so long, the love has faded. I do remember that I was quite willing to give up my dreams of moving away in order to marry Jared."

"Why?"

"For his family. They were already my family—almost—and that was something I craved."

"And then you lost them when you lost him."

"Yes." She tilted her head, eyes narrowing. "Are we having a conversation, or are you studying me as a psychologically interesting subject?" She didn't wait for his answer. "Come inside. Let's sit. Would you like coffee, cocoa or something with a bit of a nip?"

"Hmm. Do you bite, or only nibble?"

"Me?" She hooted in laughter, then was even more appalled by the shrill sound she'd made. Pressing her palms to her cheeks, she dropped onto the sofa beside him. "God, Connor. You embarrass me. I'm thirty-two years old—I shouldn't be feeling like a schoolgirl."

"Why not?" He covered her hands and dragged them off her face, keeping hold of them as he pulled her closer. "That's the fun part of discovering a mutual attraction—the newness, the nervous excitement. We both get to feel like teenagers again."

He nuzzled her cheek, her hair, not kissing her yet, but making the anticipation of it course across the surface of her skin like a thousand stinging needles of rain. She shivered into it, wanting to know the feel of his hands and the taste of his tongue.

"I haven't felt like this in so long." His breath was warm on the side of her neck.

She murmured, vaguely remembering his promise to answer all questions. "Are you trying to distract me again?" She didn't really care. She wanted to be distracted.

They sank deeper into the plush sofa. Connor's hands were at her waist and the small of her back now, holding her like a fragile vessel. That was wrong. Tess wanted…strong passion. Unbreakable, undying need.

She threw her arms around his shoulders. When he wrenched his head back in surprise, she kissed him. Resoundingly.

"Tess!" he said, his eyes flashing at her boldness

before he let out a low grunt and returned the kiss tenfold.

If their kisses atop the lighthouse had been a soft, floaty dream, they plunged directly into the deepest water now, hungry and raw. They drank from each other's mouths in long, greedy gulps. Their tongues tangled. Their legs, too. His hands were on her the way she'd imagined—sure and strong and holding her firmly, when they weren't exploring new territory. He cupped one breast during a long, brain-numbing kiss, then slipped his hand up beneath her shirt and directly inside her bra without unhooking it.

The shock of his fingers on her nipple was electrifying. She sucked in a quick, audible gasp of air.

Immediately he drew back, jerking his hand away from her breast. The elastic of her bra snapped against her rib cage. She winced.

"I'm sorry," he said. "Did I hurt you?"

She blinked rapidly, struggling to make a coherent response. "Y-you didn't...or if you did—" She licked her burning lips. "It hurts so good."

"No, I rushed you." He sat forward on the edge of the cushions, his head in his hands, fingers knotted in his hair. "I'm sorry."

"Sorry?" she squeaked.

"You need time," he said, not looking at her.

"I've had nothing *but* time!"

"All the more reason to take this slow."

"What?"

Connor stood. "I have to go."

"Go?"

He leaned down and kissed the top of her head. "See you soon."

She sat without moving as he walked out of the living room. She heard the front door, the light patter of rain, the car's engine, the squelch of mud as he drove away. Then silence.

He'd kissed her like he meant it and then he'd picked up and left. She was stupid with hormones.

Damn, she thought, staring at the walls of her living room. They were a lovely sunlit cream in the daytime, but seemed dingy with shadows this evening. There were no curtains. The windows looked like black holes, streaked with rain.

She replayed Connor's sudden exit. *What was that about?*

Take it slow, he'd said.

She sat and thought that over, but her mind wasn't clicking the way it normally did. Too many residual tremors going on below the neck.

Well, as long as they were taking it *somewhere,* she decided at last, and got up to make herself a cup of warm milk. She'd never sleep otherwise.

NOAH SAARI WAS a big man, muscled so thickly he resembled a tree trunk. He wore a flannel shirt and work boots with wool socks even though it was the tail end of June, his only concessions to the season being a pair of khaki shorts and the frayed armholes where he'd torn off the sleeves of his shirt. His biceps were huge. Connor felt like a city-boy flyweight by comparison.

Emmie Whitaker had gladly given permission for Noah to halt progress on the Bay House rehab in order to do a rush job on the most vital repairs at the lighthouse. A plumber had already been by to make emergency repairs to the pipes. The rewiring job could wait.

Today Noah was replacing the rotted trim around several of the windows while Connor followed, caulking, filling and sanding. They'd made good progress in the past week, repairing the roof and installing new windows. After today, the lighthouse cottage would be watertight again. Once the rotted floorboards were replaced, the lighthouse would be adequate for Sonny's inspection, should they need to push up the visit. The old man would be damn proud.

"So," Noah said, "you remember the Lindstrom brothers? They were the leaders of the crowd, one way or another."

Connor and Noah had figured out that they had probably met as boys, although Connor couldn't remember much beyond the pack of kids who'd gathered at the public beach and hung around the Berry Dairy ice-cream stand. "I remember Terry—he was closest to my age. He still around?"

"Not at the moment. There was some trouble...."

"What happened?"

Noah answered after a pause. "I guess it's common knowledge. Terry had a problem with alcohol. He's at a treatment center."

"I'm surprised at that. I remember him being very responsible, as the oldest brother and all."

"He took Rick's death hard."

Connor nodded. They went back to hammering and puttying. Noah had already explained about the middle Lindstrom boy, Rick, perishing in a fire out West.

"Wasn't that the baby brother, Pete, at the Scrabble tournament?" Connor asked after a while. "The young blond guy? I don't remember him at all."

"He's the youngest, about twenty-five. Comes back to town for the summers."

Connor picked up a piece of sandpaper. "Can't say I recognize anyone from my days here. At ten, I was most impressed with the boats in the marina and the time I ran across a black bear in the woods."

"You'll learn the faces soon enough, whether you want to or not." Noah glanced sideways. "Depends how long you stay."

"Emmie and Claire put you up to that question? Do they want the room back?" Connor suspected that wasn't the case. His sojourn in the bridal suite had been the source of much gibing at the lumberyard and the hardware store. He'd even been offered a piece of "wedding cake" at the diner when he'd stopped by for a quick meal.

"Hell, no." Noah fit a length of quarter-round trim into place. "They're just being nosy. Feel free not to answer."

"Nosy about the lighthouse?"

"About that, and…you know."

"Tess Bucek," Connor said under his breath. Heat shot up his throat and south to his groin. Merely her name was enough to get him going. He hadn't been

able to keep her out of his mind—or his dreams—
since those last, wild kisses on the night of the rainstorm.

He'd returned to her house early the next morning
and they'd managed the car switch without attracting
any notice. She'd been strictly friendly, and he
couldn't help wondering whether she'd taken a second, less emotional, look at his track record and decided it was a mistake to become involved. At the
back of his mind, he knew that was only his shame
talking. Tess's word was solid.

In the past week, he'd run into her a couple of
times at the retirement home, and they had gone for
coffee afterward. They'd discussed his grandfather's
progress. Other conversation was kept light and amusing by an unspoken mutual agreement. He'd kissed
her again, just once, in the parking lot, but separate
cars helped stop the moment from escalating. Even
though he'd had to wrestle the steering wheel of his
Jeep to keep the vehicle from following her home of
its own volition.

"I oughta warn you the women are conspiring.
They think of themselves as matchmakers. In fact,
I'm supposed to see that you're back at Bay House
on time for supper, because there'll be a special
guest." Noah scratched his jaw. "Sorry. You know
how females get when any hint of romance is
roused."

"The wedding curse isn't enough for them?"

"You think of it as a *curse,* huh?"

Connor rubbed a thumb across the puttied nail.

Smooth as silk. "That's what the old guys at the diner called it. I was recently treated to a retelling of the legend and a recitation of the famous ditty."

Noah had stopped hammering to gaze out the window at the rolling lake. "Claire stayed there when she first came to town, you know."

"Uh-oh."

Noah shrugged his massive shoulders. "I tumbled without a push."

"You sorry sap." The two men rapped knuckles, laughing.

"We went through the same speculation. It only let up when you checked in to Bay House." Noah shook his shaggy head, looking unperturbed by the extended teasing. "I'd just as soon get married quick and have it over with, but Claire's not letting anyone rush her into a decision."

"Maybe there'll be a double wedding."

Noah almost dropped his upraised hammer. He caught it by the head and tucked it into his tool belt. "You're kidding me. Man, you work fast."

"Not me, not me." Connor backed off, palms outturned. "Haven't you noticed that Bill Maki has a crush on Emmie?"

"Bill? How could you tell? He never talks."

"I've seen signs. Subtle, I admit. Mostly, he watches her a lot."

"Interesting," Noah muttered. His expression became speculative. "What are you suggesting?"

"Nothing. Except—"

"Payback."

"That would be—"

"Devious," Noah said. "But Emmie deserves it. She's a bossy wench. Claire, too. Could be amusing to watch their reactions when the table's turned."

"What do you have in mind?"

"We'll see." Noah moved on to the next window, in the kitchen, but after a while, he came back into the front room and said, "Come to supper. Follow my lead."

They grinned at each other.

"I guess I can do that." Connor scooped up a dollop of putty and put the jar on the windowsill. "Hell, just listen to us. We're as bad as the women, letting the Bay House mystique play games with our heads."

"Yeah. We should be talking about baseball. Has living in New York made you a Yankees fan yet?"

"Not on your life. Detroit Tigers, all the way."

They continued working. Eventually, they took a break and went out to retrieve the six-pack they'd dunked in the lake, anchored by a heavy stone.

Gulls scattered as Connor kicked off his shoes and waded into the water to pull up the beer. There was no sandy bottom out here, only flat shale and red sandstone, layered by the smooth round pebbles flung to shore by the waves. The water was frigid. The footing was slick and uneven, but it felt so good he stopped and admired the view: the picturesque lighthouse, the dark green hillside and steep rocks on the other side of the bay, the deep curve of blue water in between.

Not such a stretch of imagination, to think of living here.

Connor's toes started to sting. He climbed onto the rocks, pulling apart the six-pack. He tossed one of the icy, dripping cans to Noah, who was sitting nearby sprawled in the sunshine.

"Life doesn't get much better than this," Connor observed. "Even if that does sound like a beer commercial."

"Nope, it doesn't." Noah's can spritzed as he popped the tab. "Hard work, a good woman, hot supper waiting at home and peace of mind. That's all I need."

"Hell, I'd be happy to settle for two of the four," Connor said, realizing that once he had finished with the lighthouse, said goodbye to Tess and checked out of Bay House, he'd be zero for zero.

Maybe it was time to think seriously about exploring his options.

CHAPTER TEN

AT TESS'S KNOCK, two plump, wrinkled faces appeared in the doorway to Bay House.

"Welcome, Tess!" Emmie beamed. "It's been too long since we've had you to Sunday dinner."

Toivo chortled. "You're a sight for sore ice, girlie."

"What a coincidence," Tess said, interpreting the mangled phrase as she exchanged brief hugs and cheek smacks with the sibling innkeepers. "I brought ice cream—the rich, creamy, decadent kind."

"With chunks?" Toivo asked, taking the freezer bag and peering inside. The wisps of white hair that usually floated around his head had been wetted and combed behind his ears.

"One quart of plain French Vanilla, one quart of Moose Tracks. With double-fudge chunks."

Emmie said thank-you and gave Toivo a push. "Go on then, cabbage head. Get that ice cream to the freezer before your hot breath melts it into a puddle."

"Bay House is looking grand," Tess commented, taking in the gleaming floors and freshly painted walls of the foyer. In Claire's first act as the new manager, she'd ordered the ghastly wallpaper stripped, the old rug taken up and the wood floors refinished. The renovations team had moved upstairs to bring new life to the run-down guest rooms, though Emmie had decreed that Valentina's bridal suite was not to be touched.

"Our Claire has the fancy ideas," Emmie said, exuding mixed emotions about the changes.

"Business has picked up?" Through Claire, Tess was aware that the B and B had been running on the brink of disaster for years.

"Full house," Emmie said. She winked. "That's the *only* reason I was persuaded to put Connor into the bridal suite."

"I'm sure."

"Because I don't believe in exploiting Valentina's legacy."

"Of course not," Tess said. Everyone in town knew how much Emmie treasured her family history, particularly the tale of how her dear mother, Mae Koski, a lowly Finnish housemaid, had married the only grandson of the illustrious lumber baron Ogden Whitaker and become the mistress of Bay House. The tale about the presumed suicide of Ogden's haughty sister, Valentina Whitaker, was also valued, though more for its history than as a source of family pride. Emmie turned down most every attempt interested parties made to get into the supposedly cursed room, which only fostered the legend.

"Has it occurred to anyone here that Roxy is unmarried?" Tess asked. "Maybe Connor has his eye on *her,* now that he's destined to be a bridegroom."

Emmie folded her hands over her middle and frowned as if she hadn't thought about the wedding prophecy getting twisted in a direction other than the one she'd planned.

"Ha! Roxy would brain us if we tried to set her up." Claire entered from the front parlor to greet Tess. "The men aren't back from the lighthouse yet. How long can you hold dinner, Em?"

"Mama Mae always served Sunday dinner on the dot of 1:00 p.m. and you know that I do the same. If they'd bothered to consult me, I could have told Noah and Connor it was a bad idea to squeeze more work in on a morning meant for worship. Noah has a head on his shoulders, but that Connor—" Emmie *tsked* her tongue. "Eh, I swear he gets so involved in that lighthouse he overlooks all bodily comforts. Even eating!" A buzzer rang and she hurried off to the kitchen, the tail ends of her apron strings bouncing on her round behind.

"May I help?" Tess called, but Emmie was gone.

"We managed, thanks," Claire said. "I made the salad, Roxy peeled potatoes and Cassia set the table. Toivo and Bill—well, they sat around the kitchen and snitched croutons and crisp bits of chicken fat like a couple of old billy goats."

The aroma of roasted chicken and baking-powder biscuits had wafted into the open dining room. "Suddenly I'm starving," Tess said.

Claire's laugh rang hollow. "You think you came here for *food?*"

"Why else?" Tess dropped the innocent act and

shook her head, exasperated with the conniving. "You know, it's not truly a prophecy if you guys have to work to make it come true."

"What work? This is the regular Sunday-after-church dinner. Emmie decided you and Connor needed a nudge, that's all."

"Emmie, huh?"

"And Cassia," Claire said.

"What about you?"

"Maybe me. I was in charge of seeing that Noah got Connor here on time."

Tess laughed. "Isn't one bride per year enough for you people?"

"Here comes Noah and Connor," Cassia called from the parlor. She appeared in the doorway, dressed in a flattering gauze blouse with wide pleated sleeves and a matching broomstick skirt that fluttered against her legs and the wheels of her chair. Her red hair was piled on top of her head, knotted with a bit of lace. She even wore makeup, including artful eye shadow that brought out the green tinge of her hazel irises. "I just spotted the Jeep coming up the driveway."

"Wow," said Claire, looking the younger woman over. "I've never seen you so dressed up."

Cassia brushed off the compliment. "Oh, you know. I just felt like it, for a change."

Claire made an odd face, but Tess scarcely noticed. Connor's arrival had given her a fluttery feeling. Hunger pains, she named it, though she could feel her eyes widening in anticipation. Connor was *her* sight for sore ice. And rain, sleet, snow, thunder and hail.

She'd been to Sunday dinner at Bay House many times before. Most frequently during her first few years on her own. Emmie's sharp eye spotted the souls in need. The dinner was always lavish and traditional, colorful and chaotic. Comforting in every way.

Yet Tess found it hard to imagine Connor feeling comfortable amid the typical hubbub. She reminded herself that he *had* showed up for the Scrabble tournament. Perhaps he was becoming acclimated to Alouette-style society and felt less ill at ease, even being the center of attention. It might take a while, but she was sure that people would get over his celebrity and accept him as a familiar face. Not quite one of their own, but not one on his own, either.

Noah came in first, filling the foyer with his tall frame and wide shoulders. Tess hung back, looking for Connor. He slipped in behind the big woodsman, unobtrusive to everyone but her. He said hello to the group as a whole and bounded up the stairs to clean up, disappearing in an instant like a wild creature. Even so, the brief sight of him made her heart leap.

For the first time, Tess allowed herself to wonder if she was falling in love.

Oblivious, Claire took her arm as the assemblage moved into the dining room. Toivo and Bill were already seated at their customary places. Cassia wheeled into her empty spot, her face lowered while she fussed with her skirt. Right on time, Emmie came out with the biscuits, and Tess and Claire followed her back into the kitchen to fetch the heaped serving dishes.

Noah was washing at the kitchen sink with his shirt off, splashing like a golden retriever. Tess saw the pale scars that had once caused such a fuss among the locals' gossiping tongues. Like many previous instances, the severity of the scars had been greatly exaggerated.

Laughing and scolding, Claire approached her man with a towel. When he turned to scoop her up into a nuzzling bear hug, Tess picked up a platter of corn on the cob and made a discreet exit. Someday…

They all gathered around the table, Noah and Claire on one side with Cassia, the Whitakers at the ends, and Tess in the middle of the other side between Bill and Connor. "Where's Roxy?" she asked after Emmie had said grace and the ritual passing-of-the-dishes had begun. Tess had halfway expected there to be at least a few of the B and B guests at the dinner as well—hospitality was a religion with Emmie—but they all seemed to be out of the house for the afternoon.

"She's berry picking," Emmie said. "No sense in that, the best time to go is in the morning before the sun's hot. But there's no reasoning with Roxy. Too hardheaded."

"Wonder who she gets that from," Noah said, carving the roast chicken. He put a drumstick on Toivo's plate.

Emmie ignored the comment.

Bill, to her left, spoke up from behind a biscuit slathered in butter. "Too early for blueberries."

"She went after raspberries," Emmie said. "The thicket near the Robbins' stone cottages is chock-full of 'em."

Toivo was eyeing Bill with some suspicion. "You been checking our patches?" They were known to have a great blueberry-picking rivalry, egging each other on to spend entire days in the bush during the hottest days of July and August. Emmie usually ended up with so many quarts of the fruit, she canned for days on end. Claire had begun offering jars of sweet jam to Bay House guests for purchase, complete with quaint computer-designed labels.

Bill's eyes flickered. He smiled slyly and bit into the biscuit.

Noah cleared his throat. "Bill, this year, why don't you take Emmie out berry picking?"

Air expelled from several sets of lungs. The guests put down their forks and leaned forward with interest.

Bill stared at his plate without responding, though his gaunt cheeks were suddenly tinged a mottled pink.

"Get her out of the kitchen for a change," Noah added.

Toivo chuckled. "She couldn't take the heat out there. Me 'n Bill practice power berry picking."

Tess looked at Connor, expecting him to be tolerantly bemused by the Yooper sport of berry picking. Instead, he chimed in with Noah. "I agree. Emmie deserves a day out in the sunshine."

The two younger men exchanged a look. Both Tess

and Claire intercepted it. They looked at each other and nodded in understanding.

"Make it an outing," Claire said.

"With a picnic basket," Tess added.

"Like a date!" Cassia sang.

Silence fell. They all looked toward Emmie, sitting at the head of the table nearest the kitchen door. It wasn't like her to hold her tongue for so long.

Emmie's flush matched Bill's, but she dabbed her lips with a napkin and carefully set it aside. She dusted off the shelf of her full bust, garbed in the gaudy sunflower-print dress that was her Sunday best. "Nonsense," she said. "I have more important things to do with my time than chasing after blueberries with these two scalawags."

No one said a word.

She surveyed the table, avoiding stares. "Goodness. We're almost out of biscuits." With that, she popped up and fled to the kitchen.

Toivo sputtered, looking alarmed.

Bill chewed like a cow, showing no expression, as usual.

The rest of them, the younger generation, elbowed each other and tittered and made funny faces.

Emmie returned and plunked a second basket of biscuits on the table. There was fire in her eye as she glared up and down the rows of dinner guests. "We'll have no more of that nonsense. Eat up while it's hot," she commanded, and they all dropped their chins and fell to the task with seemly haste.

WHEN THE MEAL was finished, Bill was the first to take off, snatching his cap from the peg by the kitchen door and skedaddling with only a mumbled "Good dinner" for Emmie.

Soon after, Noah and Claire left for their cabin in the woods, where they were living in rustic happiness without modern conveniences. Several weeks ago, when Claire had come into the library for books on homesteading, she'd confided to Tess that though she preferred her electricity and water at the flick of a switch and a twist of the tap, there was something very romantic about their little love nest beside a small inland lake. Tess had thought that Claire was too besotted to see straight, but now she had an inkling of how falling in love might change one's perspective.

She wouldn't say no to a nice long interlude with Connor at the lighthouse. Over the past few reading lessons, the bits and pieces she'd gathered from Sonny's comments about his married life at Gull Rock were enough to melt even a woman less prone to fantasy than Tess.

She suspected that Connor, once smitten, would be as devoted a partner as his grandfather had been. It was that obsessive, single-minded streak, and the depth of feeling. Which, unfortunately, could lead to torture and despair as easily as rapture.

As the remaining group moved out of the dining room, Cassia announced that she intended to practice for the Scrabble tournament, having found a cheat sheet of lesser-known two- and three-letter words on the Internet. "Give me the list. I'll drill you," Emmie offered. "But we should go outdoors to the garden. You're looking pale, *pikku.*"

"What do you expect? I'm a redhead!" Cassia efficiently maneuvered her chair toward her room on the ground floor. "Hold on just a sec, I'll get my sunscreen."

"And a hat," Emmie called. She turned to Connor and Tess. "Will you join us?"

"I know plenty of words, thanks," Connor said.

"Not *aa* and *udo,*" Cassia said, backing out of her room. She smiled saucily at him, and Tess was struck by how pretty the girl was. And that she was flirting with Connor. "But never mind. I forgot that you're one of my opponents."

They departed, making their way through the sunroom at the back of the house, leaving Tess and Connor with Toivo. He rocked on his heels, blueberry eyes narrowing as his mischievous grin sprang up. "Hey, I've got one for youse two. I was coming outta Maki's Pasty Shop with a bag of pasties when my friend Eino walked up. He was something hungry, so he says would I give him a pasty if he guessed how many I got in the bag." Toivo peered at them. "Have you heard this story before?"

Connor said no. Tess, who recognized an Eino and Toivo joke when she heard one, just smiled. "Eino and Toivo" were a fictional pair, the legendary butt of a series of dumb Finn jokes.

"So I tell Eino that if he can guess how many I have, I'd give him both of them." Toivo's eyes danced. "And that Eino, he goes, 'Holy wha! Then I'm guessing you have five.'"

Connor snorted air through his nose, then broke into a chuckle. Toivo bounced with excitement at his joke's success. Tess rolled her eyes, but she was smiling.

"You know," she said, "I'll bet Eino—I mean, Bill is already at the blueberry bush, checking for ripeness."

Toivo couldn't get out the door fast enough.

"Eino and Toivo?" Connor said once they were alone.

"Yooper jokes. You don't want to get Toivo started. He thinks he really *is* the legendary Toivo, and sometimes the rest of us agree." She cocked her head back. "So it's down to just you and me. What do you want to do?"

Connor's black eyebrows knitted. "Should we go out to the garden and spend a lovely Sunday afternoon practicing Scrabble words?"

"Hmm." Tess pretended to think. All she really cared about was being with him. It didn't matter what they did. "You're not in a rush to get back to the lighthouse?"

"We've accomplished a lot. I'll be painting next, but I can afford to take the rest of the day off. What I should do is go and visit Grandpa. Maybe take him out, if he's feeling well enough."

She patted his arm. "You're such a good grandson."

Connor turned his hand over to hold hers, fingers

twined. "Want to come along? Or have you had enough of me and my troubles?"

"I'd love to go," Tess said. "If you'll agree to help me with the notes I mentioned. You know, the interviews with Sonny. So far, I'm doing all the work."

He frowned. "Don't think I can't see what you're up to."

Her smile was undaunted. "Never fear. My motives are purely altruistic."

The afternoon did not turn out the way she'd hoped. An odd tension was in the air from the moment they arrived at the nursing home. Two female aides in powder-blue uniforms stared hard at Connor when he walked through the hall to Sonny's room, then huddled together and whispered behind their hands, throwing daggers at him with their eyes. "Heinous," one of them said, making sure to be loud enough for Connor to hear. "What is the world coming to."

Tess was appalled by their rudeness. No wonder he was so prickly around strangers.

Connor's step didn't falter. His eyes betrayed nothing, but she saw the set of his jaw, the deepening of the hollows in his cheeks and the lines around his mouth. She slung an arm around his shoulders, cozying up more than she normally would in public, but his arm remained hanging lifelessly by his side. She squeezed him anyway, offering support even if he didn't want it.

A nurse with a similarly foul air greeted them outside Sonny's room. "Mr. Mitchell's had a bad day," she said. She scowled at Connor. "You can sit with him for a while, but I'd advise not turning on the TV set. We don't want him to get agitated."

Connor shrugged. "That's fine. We don't usually watch TV during our visits anyway."

The nurse gave him a curt nod. "Keep the visit short." She departed.

"They're not always this frosty with you," Tess said, mystified. "Are they?"

"Maybe they weren't sure about who I was before."

She wrinkled her nose. "I'm sorry that I dismissed your concerns so lightly. I thought you were too sensitive to every slight. That maybe you even looked for disapproval."

Connor was walking around the bed. "You might be right about that."

"No. It's real." Of course it was. Hadn't she seen the media coverage? Experiencing the censure firsthand was different, though.

Connor didn't seem to want to talk about it. His concern was all for his grandfather, who lay flat in the hospital bed, gnarled fingers clasping the covers drawn up to his chest.

"Grandpa?" he said.

Tess thought Sonny was sleeping, until she got close and saw that his pink-rimmed eyes were wide open and staring—unfocused—at the ceiling. His pallor was disturbing, particularly after he'd seemed so vigorous just recently when he'd made good progress on the reading lessons. Blue veins drew a road map beneath the parchment of his skin.

Gently, Connor touched his grandfather's skull.

No reaction. The room was utterly silent.

Tess faded back from the bed, intending to leave them alone.

"Mary Angela," the old man suddenly said. He lifted his head off the pillow. "Don't go."

Connor motioned Tess over.

She hovered over the bed, letting Sonny see her face. His fingers clawed the air, and she gave him her hands to hold. His fingers clamped over hers. "It's Tess Bucek, Mr. Mitchell. I'm visiting with Connor."

"Mary Angela?" he said, gazing at her.

She opened her mouth to correct him, but Connor shook his head no. "It's good to see you," she said instead, hoping her voice would prod his memory. "How are you feeling?"

Sonny mumbled.

Connor leaned over the bed. "Is there anything you need, Grandpa?"

"Tell that girl of yours to come back."

"I'm here," Tess said, not wanting to mislead him.

Sonny looked at her and she thought there was recognition in his eyes before he closed them in exhaustion, letting his head fall back on the pillow. His mouth opened as he fumbled for words. He clutched her hands and croaked, "Stay with me...."

"I will, I promise."

Connor got her a chair. For fifteen minutes, they sat on either side of Sonny's bed. Now and then he spoke coherently, seeming to understand who she was. Other times he became agitated and Connor calmed him by speaking of the lighthouse, the lake, their summers together. When Sonny finally slept, they disengaged and moved quietly out of the room.

Connor went to find the nurse to ask what was going on. Tess waited in the lobby, watching a family arrive with a fruit basket, a bouquet and a birthday balloon. She'd brought Sonny flowers last week, the daisies he'd said Mary Angela liked, but he'd acted as if they embarrassed him.

Connor was back shortly, offering only a shrug. "It's the meds, according to the nurse. He's had a lot of pain from the arthritis and they're worried about his other ailments, too. They had to up the dosage on some of his pills and that's making him foggy."

"Do you think we should stay longer to keep an eye on him?"

"He'll be sleeping. I'll come back in a few hours and see if he's any more alert." Tiredly, Connor swiped a hand over his face. "I hope he improves, or…"

There was no need to finish the thought.

Tess hugged him. After a moment, he returned the embrace, burying his face against her hair. "It's going to happen," she said. "Sonny will live to see Gull Rock again." She thought of the way Connor had talked about the lighthouse over his grandfather's bed, painting a picture with words as only a talented writer could. "One way or another."

Connor muttered. "I'm not sure anymore if it's him or me that needs this."

She pulled back a little, framing his face in her hands. "Maybe both?"

"Maybe." He touched a kiss to her lips. "And maybe we both need you."

Tess smiled into his stark, hurt-filled eyes, silently sending him a share of the strong emotions that had made her heart open like a blossoming rose.

THEY RETURNED to Bay House so Tess could pick up her car and Connor could load his Jeep with the gallons of primer and paint he'd need to begin the next stage of the lighthouse project. She seemed absorbed in her own thoughts as they approached the inn, its sandstone facade a deep golden red in the afternoon sun. He hoped he hadn't insulted her by turning down her offer to go and help him paint.

At the moment, he felt too raw to have her near.

Without his armor of cynicism, he had no defense against the warmth and brightness she brought into his life...his heart. Part of him recognized the perversity of not wanting that. But he wasn't ready. He wasn't worthy.

Although Connor repeatedly told himself he'd made the technically correct choice when he'd reported the evidence that the police had coerced a witness to implicate Roderick Strange, the result hung over him like a pall. As long as the man was free, Connor wouldn't be at ease.

And as long as he was stuck in this hellish limbo, he couldn't love Tess.

"I'll go in and say hi before I leave," she said.

He followed her.

A huge pile of vacation flotsam had been dumped in the entry hall—life preservers, goggles, swim fins, damp swimsuits and sandy towels, a canvas carryall, one of Emmie's picnic hampers and even a blow-up sea horse. The sliding doors to the parlor on the left were pushed open. Inside, Cassia and Emmie talked to the family of four who'd rented a couple of rooms while they visited relatives in the area. Connor would have avoided the gathering if it had been his choice. The father of the clan had trapped him on the stairs a couple of days ago and told him all about Uncle Chick's penchant for booze and casino gambling and Grandma Ruth's sciatica.

Tess raised a hand. "Hi, we're back. I just popped in to say thanks for—for, um, Sunday dinner...." Her voice faltered, then faded altogether. She glanced over her shoulder at Connor.

Everyone in the room was staring at him.

The mother of the guest family hopped up and hustled her children past Tess and Connor. "Let's get you two upstairs. We're going to a barbecue at your cousin's house. Won't that be fun?" She grabbed at the beach gear. "Herb!" she screeched, pushing the kids toward the stairs. "Get a move on."

"Hey, that's one of those men," the older boy said.

Herb, the paunchy father, sidled by still staring at Connor. "That's one of 'em, all right."

After the family had jostled their way upstairs, the silly sea horse bobbing its plastic head, Tess moved into the parlor. Connor stayed where he was. Dread had rooted his feet to the floor.

"What's going on?" Tess said, looking around the room. It seemed that Emmie and Cassia had been interrupted—or startled. An abandoned Scrabble dictionary was splayed upside down on the floor. A cookie with a bite out of it lay on the coffee table. Emmie held an open tube of lotion in one hand. Cassia's face was pink.

The small TV on the credenza was blaring.

Tuned to a twenty-four-hour news channel.

Connor heard the name Roderick Strange and his heart sank.

"Emmie? Cassia?" Apparently Tess hadn't paid attention to the TV announcer. "Is there something wrong? Did the nursing home call? Did—"

She abruptly fell silent, turning to Connor. He took note of her confusion somewhere in the back of his brain, even though his gaze was locked on the television screen.

"To repeat, a young woman was believed to have been abducted early this morning from a roadside rest stop outside Dayton, Ohio. Eyewitness reports of a loiterer in the area have led police to launch a manhunt for Roderick Strange, age thirty-one, last known residence Ashland, Kentucky. Strange was involved in the tragic case of Elizabeth Marino, the college student kidnapped and murdered three years ago in…"

Connor's mind went blank for a moment and then the words and images crashed in on a tidal wave: the bedraggled yellow ribbons on the trees of Elizabeth Marino's hometown; the horror of the discovery of her body; the grim crime-scene photos; the deserted truck stop where she'd been abducted weeks before, ribboned with crime-scene tape; Elizabeth's weeping mother; Strange chained to his chair in the courtroom, smiling like a serpent as the conviction against him was overturned.

"Oh, God, no," Tess said, snapping him out of the trance.

She was staring at the television set.

The news announcer droned on. "Despite the original conviction, Strange was released from prison after serving less than a year of his sixty-year sentence when Connor Reed, a true-crime writer working on a book about the Marino murder, discovered that the testimony of an eyewitness was coerced by police. An investigation was launched…"

"No," Tess breathed.

Connor was shattered. He tried to shut out the news report, but the narration went on and on as the screen flashed morbid photos of young, bright-eyed women who were all presumed dead.…

"Reed, bestselling author of *Blood Kin* and *Savage Bounty,* could not be reached for comment. At age nineteen, Roderick Strange was convicted of—"

Emmie reached out and snapped off the TV set. "I can't bear it," she said, shuddering. "To think of that poor girl—"

Cassia hushed her.

Tess's spine was rigid. Connor could feel, even taste, the horror and disgust radiating from her. If learning that Strange had struck again hadn't numbed him to all pain, her repulsion would have cut him into pieces.

Tess began to turn toward him.

Time slowed.

Her hand rose, flipping her hair away from one cheek. He saw her frown, the tiny freckles sprinkled across her nose, the pale red fan of her lowered eyelashes....

He did not want to see the disappointment in her eyes.

She was shaking her head. Her lids squeezed shut. Before she could blink them open, he turned and bolted out of the front door.

CHAPTER ELEVEN

THE SLAM OF THE DOOR reverberated through the house. Tess wavered on her feet. "Oh, God," she said, lifting a shaking hand to her mouth.

Emmie grasped her elbow. "Come sit down."

"But I have to go after him."

"There's time for that. Right now, you need to get off your feet before you keel over." Emmie patted Tess's arm, leading her to the sofa. "It's a shock to all of us. To think we know an author who's involved in a murder case, and now this terrible kidnapping. *Tch,* such a shame."

"It's more than that." Tess sank onto the stiff cushions. Connor...poor Connor. Never mind the scornful reprimands from strangers. It was his own sense of guilt that would beat him black and blue.

"Of course it's more," Emmie said. She was interrupted by the shrill *beep-beep* of the telephone in the front hall. "Oh, dear, not again. That thing has been ringing off the hook all afternoon."

"And not with people making reservations," Cassia said as the innkeeper hurried off to answer it.

"Who's calling?" Tess asked sharply. "Reporters?"

"I don't think so. There were a few messages for Connor, but mostly it's been our own nosy friends and neighbors. They should know that Emmie won't rat on her guests."

"Toivo will." Emmie's brother was part of the group of senior citizens who hung out at the coffee shop, telling tall tales and bad jokes, keeping their collective thumbs on the pulse of Alouette.

"Probably, but he won't do it out of malice," Cassia said. "Just, you know, running off at the mouth like always."

"It's no secret. People had already judged Connor guilty by his association with Strange. This latest kidnapping will only worsen public opinon." Uncomfortable with the thought that she'd been almost as quick to judge, Tess found the remote control beneath the Sunday paper and clicked the TV on again. The news channel had moved on to another story, but she knew they'd return to Roderick Strange soon enough.

Emmie came back into the room. "Now we'll get some peace. I left the phone off the hook." She looked askance at the TV.

"Who was calling?" Tess asked.

"A lady for Connor." Emmie carried several pink note pages. "Called herself Ms. Krissa Picton. She said she's Connor's editor in New York City." She shuffled to another note. "A man claiming to be Connor's agent has called three times since the news broke. He was almost rude the last time. Shouting in my ear, demanding to know why he couldn't get through on Connor's cell phone. I hung up on him."

"Does Connor have a cell phone?" Cassia asked Tess.

"Not that I've noticed." Which was odd, come to think of it.

Or not, Tess decided. When Connor had arrived, he'd been doing his best to cut himself off from the world. It was she who'd pulled him back in, what with solicitous innkeepers, Scrabble games and Sunday dinners with the folks.

He'd been on the verge of liking it, too.

And now...

She winced, thinking of the torture he must be putting himself through.

"Do you think Connor will come back?" Emmie asked. "I promised to give him these messages as soon as he returned, but he ran out so fast I didn't get the chance." She thrust the note papers at Tess. "Will you see that he gets them?"

Tess took the messages. She paged through them and found one from his father and mother that he might want to return. She put that page on top and tapped the small pile against her knee to align them, imagining the onslaught if the national media learned of Connor's whereabouts.

"He's probably at the lighthouse." Tess looked up. "If he stays away very long, I'll go out there and give him the messages."

"Tell him to come home," Emmie said. "It's not good for a man, keeping to himself and brooding all the time, even if he has got the light keeper's solitude in his blood. Look at how Sonny Mitchell became an old crank after Mary Angela died. Lord knows I tried with the man, but he just wasn't comfortable, even at my table. He wouldn't discuss the Sunday paper, he wouldn't join in our board games. After two visits, he never accepted another invitation. Imagine."

All that Tess could do was shrug.

Emmie cocked her head. "I hear from Alice that you've been visiting Sonny several times a week."

"Connor brought me to meet Sonny the first time," Tess said. "We've gotten to know each other. I'm recording his memories of life at the lighthouse. I may do an exhibit about Gull Rock at the library."

Emmie nodded. "Good idea. There'll be plenty of community interest, what with Connor fixing up the old place."

Tess held up a hand for silence. A graphic with Roderick Strange's face on it had flashed on the screen. "Beware of Strange, R.," the report was called. She grimaced. Great, they'd already come up with a catchphrase and packaged the terrible developments for full entertainment value.

Emmie plopped beside Tess, taking hold of her hand throughout the report, which was essentially the same as the one she and Connor had walked in on earlier. This time, though, she caught clips of an old network interview with Strange, an average Joe in appearance except for the evil smirk that hovered on his face now and then. A brief rehash of Connor's involvement in the saga followed.

Tess shuddered. The linking of Connor's name with Strange's was disturbing to her. The covers of his books were shown, then a sound bite from his publisher about the forthcoming book, *Strange Mind,* its publication having been "understandably delayed because of the shocking developments," according to the publisher, who hinted that all sorts of juicy insider details would be revealed.

News to Connor, Tess thought. No wonder his editor was desperate to get in touch.

Unless he'd lied to her and the manuscript was already written. She tried to remember if he'd said that he'd quit before or after. There'd been something about breaking the contract....

"Jeez," Cassia said when the report concluded.

Emmie clicked the TV off again. "We've had enough of this for the day."

"It's not what you think," Tess blurted. "I mean, what else could Connor have done, really? He discovered corruption in the system. He had to report that. It's not his fault that Strange was set free…is it?"

"Heck, no. It's the fault of the ones who messed up the case," Cassia said with a staunch air that appeared to be founded more in solidarity than in a firm belief of Connor's innocence. Tess threw her a grateful look anyway.

Emmie squeezed Tess's hand. "I'm sure that Connor did what he felt was right."

"I don't suppose that the families of the missing or murdered women are as charitable." Tess's voice broke. She dropped her forehead against her fist, crushing the notes clutched in it. "If only they knew how torn up he is."

"You tell him to come home," Emmie said.

Tess looked up.

"I feel so bad for staring at him. I probably looked like I was horrified or something." Cassia bit her lip, her eyes gone so large they'd taken over her small face. "I know what that feels like, being singled out. But I was shocked, is all. I don't *blame* him."

"Thank you," Tess said, including both of them. She gathered strength from their goodwill. Perhaps it would be okay. Perhaps Strange would soon be arrested. Whether or not he was, she wanted Connor to realize that he was among friends. "I will tell him. I'll do my best to bring him home."

FIRST, TESS DROVE OUT of her way to the Buck Stop, a roadside convenience store with one lone gas pump a couple of miles outside of town. She could have easily shopped in the small sporting-goods store in town, but there was the possibility of encountering curiosity and questions.

The Buck Stop was far less public. Most likely, she'd be the only customer. And Rose Robbin, the primary employee, wasn't the type to blab. During the years that Noah Saari had been living in his cabin in the woods as a supposedly scarred and half-crazy hermit, he'd bought his supplies at the Buck Stop and never a word had passed Wild Rose's lips.

Tess parked outside the run-down shack of a store. Sure enough, the only other vehicle in the parking lot was the rattletrap pickup truck owned by Rose's widowed mother, Maxine Robbin.

The screen door wheezed open and shut as Tess made her way inside. She had had little reason to stop by over the past few years, but the Buck Stop never changed. There was still the same scuffed-up wood floor, dingy shelves and a checkout counter plastered with cheap decals from beer and cigarette companies. The freezer at the back of the store hummed in counterpoint to the whir of the ceiling fan.

Wild Rose sat behind the counter, her head bowed over a book. Tess wasn't surprised by that, either. Rose was a frequent patron of the library, slipping in and out during the quiet times, checking out stacks of every genre of book imaginable. Despite their overtures, Tess and Beth never got much conversation out of Rose. But she'd continued to steadily read her way through the library's collection.

While Tess had made up a number of scenarios to explain the woman's reserve, the truth was simple enough. Wild Rose Robbin was a misfit. She'd been one year ahead of Tess in school, and they'd known each other in the usual friendly, small-town way. As a girl, Rose had been very shy. That had suddenly changed during her teen years, when she'd begun smoking and drinking and carrying on with boys. Her nickname referred to her wild reputation that had been escalated by talk in the boys' locker room and at girls' slumber parties. Then, at sixteen, Rose had suddenly dropped out of school and disappeared from town. An arrest that had led to juvenile hall had been the hot rumor.

No one had heard from Rose until she'd returned for her father's funeral. And since then, she'd kept to herself, working long hours at the Buck Stop and helping her mother rent out their cottages during the summer. She was considered to be rough and uneducated, but Tess knew better.

"Good book?" she said.

Wild Rose looked up, startled. "Tess Bucek. I didn't hear you come in." She shoved the book under the counter, then straightened, brushing her disheveled black hair out of her face. Her eyes narrowed. "What brings you here?"

That was Wild Rose—straight down to business.

Tess followed suit. "I need a pair of waders. Do you have any?"

"We might." Wild Rose came out from behind the counter. "Going fishing, huh?"

"Nope." Tess hadn't fished since her outings with Jared.

Wild Rose hiked up baggy jeans shorts and led the way to the back of the store, her cheap sandals slapping the hardwood floor. Her voice floated back to Tess, carrying an unusual hint of curiosity. "Boating?"

"Nope."

"In here." The other woman entered the bait shop, an even dingier lean-to addition to the main room, where buckets of bait and cartons of worms were sold, along with a meager supply of fishing gear.

"I'm pretty sure there's a pair of waders somewhere in this mess." She glanced at Tess's outfit—a blouse and skirt and strappy sandals. "You'd better stand back. It's dusty in here."

Wild Rose rummaged until she emerged with the boots. "Gonna be big on you," she said, eyeing Tess's petite frame.

"That's okay. I'll take them."

"Huh." Wild Rose toted the boots back to the front of the store. "Okay, I've got it," she said, ringing up the price. "You're going to search for beach glass with Noah and Claire and you don't want to freeze your toes off in the lake."

Tess grinned. "Nope." She opened her purse. "I'll tell you why I need them if you'll just ask me."

Wild Rose made change, her mouth pulled into a pucker. The screen door banged open and a couple of boys raced inside, heading for the freezer section. "No running!" she yelled, and they skidded to a sliding stop, yelping like puppies.

She looked at Tess. "Okay, so what's up?"

Tess folded the rubber waders over her arm. "I'm going out to the lighthouse. That night of heavy rain we had washed out even more of the causeway. Connor said the water's almost up to his knees in some spots."

"Yeah, I see." Wild Rose weighed various options. "Except you could have bought waders in town."

"Right. But then everyone would have known."

The corners of Wild Rose's mouth twitched. "Everyone already knows."

Tess rolled her eyes. Of course everyone knew. Even Wild Rose, who didn't gossip, but certainly seemed to listen and pay close attention to town happenings. She was often in attendance at the high-school basketball games, hovering around the edges, never quite part of the crowd. Tess had never been able to figure out Rose's motives.

"Have you met Connor Reed?" Tess asked.

"He stopped by a few times for gas. Seems like a good guy. No trouble, anyhow."

"Would you like to help him out?"

Wild Rose crossed her arms over her T-shirt. "Dunno. What would I have to do?"

"It's like this," Tess said, and launched into her plan.

CONNOR THOUGHT he might go mad. The pictures wouldn't get out of his head.

He'd been trying to shut it all out and concentrate on work. Mix paint in bucket, pour paint in pan, load roller and apply. But gazing at the growing whiteness of the wall in front of him had only made the pictures in his head sharper, brighter. Yellow crime-scene tape, orange prison coveralls, the stark contrast of flashbulb photographs, the ugly stains of blood-spattered clothing, as black as Strange's soul....

With a curse, Connor threw down the roller and raced up the spiral steps of the lighthouse, his gut twisting even tighter as he progressed. He knew he couldn't outrun his demons. Even though he'd been attempting to for months.

He threw open the door of the lantern room and stepped onto the deck. Superior spread before him in the early-evening light, rippling like a bolt of discarded satin. He gripped the railing, imagining diving from the tower, arching across the rocks into the water. The lake would enfold him in numbing cold. No more garish pictures in his head. No desperate voices. No guilt.

He pushed away, circling the catwalk in long strides. Once, twice, three times around.

He would leave. He would go to Ohio, where the girl had been abducted, and he would follow every lead, speak to every witness, until he had enough real, hard evidence to see Strange arrested. For good, this time.

But there was Sonny…and even Tess.…

A movement in the forest across the way caught Connor's eye. He heard the sound of a car approaching the wooded edge of the shoreline where the narrow causeway was all that connected Gull Rock to the mainland. After a minute a figure emerged, walking along the rutted path that led to the lighthouse.

Tess, he thought, even before the burnished copper cap of her hair caught the soft evening light. Who else?

Sweet Tess. She would be coming to comfort him.

Didn't she know that until Strange was taken care of, Connor would never be at peace?

She was wading through the water, arms outstretched for balance, not looking toward the light-house until she reached the dry path again, where it veered sharply upward. Then she looked up, saw him, and waved before starting to climb. He watched until she disappeared beneath the trees.

His chest hurt.

He went inside and descended the steps, wanting her with every molecule. She was crossing the yard when he threw open the door at the base of the tower.

"You shouldn't have come," he said, intending to discourage her sympathy before it started, when he saw that her skirt was tucked into a pair of ungainly waders that wobbled and squelched with every step she took. The black rubber was as shiny as a wet seal and there was enough of it to wrap twice around each thigh. Amazingly, he found himself laughing. It felt damn good.

She peeled the suspenders off her shoulders. "Never mind the welcome. Help me get out of these."

The baggy boots slithered down her legs. He offered a hand and she kicked out of the piles of scrunched rubber, revealing bare legs and dainty sandals. "How did you ever manage to walk?" he said.

"Not well. I almost fell—caught myself on one hand." She lifted and gathered her long skirt, wringing the fabric. "I'm all wet. When are you getting the causeway fixed? Or are you discouraging visitors?"

"That seems like a good idea—especially now."

She shook her head, but didn't argue.

"Why did you come?" he blurted.

She looked at him with eyes like a bed of moss, sincerely mystified. "How could I *not?*"

"You saw the reactions I got."

"Shock," she said. "Horror. But not directed at *you*. Not on my part, anyway, or anyone who knows you."

"How very Pollyanna of you. Reactions aside, the truth is that I carry a share of the blame and that's all there is to it." He remembered her using similar words. "Like you, with the accident."

"But I was actively involved in that. You came in after the fact and—"

"Semantics," he said, backing away from her rational reasoning. It was a seductive thing—making him hope that he could feel free and alive again.

She stood watching him with her red skirt wadded in her hands. Her chin puckered. Her eyes snapped. "Then, for God's sake, *live* with it, Connor. Accept that you made a choice, but that even so, you have no control over what's happening now. Give yourself a break. Believe that you are not responsible for Strange's crimes."

A sardonic twist of a smile took hold. "Overlook popular opinion, you mean."

She let the skirt go and set her hands on her hips, an imitation of Emmie in bossy mode. "Who gives a flying fig about popular opinion? It's the people you love who count. Your friends, your family."

"They have to support me, no matter what they really think. It's in the job description."

Suddenly Tess's gaze dropped. "No, they don't, Connor," she said in a strained voice, and he saw the pain that crossed her face.

Too late, he remembered that she'd been abandoned by the people she considered family. He may have been the Police Turncoat poster boy, even the target of slings and arrows from his own kind, but at least he'd never dealt with losing the support of his family. When he'd been struggling with what to do about the information he'd uncovered, his parents had been there to listen to his dilemma. They'd sworn they would stand by him, come what may.

And here he was, acting like a mope, running and hiding to nurse his wounds instead of facing up to his detractors like a man.

Like Tess. She'd stayed in Alouette despite what must have been extremely hurtful gossip to a vulnerable young woman still in grieving for her loss.

Connor let go of his black mood and went to her. "Tess, you are loved." He put his hands on her arms, kissed her forehead. It didn't take any special insight to see her value to the community and to her friends. The Johnsons had doubled their loss when they'd turned their backs on her.

"Yes, I am." She touched her cheek to his. "You are, too."

"I am," he echoed, though he preferred to go in another direction. Not everything was about him. "You know, it won't take much for me to become a lifetime member of the Tess Bucek fan club."

Her laugh was light and sparkling, almost hiding

the catch of her breath. "We'll have a mutual-admiration society."

"You can say that, even after I've been such a self-indulgent, sullen crank?"

"Oh, I forgive you that. After all, those traits run in your family."

"You've charmed both of us, you know. Sonny's got a crush on you, too." Connor spoke into her ear, breathing her scent, her shampoo. Her hair feathered across his lips as he lowered his head.

"Only because I remind him of Mary Angela," she said, shivering a little.

He smiled against her neck. "What's my excuse, then?"

She wound her arms around his waist, snuggling in closer. "You don't need one."

"What happens if I'm falling for you?"

She squeezed. "I will catch you."

He ran his hands over her body. "You're too small. I'll hurt you."

"Hurt me? Connor…" She tilted her head back to see his face. "Are we talking about what I think we're talking about? For a man who has made his living with words, you seem to avoid using them."

"Do you need the words?"

She nodded vehemently. "Yes, absolutely!"

"I can give you three of them."

Her eyes widened, shining with an obvious expectation that hit him like a thunderbolt. A few seconds too late.

Damn, he wasn't thinking, only speaking. It was

too soon to be offering commitment when he didn't know what to do with himself. But her parted lips were so ripe and kissable he didn't want to walk away.

He'd offered her three words. It was obvious what she expected, but all he could come up with was his original intent. And so he kissed her, holding on tight as if it was she who might run away, lingering over the taste of her until retreat was impossible. ''Let's…make…love,'' he whispered across her soft lips.

If Tess was disappointed, there was no sign of it except a lightning-fast blink. Perhaps she knew he needed the healing before he could go any further. Perhaps she wanted him as badly as he wanted her.

''Here?'' she said, blinking again.

''Why not here?''

She looked around at the wild grass and rampant bushes, the straight-shot view to the harbor. ''You've got to be crazy.''

''Guess so.''

He would have pulled away, but she locked her arms around him. ''Okay.''

He shook his head. ''Now you're the crazy one. I don't know what I was thinking.''

She kissed him. ''You were thinking that you need to feel *alive*. The best way to celebrate life is by—''

Making it, he thought, leaping ahead of her. What if she was one of *those* women—looking to get pregnant without bothering to keep the father around for the long haul? Tess had never even hinted at that, but...

He closed his eyes, imagining it. Tess would make a remarkable mother. Oddly, the idea of her growing round with his child wasn't too alarming. Not that he wanted it, of course.

But maybe someday.

"By making love," she said with a velvety purr, rolling her shoulders against his chest. Her breasts were pressed into firm mounds and he forgot the out-of-left-field ideas about mothers and babies as he brought his hand up to the side of one breast, his fingers slipping over the sheerness and intricate patterns of her lacy blouse. Red and white and lace—she was done up like a Valentine. And offering her heart to him.

Of all people, Tess Bucek had chosen him.

"This isn't the best place to do this," he said, kissing her with more heat.

She eased out of the kiss, running her knuckles over his jaw as she withdrew. "I think it's perfect." With a whirl of her skirt, she turned and walked around the cottage to the other side of the peninsula, where the grass sloped more gently to the rocks and everywhere you looked there was only the wildness of the pounding surf and the wheeling gulls.

Connor made a quick detour into the cottage for the blanket and sleeping bag he'd stowed in one of the empty bedrooms upstairs. He stopped and glanced out the window.

In the yard below, Tess was bent at the waist to

step out of her skirt. The breeze molded her silk slip over the erotic curve of her backside, sending any thought of hesitation up in flames. He stood admiring her for a long moment, and then bolted out of the room. If Tess's intentions were to distract him from his problems, she'd gone all out.

He found her in bare feet, spreading the red skirt over a bramble bush. "The sun will dry it," she said, going pink when she saw the sleeping bag.

She turned and stared across the water, absently fingering the lace collar of the blouse that hung loose over her slip. It was made so that what he saw through the see-through fabric was the matching lacy top of her ivory slip and modest hints of skin—shoulders, arms, the slightest shadowing of the hollow between her breasts. The slip fluttered over her thighs.

She must have felt him looking. With a secret little smile, hovering halfway between alluring and shy, she gazed at him from the corners of her eyes. Her hands lowered to the buttons of her blouse. It floated down her arms and landed at her feet.

She beckoned him to her with a come-hither lift of her bare shoulder.

Connor found himself moving without conscious effort. There had never been a woman who looked sexier than Tess at that moment.

He swooped her up into his arms. Even now, there was no forgetting the grief and suffering in the world, particularly that which he'd had a hand in, but a part of him exalted. He had Tess. He was blessed.

They kissed until they were too weak to stand, then

slid to the ground in a heap, laughing together when they hit the grass and were jarred apart.

Tess was amazed.

"I never expected this in a million years," she said, though part of her had dreamed it. They knelt and spread the sleeping bag and the blanket in a hollow of the hillside that overlooked the rocks and surf. It was as private as possible, considering they were outdoors and open to the sky and sun and anyone who happened to sail by. "My days of making out at Gull Rock were supposed to be over a long time ago."

"I'm your second chance." Connor stripped off his paint-streaked T-shirt and stretched out on the bag, holding the blanket up for her to slide beneath.

She hesitated for one heartbeat before she recognized the truth: she would risk anything to be what he needed—a second chance, a pure gift of love, even just one fleeting moment of forgiveness.

She pressed a hand to the neckline of her slip and crawled into his arms. His chest was hard with muscle and bone, but oh, so warm, and his skin was scented with a male aroma so distinctly arousing she wanted to crawl all the way inside him and live there in mindless bliss. The moan that came from her mouth as he hugged her was embarrassingly revealing. She buried her face against his chest, still not quite sure about the logistics of actually *doing* this, but knowing she'd made the decision and couldn't stop now.

Full throttle, she thought, and released the front catch on her bra.

Connor's fingers danced across the back of her

thighs, where her slip had risen to an immodest height. He stroked, pushing it higher, past her hips. She squirmed, unable to keep still when he took hold of her bottom and rolled her on top of him, their legs tangling and their mouths colliding.

Oh, yes, she was going to do this!

He skimmed the straps of her slip off her shoulders, dragging the bodice low enough so the lace caught on the tips of her breasts. She'd braced herself on her arms, giving him access. He took it, his eyes espresso-hot as he curved a palm beneath one breast, lifting it free.

The blanket was down around her waist. She didn't care. She flung back her head, loving the tickle of the breeze, the tug of Connor's fingertips. One of his thighs nudged between her legs. She pressed against it, and he raised it even higher, urging her to inch upward until he could reach her breasts with his mouth.

With a deep sigh, she sank into the sense of swirl-ing pleasure. Let it overwhelm her. She wanted to know what letting go was about—completely and un-apologetically letting go of all that she knew and all that had kept her safe. Making love wasn't only for Connor, it was for her, too.

He rolled her onto her back, taking a moment to shuck his jeans and shorts before he settled on top of her, loving her with his mouth and his hands and the sweet words of praise he whispered against her skin. She acquainted herself with his body, alternately laughing and shivering with delight as she tasted and licked and stroked until the temperature and electricity between them was crackling hot.

"Do you have protection?" she remembered to ask.

He nodded and pulled away just far enough to reach his jeans. Her hand stayed on his ribs, feeling them through his satin skin. When he returned, sliding into place between her thighs, she raised both hands to his face, wanting to hold him there so she could look into his eyes and see the love—she believed in her heart that's what it was—as their bodies joined. She didn't need the words, did she, when she could read them for herself.

"Okay?" he said, and she nodded, involuntarily closing her eyes as he slowly pushed inside her and the wondrous sensation of it became too much for her heart to contain without spilling over into tears.

"Don't cry." Connor held her, kissing the moisture that seeped from her eyes.

She blinked them open. "It's not sadness."

"I know."

She studied his face through the blurry tears. "Of course you do," she said, just before losing her breath when he moved inside her, striking a thousand sparks off her nerve endings. She gasped, winding her arms around his neck, clutching tighter, arching up to meet his thrust again and again. At the very last instant before the pleasure exploded into white-hot fireworks, he raised his head and she saw the emotion that stripped away his armor. He loved her—oh, he really did!—maybe even as much as she loved him.

CHAPTER TWELVE

TESS PUT the telephone receiver in its cradle. "Well, that's finally confirmed. I've got a bulldozer and three loads of fill and gravel arriving at 7:00 a.m. tomorrow morning. By early afternoon, the rest of the workers will be able to safely cross the causeway."

"Randy's coming," Beth said. She patted Bump. "Mostly to keep an eye on me for incipient labor pains, but you might be able to get some work out of him."

Tess surveyed the library. The only patrons were a tourist reading newspapers and Wild Rose, who was lost in the stacks. It was the lull before the storm—the children's hour started in ten minutes and any moment now parents would begin dropping off the little demons. "It's not necessary for you and Randy to be there. Why don't you two stay home? You're not allowed into the lighthouse while we paint and varnish anyway. Fumes, you know."

"That's okay. I'll be outside, helping Emmie with the lunch."

"But there are plenty of volunteers," Tess protested. "Once I put the word out—"

"*For*-get it, boss." Beth grinned hugely. "There's

no way I'm not coming. Imagine—Tess Bucek, wearing her heart on her sleeve. And parading it in front of half the town, too. Oh, no, I wouldn't miss this for the world. I'll be at Gull Rock even if I have to superglue my knees shut to keep Bump in!''

Tess gazed fondly at Beth's immense midsection, clothed in a pastel striped trapeze top that made her look like an Easter egg. ''Any chance of an early labor?''

Beth rubbed her belly. ''First babies are usually late, not early.''

''No Braxton Hicks contractions? Urges to nest?''

''I cleaned out all my kitchen cupboards and sterilized the dishes. Does that count?'' Beth chuckled. ''You should have seen Randy's face when he got home from his route and saw the pots of boiling water. He thought I was preparing for a home birth.''

''Why do the doctors always ask for boiling water?'' Tess said absently. Anything was better than putting up with the teasing Beth had subjected her to ever since she'd come home from Gull Rock several days ago with a smile on her face and a hickey on her neck.

Evan and Lucy walked into the library. Tess waved. ''Hi! You're the first to arrive.''

''I want to see if my 'stershum needs water,'' Lucy said as she hurried to the children's room.

''Luce,'' her father said. ''Did you forget something?''

She stopped and retraced her steps to the desk. ''Good morning, Miss Bucek.'' Evan came over and helped her free the storybooks tucked into her backpack. Lucy placed them on the desk and ran off again.

Beth followed, one hand pressed to the small of her back, the other wielding a watering can. "I'll go along." She tipped the can. "Save the nasturtiums."

"So, Evan," Tess said. She eyed him hopefully. "I'm getting together this crew…"

"Say no more. I'll be there."

She smiled. "Word's spread, then? Do you think I can get any of your coworkers to come?" Evan was part of a carpentry crew working on a new house in town. She'd already gathered quite a labor force, but not a lot of it was experienced.

"Hard to tell. Connor and Strange have been a topic of conversation among the guys. Some are hardliners, especially about the issue of police corruption. My boss's son is a cop and he's not happy with the public criticism, and even though it may not be fair, Connor gets the blame for starting it." Evan shrugged. "You know how it is."

"I guess so." Tess had run into similar opinions here and there. "If there's ever a librarian scandal, I'm blaming no one but the librarians at fault."

"Tell me when that happens. I'd like to see what a renegade librarian looks like."

Tess laughed. "I'll bet." She spotted the top of Wild Rose's head, lurking among the first rows, almost as if she was eavesdropping. Tess pretended not to notice. Calling the woman over would only send her off in the opposite direction.

"You can count on me to help out," Evan said, heading for the door.

"Thanks a lot. We're going to need you."

Five seconds after Evan had gone, Wild Rose was at the desk. She had only one book, but seemed in a hurry, so Tess checked her through quickly. "You're still coming tomorrow, right, Rose?"

"Um, maybe."

"It'll mean a lot to Connor. Please try."

"It's not like I'll be missed," Rose said, holding the thick botany text against her chest as she backed toward the door.

"Why, of course I'd miss—" Tess started to say, but just then a young mother with three children in tow arrived, and in the bustle, Rose slipped out of the library unnoticed by all but Tess.

CONNOR DROVE OUT to Tess's house early that evening. He listened to news reports on the car radio—he'd been checking in all day, in fact—but there was no progress in the search for Roderick Strange. At the least, the man had broken parole. The police had reported that the apartment he'd recently rented was empty. Estranged family members had been swarmed by the media, but swore they knew nothing. Although the alerts and all points bulletins had gone national, police were said to be concentrating on a three-state area. Meanwhile, the missing woman's mother had appeared on TV, pleading for her daughter's release. And every news program in operation was rehashing the details of Strange's criminal history.

Connor's mind raced over every detail, looking for clues. There had to be *something*....

He pulled up to Tess's bungalow. She was home. Mellow jazz floated from windows glowing with golden lamplight. He got out of his Jeep and waited near it for a minute or two until he saw her, moving from one room to another with a glass in her hand.

He hadn't said much about his plans after they'd made love at Gull Rock. And she hadn't asked, either, except to speak about his grandfather and how wonderful it was going to be when he saw the lighthouse again.

Whether or not she meant to pressure him with that, she had. Or rather, it had. Tess was only an innocent bystander.

Who would be hurt to hear that he'd decided to leave.

Regrettable, but she was not the first innocent to be harmed by his decisions since Roderick Strange entered the picture.

The front door opened. Tess appeared. ''Connor, is that you? I thought I heard someone drive up.''

''It's me.'' He crossed the cobblestone walkway.

''Hi.'' Her smile was sweet and a little bashful. ''I made dinner. Enough for two.''

His edginess eased, just a little. And he welcomed that. ''What are we having?''

''Steak fajitas. And for starters, I have blue-corn tortilla chips with some yummy cheese-and-spinach sauce for dipping.''

He followed her inside, unable to resist the urge to

put his hand on her hip. And then when she turned to look at him, a quiet delight lighting up her face, he also had to slide his arm around her and pull her close and brush his cheek over her hair.

She breathed, holding on to his button-down shirt with both hands. "I'm glad you came by."

"Couldn't stay away."

"Then don't even try, okay?"

That, he couldn't agree with.

He pressed his fingers beneath her chin, tipping her face toward his kiss.

She said, "Mmm," and darted her tongue over his lips.

He released her, using up a good amount of his available willpower. "Smells good," he said, even though he was only aware of her scent, her softness, her smile.

All of it seductive.

"I'll be right back." Her expression was faintly quizzical, but she stayed cool. "No margaritas," she called on her way to the kitchen, "but I do have wine. It's on the table. Pour yourself a glass."

Connor went into the adjoining dining room and found the open wine bottle and her half-filled glass. He took another from a built-in oak cupboard with leaded-glass doors.

Tess emerged with a tray. "Let's go in the living room. You take the wine, please."

This isn't right, Connor told himself as they settled on her couch. He couldn't sit here in domestic bliss as if nothing was on his mind. But his voice stuck in his throat every time he looked at Tess.

"Norah Jones," she said, tilting the wineglass to her lips before returning it to the coffee table. She closed her eyes, smiling as her head wove slowly back and forth. She seemed to have total peace of mind.

It made Connor envious. He had forgotten what peace of mind felt like.

Without opening her eyes, Tess took his hand. "The music. It's Norah Jones."

He tried to speak again, but she said, "Shh," and held tightly on to his hand. "I know. Your head is filled with horror. But you can't do anything about it tonight, so you should try to relax, all right?"

Not all right.

"Take a sip of wine."

He took more than a sip.

"And close your eyes."

With a groan, he slumped lower in the cushions and let his head fall back. Closing his eyes never stopped his mind from racing, but he did it anyway because Tess had asked. He would do just about anything she asked.

"Don't think," she whispered. "Listen."

He tried. For a full minute.

"Sorry." He wrenched forward to sit on the edge of the couch. "Nice try, but it's not going to work." He looked around the room. Cream-colored walls, cushy armchair, nubby moss-green rugs, built-in bookcases packed full to the brim, with the excess volumes stacked around an art nouveau tile fireplace. Every lamp was lit, but the lighting was soft, not harsh. She must have dimmers.

He didn't see what he wanted. "Do you have a TV?"

"In the bedroom."

"Um…"

"No," she said, sliding forward beside him. "Eat some chips. Drink your wine. Talk to me about anything you want except what's on your mind." She dipped a chip into a small dish of gooey cheese and fed it to him, holding her hand under his chin. "You can go a few hours without beating yourself up."

When he was with her, maybe.

But he couldn't stay here forever.

MINUTES PASSED, time flowed; Connor didn't care. They were in the bedroom and Norah was singing "Come Away With Me" and Tess's lips were beckoning him with promises that it would be all right, *he* would be all right, if only he came away with her into a sweet neverland of soft jazz and warm loving. He closed his eyes. Sank with her, twined in sun-dried sheets that coasted over their naked bodies each time the night air breezed through the dark room.

He breathed the scent of her skin. Sang her name in his head as she rose over him, sliding into an intimate caress that seemed to enfold his entire body in slippery warmth. Pleasure doubled and then redoubled, becoming too much for him to contain.

She sat taller, threw apart her arms, embracing the

entire world. The sheet billowed out like a sail, then drifted to the floor when she released it.

He reached for her hands. She gave them, leaning into his support as her thighs flexed and her hips rocked. Together, they dissolved into the heat.

And Tess was looking at him all the while, her eyes wide open and wondrous. For a moment, he believed they flickered with stars. Just like heaven.

"THIS IS ABOUT the fifth time I've heard this song," Connor said against Tess's back when "Cold Cold Heart," a Hank Williams cover, began to play. They were spooned in her bed, and Norah was still singing in the other room. Outside, a whippoorwill fluted in harmony.

Tess roused herself from the edge of sleep. "Auto replay."

"You'll wear out the CD."

"Wouldn't be the first one."

She patted his arms where they wound around her, and closed her eyes. Her mind drifted, but never far from one thought: how good this was.

Just this.

Simple, pure, easy.

"Any steak left?" asked Connor.

She nearly laughed. Thinking of his stomach. So like a man.

Though not Connor, usually. She hoped he was getting his appetite back.

"We ate it all. But there's dessert—homemade almond cookies and raspberry sorbet."

"Mmm."

Smiling to herself, she waited, not twitching a muscle or blinking a lash.

"I'll get it," he said, and slowly, slowly slid his leg from between hers.

She tangled their ankles. "Let me."

"Stay."

"No, really."

"I insist."

She pressed her smile into the pillow. "Spoons are in the drawer on the far right."

Two minutes later, he was back, holding a cookie in his mouth. He crawled over her, balanced on his elbows with his hands full, his face ducking near hers. She bit into the cookie and they had a tug-of-war until it broke in half. Crumbs scattered over her bare breasts.

"Uh-oh," Connor said.

She started to brush them away and he stopped her, dropping openmouthed kisses up and down and all around, his tongue picking up crumbs as he covered all territory. He flicked the rosy tip of one breast. "Tasty."

She giggled. "Homemade."

"Emmie would be proud." He put a dish on the bedside table, pried off the lid of the sorbet and handed her a spoon. They dipped into the icy dessert, lying flat in bed. From time to time, Connor added cold, fresh raspberries from the dish. Tess was strangely touched at his thoughtfulness.

She arched her throat. A tangy dollop of sorbet slid down it. "You forgot to change Norah."

"I'm getting to like Norah. It's the whippoorwill outside the window that's driving me crazy."

"What? The whippoorwill's *romantic*."

"Oh."

"You don't agree?"

"I thought the crumbs were romantic."

"The crumbs were…sexy." She licked her sticky spoon.

He crunched a cookie near her ear.

"Now you're getting crumbs in my hair," she protested.

"You're a mess. Sticky chin. Berry stains on your lips. To say nothing of the crumbs. I'll have to wash you clean in the shower."

Lick me, she thought, but was too modest to say it. Anyway, the double shower didn't sound bad. She'd make the sacrifice to keep him occupied.

SHE WOKE ONCE in the middle of the night to a soft blue light. After a couple of hazy moments, she recognized Connor's shape, hunched at the end of the bed, naked except for boxer shorts. Moonlight highlighted the bumps of his vertebrae. His mussed hair gleamed blue from the electric illumination of the television.

She squinted at the harsh strobe effect as he changed channels, one after the other. *Click, click, click.*

"Connor?" she croaked. Her mouth was cottony from the wine.

"Sorry."

"Tha's okay." She lifted her head, trying to see the screen. "Any news?"

He sighed with the weight of the world. "No."

"Maybe tomorrow."

"It *is* tomorrow." He sounded so sad. As if with tomorrow had come the end of the world.

"Maybe in the morning…"

He clicked off the TV. But didn't move, except to bow his head. His prominent shoulder blades threw shadows over his pale back. In daylight, he was tanned. In moonlight, as silvery as a fish.

She plumped his pillow. Straightened the sheet. "Come back to bed. I miss snuggling with you."

After a long pause, he pushed off from the floor, falling straight backward so the mattress jounced. His eyes were squeezed tightly shut. "I have to tell you…"

"In the morning," she whispered, running her palm over his chest.

He placed his hands over her arm, almost as though he meant to push it away. She held her breath. And then he relaxed, air whistling from his mouth, lonesome as a whippoorwill.

She kissed his shoulder. "I'm here."

His fingers tightened on her. "You are. I'm—"
Not.

She felt the words in her heart. She could almost hear him say them. *I'm not.*

But she didn't know how to prove otherwise. He'd have to find out the truth on his own. He'd have to believe in himself again—and in her.

CONNOR WAS UP EARLY, in time to see the sun rise over a field of yellow grass across the way. He sat on Tess's front doorstep to tie his shoes and noticed the dewdrops glistening on the lush green lawn. The grass was raggedy and thick, a couple of inches too tall. Tess needed it mowed.

She probably did it herself, in a sun hat and shorts, her bare limbs oiled with sunscreen. Tiny red and brown and copper freckles dotted her entire body, he'd discovered. Connecting them could grow to be his passion.

If he wasn't leaving…

But not for good, whispered a voice inside his head. Tess would be here when he came back.

He smelled the coffee in time to make a coward's getaway, but he couldn't do it. Bad enough he'd let her entice him from his intended purpose with peppery steak and tortilla chips, smooth jazz, floating sheets and her body like speckled cream.

''Brought you coffee,'' she said from the other side of the screen door. She nudged it open with a foot clad in a hiking boot.

''Planning a rigorous morning?'' he asked as he took the cup she lowered. She was dressed in splotched white painter's pants and a skimpy gray T-shirt, slightly wrinkled from being folded in a drawer.

She sat beside him. "There's something I have to tell you."

He took a deep breath. "Me first."

Her nose tipped up, her lashes fluttered halfway shut. "Yes?"

"I have to go."

She dropped one word into a well of silence. "Where?"

"New York, first. Then Kentucky…Ohio…"

Her face went white. "Connor—*no.*"

He fought for words, but they all sounded weak and stupidly useless in his head. Finally he shrugged. "I have to."

"But you can't *do* anything. This isn't like TV, where amateurs snoop around, overturn a few leaves and right after the last commercial break, presto, they solve the case the professionals have botched."

"I am aware of that."

"Then why go? What about me?" She grabbed his arm, splashing coffee from his cup. "What about Sonny?"

"I know, I know." Connor scrubbed at his prickly jaw. "Keep an eye on him for me, okay? I'll be back as soon as I can."

She shook her head vigorously. "No, I won't help you leave."

He hardened his heart. Made it detached, objective. Cold. "Doesn't matter. I'll leave, either way."

"Why go?" she cried again. "You don't have to."

"I trashed my manuscript, but not my research notes. I still have the taped interviews I did with

Strange in prison. There could be something in them. A clue. He liked to talk. Bragging, really. Maybe there's—'' Tess's eyes had welled up. Looking into them, Connor's voice failed.

He swallowed. "It's a long shot, but it's all I have."

She dropped her face into her hands, surrendering with a shudder. "Promise me you won't get involved in the manhunt. I mean, not physically. Don't go chasing down back alleys or deserted warehouses. Don't—" She broke off, laying her head against his shoulder as she pulled in a ragged breath. "Be safe, that's all. I'm not finished with you."

He took her hand. "I'll come home."

"Home?"

"To the lighthouse," he said, because he couldn't make the leap all the way to her, not when it took every shred of his control to keep himself detached.

Tess sat up. "The lighthouse!"

"What is it?"

"That's what I was going to tell you. I've arranged for a crew of workers. Volunteers. They're coming to the lighthouse—*today*. To help you get it fixed up. I was worried about Sonny's health, and then you— when you heard about Strange, I thought you needed to know how much we support you, and so I—oh, damn. What time is it?"

"Early yet. Sun's barely up."

She jumped to her feet. "The gravel trucks are arriving at seven. We have to go."

"But I can't—"

She tugged on his arm. "Tomorrow, Connor. You can leave town tomorrow." She pleaded, weakening him. "Isn't that soon enough?"

He shook his head. But he let her pull him up, and he let her prod him to his Jeep, and he let himself notice the way the sunshine turned her hair to melted copper and finally, damn if he didn't let go of his anguished isolation and accept the inevitable. She was making him live again.

EVERY TIME TESS SAW Connor throughout the day that followed, he wore an expression of amazement, whether he was getting his hand pumped or his back slapped by a new arrival, fitting safety goggles over his eyes before switching on the belt sander, or nodding patiently while a sweet old lady recited her memories of visits to Gull Rock. A couple of times they'd connected, and with awe in his voice he'd asked Tess how many more people she expected. She'd laughed and admitted she had no idea. All she'd done was tell a few people to spread the word that everyone was welcome.

The causeway had been filled and tamped by noon, which made the crossing much easier. Soon after, groups of two and three had begun arriving, armed with their own tools, rollers and paint pans. Wild Rose dropped off a load of supplies she'd donated from the Buck Stop and made a hasty getaway. A generator was hauled over in the back of Jimmy Jarvi's pickup truck. Once the painting was well under way—overstaffed, in fact—other projects were begun. Weed removal, floor sanding, shingle repair. Several of the men made plans to come back when there was less of a crowd to sandblast the painted graffiti off the bricks. During lunch—a sandwich and soft-drink feast run by Emmie—several members of the historical society started planning what furnishings they would donate, keeping in mind the proper historical significance. One woman remembered that she'd seen a lovely old daguerreotype of the lighthouse among her great-grandmother's belongings and vowed to search for it.

Tess was thankful for the enthusiasm, but she reminded everyone that the lighthouse might remain in private ownership. That Connor had made no promises there.

By late afternoon, so much work had been accomplished that a number of volunteers called it a day. The hardiest among them stayed on determined to finish various tasks. Emmie had packed up her picnic hampers and was cheerfully haranguing Toivo and Bill as the trio of them traipsed down the slope to the causeway.

Tess stopped work long enough to say thanks and goodbye then she looked around, checking progress as she wiped paint from her hands with a damp rag.

"Hey, you," a voice called from above.

She stepped back, shielding her eyes as she looked up.

Connor was straddling the peak of the cottage roof like a cowboy on a Brahman bull. He lifted a hand, flashing a big grin at her. "Don't leave yet. We're almost done."

"I'm in no rush," she shouted. "Be careful!"

Evan Grant passed Connor a last packet of shingles. There was another figure hunched on the roof, wielding an air hammer. Tess squinted against the brilliant sky. For an instant she thought it was Noah. But no. The man turned and recognition pierced her, as cutting as ever despite the decade that had gone by.

Erik Johnson.

She'd known he was a roofer, but never in a million years had she expected him to help out.

"Tess? You okay?"

Tess wiped a hand across her eyes before turning to answer Beth. "Yeah, sure. Just daydreaming."

"You've got to be beat. Come sit down." Beth was ensconced in a webbed lawn chair beneath a pine, looking relaxed and content with one hand resting on her stomach.

Tess plopped down beside her, in the grass. She dragged the bandanna from her hair and ran her fingers through it. *Erik Johnson!*

"He's been here all afternoon," Beth said. "Working on the roof."

"I didn't know."

"You were inside painting."

Tess squinted at the figures silhouetted against the sky. "I saw Gus earlier in the day, and Sarah came over with a group of teenagers. But…" She raked her

hair again, until her fingers snagged. "Was there anyone else from Jared's family?"

"His mother—she was in the garden, clearing
brush and weeds."

Tess worked a knot out of her hair. It was a hot
day; she felt sweaty and limp. The adrenaline she'd
been running on had become a sour taste in her
mouth. After Connor was gone, she'd be left alone to
face a truth that was only now apparent to her. One
that he'd spotted some time ago and had suggested to
her in his calm, nonjudgmental way.

It wasn't the Johnsons who couldn't forgive her for
Jared's death.

"I'll have to thank her," Tess said quietly.

"And Erik," Beth prodded.

"Guess so." Tess swallowed, wondering how to
face Erik again. She'd become so accustomed to
avoiding him that it wasn't as easy as walking up and
offering him her hand.

The folding chair squeaked as Beth shifted. Tess
glanced up at her friend's sun-flushed face, grown
fuller and softer since the pregnancy. "What about
you? Isn't it time for you to head home?"

Beth fanned her face. "I'm just waiting for Randy
to finish sanding the bedroom floors. It's not like I've
been really working. Emmie let me unwrap sandwiches and hand out sodas. And I trimmed the dead
blooms off a couple of lilac bushes."

"You did enough." Tess reached up and patted
Beth's arm. "It's been pretty amazing how everyone

pitched in. With his reputation, I wasn't sure how many we'd get."

"Well," Beth said with a bit of a grin, "it's possible some of the turnout can be attributed to the curiosity factor. Both about Connor as a celebrity *and* what he's been doing to the lighthouse. Nobody in this town wants to be left out of the loop."

Tess summoned a smile. "You might be right."

"So what's wrong? It's not only Erik, is it?"

There was no sense in holding back from Beth. They were too close. And Tess needed a sounding board. If she had to keep her concern for Connor inside and unspoken, she'd wind up a basket case like her mother.

"Connor's leaving. I talked him out of going today, and if I work it, I might be able to persuade him to stay tomorrow, and perhaps for the next round of the tournament, but I'm going to run out of reasons before long."

"He never planned to stay permanently, did he?"

"Not really. But I'd hoped he was sort of leaning that way."

Beth pushed up the bill of her baseball cap to better see Tess's face. "How come? Or do I even need to ask?"

Tess lowered her eyes.

"You are not just sleeping with him," Beth said. "You've gone and fallen in love."

Tess scrunched up her face, but she couldn't stop from answering in one joyful burst. "Yes."

"I knew it, of course. It's been obvious for weeks

and weeks.'' Beth waved a hand, exaggerating, but not too far off base, either.

Tess was almost afraid to ask. "How obvious?"

"It didn't go unnoticed that you and Connor arrived together this morning. That was part of the excitement all day. You might as well have made a public declaration."

"Super. Now, when he leaves, I get to be the lovelorn librarian again."

Beth made a consoling sound. "Why does he want to go, anyway? I thought for sure he'd stay for his grandfather, at least."

The dread that had been weighing Tess down like a brick became even heavier. Her shoulders slumped. "It's all about that abduction. Connor thinks he can help. And who knows, he might be right." She watched as the men gathered their tools and slowly made their way down the pitched roof to the ladder. "He doesn't miss much."

"He's going to miss you," Beth murmured. "A whole lot."

Tess got to her feet. "He damn well better."

"Here comes Randy," Beth said, and Tess offered a hand to hoist her from the lawn chair.

With a shaky smile, Tess watched Beth amble across the grass to meet Randy. He greeted his wife with a quick peck on the lips, then said something that made her laugh as he bent and pressed an ear to her belly.

Twisting the bandanna in her hands, Tess approached the cottage. Evan stepped off the ladder, his tool belt jingling. He spoke to Tess, but she barely heard him. Connor was next, and she glanced into his tanned face, seeking reassurance—and finding it. His irises were the color of maple syrup, warm and soothing. She touched his arm. He nodded once, then caught her hand in his. Squeezed it encouragingly.

She hadn't had to say a word. Connor knew. He always knew.

Erik Johnson swung off the ladder. He turned, saw Tess, and flinched. Not much, and perhaps only out of surprise. She'd avoided him for so long.

He was stocky but still fit, gone florid in his midthirties with his broad face and neck and a few too many beers under his belt. There was something bland about his open-faced heartiness. Bland in a well-meaning, cheerful, undemanding way. He was a hard worker, a good provider, a solid citizen.

He was what Jared would have become had he lived.

He was what Tess no longer wanted.

Nor feared.

She closed her lids for a moment, swallowing thickly, then took a breath and forced her leg forward. One step. Two steps. She was looking Erik in the eye now.

He was looking back at her, his cheeks ruddy.

"I wanted—" Tess's voice rasped. She swallowed again and started over. Eleven years, she thought. Gone so fast, and yet they'd hollowed out an immense chasm that it was long past time to refill.

"Erik, I wanted to say thank you." She held out

her hand. With no hesitation, Erik took it. And pumped vigorously, so vigorously that her sudden burst of laughter rattled like an eggbeater.

It was that easy after all.

CHAPTER THIRTEEN

"THE BEA-CON AT GULL…Rock…Lig—"

Tess clenched her teeth to stop from urging Sonny on.

He scowled. "Don't make that face, missy. I know what it is."

"Of course," she said, sending him a mental message: *Remember your rhyming words—fight, sight, bright…*

"Light," he read, really read, not faking it because *lighthouse* was the obvious next word. "Lighthouse."

"Mmm-hmm. The beacon at Gull Rock Lighthouse…"

"Burn-ed."

Tess gave a soft reminder. "One syllable."

"Burned." Sonny heaved a sigh. Each word was still an effort, but he had a stubborn will. "Burned for forty…years…un-der…the car—the *care*—" he peered at the page, reading the caption beneath a dramatic color photo of the lighthouse being battered by crashing waves "—of keeper Addison Mitchell."

"And there you go," Tess said, giving the page an exuberant slap. "You read it."

Sonny made a sound of disgust. "But the book got

it wrong. S'posed to be thirty-nine years. Forty? What kind of bull-hockey is that?''

Tess laughed. ''I guess they rounded off.''

''Phht, then they're wasting my time,'' he said, but she caught the glimmer of satisfaction behind his gruff exterior. He drew the book closer. ''Eh. Maybe it's a good thing I'm reading now. I've got to find out what other mistakes are in here.''

''Next time,'' she said. ''But practice all you want in between.''

She gathered her things, then rose and fluttered around the room, straightening and fussing. The decor was much improved. She'd tacked up a few magazine photos of Lake Superior on the bulletin board over the desk, replaced the flowers, brought in a couple of cushy pillows, a soft fleece blanket and a selection of paperbacks geared for beginning adult readers.

Sonny was flipping through the library books. ''Where's Connor at?''

''The lighthouse. They're sandblasting the brick this morning. He sent his greetings to you, though, and promised he'd stop by later today.''

She tried to sound cheery, but she was worried. At this rate, Connor would be able to bring his grandfather to the lighthouse any day now, and then there would be nothing left to hold him in Alouette. The unsolved alleged abduction was still in the news, and Tess's heart went out to the young woman's family, though she was grateful that the media frenzy had eased up regarding Connor's involvement. For now.

When he showed his face, all hell would break loose. But she knew that wouldn't stop him.

She'd overheard him on the phone this morning, making airline reservations for the day after tomorrow. He hadn't volunteered his plans, and so far she hadn't asked.

She eyed Sonny. "How are you feeling?"

He lifted his head. "Damn fine."

"Wonderful." She truly meant that, even if it was inconvenient that the new medication had given Sonny a boost at right this moment. Of course, Connor had been ready to go, either way. But she'd had a better chance of delaying him when she could play the grandfather card. "Has Connor mentioned anything to you about visiting the lighthouse? Soon, I mean?"

The old man shrugged. "He knows I'm raring to go anytime. I can't wait to bust outta this joint."

Tess laughed ruefully. "Looks like you'll get your wish sooner than expected."

"What do you know?"

"Only that Connor's been working very hard to please you."

"Huh. Are ya sure it's me he wants to impress?"

She blushed. "Yes, of course it's you."

It wasn't necessary for Connor to lift a finger to impress her. All she wanted was to keep him close and whole. The quandary was that to become the latter he'd have to surrender the former.

TESS CARRIED ON, glad to be busy with her projects and lists. The next round of the Scrabble tourney was scheduled for that Sunday evening, thankfully less of an extravagant affair than the opening round—which meant they were serving light refreshments instead of a full meal.

She went early to set up the tables, chairs and game boards. Only eight this time. Since they didn't run the tournament by official rules but rather in a single elimination, the two rounds tonight would pare the field to four semifinalists.

One by one, the contestants arrived and checked in with Tess. Noah and Claire came together, and Cassia was accompanied by her red-haired mother, who supplied a running stream of advice and admonition. Other friends or relatives came along for support, including Deb Johnson, who'd driven with her father-in-law, Gus. Tess dropped her pen and fumbled around with the sign-in sheet. But Deb smiled in her placid, motherly way and chatted about the lighthouse until Tess found her bearings and was able to answer in more than monosyllables. If there was a trace of sadness in the way the older woman looked at her, well, that was only natural. In a different life, under altered circumstances, they would have been as close as mother and daughter.

Connor was the last to arrive. The other players were champing at the bit, so Tess had no chance to speak to him before he was plunged straight into a game against Emma Koski, a schoolteacher armed with a degree in French literature. Perhaps if it had been English literature, she would have won.

During the break, Connor nabbed Tess. "I have news."

She inhaled, hardly daring to hope.

"No, not that," he said with a sharp shake of his head. "This is about my grandfather."

"Oh." *Damn.*

"Come with me." He led her through the double doors and into the hallway lined with old school lockers. It was empty and silent, dimly lit by fluorescent bulbs that had been installed in an ill-advised attempt at modernization.

"I hear you had a good lesson."

"Yes. In fact, there's not a lot of need to keep on." As much as she didn't want to admit that, she felt compelled to be scrupulously honest. "Your grandfather's reading level has greatly improved. He has every reason to be proud of himself—it's quite an accomplishment at his age. I'll continue if that's what he wants, but since I'm assuming the intention wasn't to make him a Fulbright scholar, we can..."

Her voice faded. How uptight she sounded.

"Relax," Connor said. "Breathe."

She leaned her head against the lockers. "Where have I heard that before?"

"Your method worked on me."

The corners of her mouth lifted momentarily. "My *second* method worked." She let out a sigh. "Okay. I'm ready. What's the news about your grandfather?"

Connor didn't waste words the way she did. "I got the okay to bring him to the lighthouse."

"That's, um, well, that's great." She clenched her hands. "When?"

"Tomorrow."

"You work fast," she said, thinking of his reservations. Wham, bam, good riddance, ma'am.

But he'd promised to come back. Why did she feel so hopeless, when so much was going right? Sonny's lessons, the lighthouse, her reconciliation with the Johnsons, being in love with Connor.

"Do you want to come?"

She blinked, missing his meaning for one heady moment. Then she got it. "To Gull Rock, you mean?"

Connor grazed her cheek with his knuckles. "Spend the day with Sonny and me."

That single, small touch was all it took. With a gut-wrenching moan, she gave up all attempts at composure and wound her arms around his waist, hugging him to her as if the tighter her hold, the longer he'd stay.

"Aw, Tess." Connor pried her arms a little looser. "Don't be scared. I'm coming back."

"Not to stay, you aren't."

"Says who?"

She looked up at him. "*You* certainly haven't! Most of the time, I don't know what you're thinking."

He put his chin on her head. "We'll talk. Eventually. Now isn't the time."

But I need words, she thought. *Three little words, that's all.* To tide her over until his return. Unless going back to his old life *was* the return, and she was the...intermission. In that case, shouldn't she be glad for him, that he'd renewed his career drive?

Nope, not *glad.* That was asking too much.

But she could be strong enough to let him go.

She sniffed and squeezed the tip of her nose before stepping back. "So, um, how are you planning to work this, with your grandfather? I don't want to be an intrusion, but I'll come along if I can be of some help."

Connor gave her upper arms a pat. "That's not your only role, Tess. You've been enough help. Hell, you've given even more than I asked for. Thanks to you, the causeway is passable now, and I can drive Grandpa across in my Jeep." His voice was as gravelly as the fill they'd poured and she thought that maybe he felt something for her, more than he said—or hadn't said—and even more than he showed.

"I've put in a few furnishings for comfort. Sonny should be fine, as long as he doesn't get too worked up."

"What about the steps?" She knew that Connor and Noah had been discussing a way to transport Sonny to the lantern room. Noah had wanted to rig a chair with hand grips so that he and Connor could carry Sonny up the spiral staircase, but that idea had been discarded. Connor was sure that Sonny would be insulted by the very idea.

"I don't know," he said. "We'll see how he does. If he's strong, he might be able to make the climb as long as he takes it slow."

"He was in fighting form this morning."

Connor pecked her forehead. "Thanks. You've made him happy."

"My pleasure."

He chucked her chin. "Dealing with Sonny isn't always a pleasure."

She shrugged. What was next, a high five and a pat on the butt? Was this Connor's way of signaling they were "just friends," even if that meant friends with benefits?

Right, so they'd stick to business. "Oh, I just remembered," she said. "I did finally speak to my friend in the Coast Guard. You were right about the light—except that you might be able to get a temporary permit if you're set on Sonny seeing the lighthouse operational one more time. He said you'd have to limit the power of the beam, and something about calibrating the lens out of focus...well, I wrote it down for you. You'll have to contact him."

"That would mean a lot to Sonny."

"I thought so."

Connor smiled, ruffled her hair. "Thanks again."

"Huh. Uh, I mean, you're welcome. Well..." She sighed. "Right. We'd better get back to the games." She dragged her feet even though she'd given up on getting a different sign out of him. "You're playing Gus in the next round."

Connor seemed oblivious, only making a bland comment about the tough match as they walked side by side. Or maybe it was just that he was so much better at withholding his emotions. Going back into journalistic mode. Forever playing the observer, out to tell a story, but not to *be* one.

Fine for him. But *she'd* had enough of storytelling.

IN THE END, though Connor had convinced her to arrange for a substitute librarian so she might join him and Sonny at Gull Rock, Tess couldn't go. An apologetic Randy Trudell called early in the morning as he was leaving on a delivery run and asked her to keep an eye on Beth, who was finally on leave from the library for her last few weeks of pregnancy.

As soon as it was a decent hour, Tess phoned Bay House, hoping to catch Connor.

"Sorry," Emmie said. "We've seen very little of him since the news reports started. He's paid up on his room, but I'm not sure that he ever sleeps there." She paused significantly.

Tess held her tongue. Connor had been with her for several of those nights, but not all of them. She remembered the sleeping bag, and assumed he'd been staying at the lighthouse. She'd hoped that the work party had shown him he didn't have to hide from the citizens of Alouette, though she supposed there was no telling where a critic would turn up.

Besides, Connor was intending to face all the critics, merely on the off chance that he could aid in the search for Roderick Strange.

And perhaps to get back in the game, she reminded herself, just to toughen herself up for his departure.

"I imagine you know how to get hold of him," Emmie went on.

"Yes, of course. But if you should see him, can you pass on the message that I'm spending the day with Beth?"

"Oh, my. *Really?* Does that mean—"

"No, Emmie, she hasn't gone into labor. Randy's boss called him in to work and Randy doesn't want Beth to be left alone."

"I'd be happy to help out."

"Thanks, but we're set. I've already got my emergency substitute taking over the library hours. I should be going though. Thanks, Em."

"Anytime, dear."

Tess was in the mood for a good old cranky men-are-dogs gripefest. She suspected that Beth would be, too. They'd decided long ago that calories consumed during such discussions didn't count, so on the way to Beth's apartment Tess stopped at the supermarket for orange juice, fruit and fresh doughnuts, then bought four pints of ice cream and sherbet from the Berry Dairy. At times like these, a woman shouldn't have to choose between chocolate ripple and kiwi-strawberry.

The Trudells' modest apartment was above the town's only Laundromat—three rooms furnished with an odd mixture of wedding gifts and hand-me-downs. The floors vibrated underfoot whenever several of the Laundromat's machines were cranked up at once and the scent of bleach and fabric softener often drifted up from the registers. Beth swore that Bump had been conceived to the *thumpety-thump* of an unbalanced load.

"Hey, there!" Tess called, and got a muffled, "In here."

She found Beth down on all fours under the kitchen sink, a bucket of sudsy water nearby. The floor was littered with everything she'd pulled out of the cabinet: folded paper bags, jugs of bleach and vinegar, a carryall of cleaning products and a half-filled tub of recyclable products.

"What *are* you doing?"

"What's it look like?" Beth snapped. She braced her arms and sawed back and forth, her rear end rocking as she put her entire body into the motion of scrubbing the inside of the cabinet.

"You're nuts. Get out from under there." Tess put her grocery bags on the counter, got out the cartons and stowed them in the freezer next to six packages of venison in brown paper wrappings. Randy was a hunter, as Jared had been. Sometimes Tess thought that being around the newlyweds was like watching a play of what her life might have become.

"Ungh. Almost finished." By the sound of it, Beth was scrubbing her way to China.

"You cleaned under the sink only last week. There's not a speck of dirt left." Tess gawped at the recycling bin. The glass jars and tin cans shined as if Beth had polished them. "This is your hormones talking."

"I cannot tell you—" Beth wiggled out of the cabinet and sat back on her heels, panting heavily "—how really, really sick I am of hearing that. It's a thousand times worse than men who smirk about 'that time of the month' every time a woman raises her voice. Like they don't give us *puh-lenty* of reason to—''

Tess held up a hand. ''I get the idea. And I apologize. Remember, I've never been pregnant. You have to make allowances for me.''

Grumbling, Beth grabbed a clean rag and disappeared into the cabinet again to wipe it dry. Tess pounced when she reemerged, catching Beth under the arms and helping her up when she would have reached for a second round with the can of Comet scouring powder.

''But I have to—''

''Tell me what to do,'' Tess interrupted. ''You sit down. I promised Randy that I'd get you to take it easy. He thinks you're going to nest yourself into early labor.''

''I *wish*.'' Beth took a chair at a 1950s dinette set that had come from her mother's attic. She kicked out the other chair and lifted her feet onto it with a groan of relief.

Tess counted in her head. ''You've still got two weeks to go, right?''

''Eleven days, but who's counting?'' Beth wiped her forehead with the back of her hand. ''For sure not Randy's boss.''

''Tough break.'' One of the drivers at Randy's company had been in an accident, so they'd called him back for another delivery run.

''I have to admit, Randy tried. He even threatened to quit, but his boss called the bluff. And we just can't afford for him to be out of work right now.'' Beth's lower lip trembled. ''That doesn't mean I'm not mad at him for going, of course.''

''Pregnant woman's prerogative.'' Congratulating herself for avoiding the forbidden word, Tess knelt near the sink and started putting items back in.

''None of the cleaning products,'' Beth said, directing Tess with dictatorial hand motions and finger snaps. ''They're going into a padlocked closet. You can refold the paper bags if you like. And scoot that bin over here. I want to check those cans for sharp edges.''

''No.'' Tess slid the bin under the water pipes. ''I won't say the H-word again, but can I point out that Bump won't be crawling for months yet? Plus there's a safety latch on this door.''

Beth frowned.

''*And,*'' Tess said, ''I would expect that this bin is going to the curb *before* your delivery.''

Beth snorted. She clamped her hand over her mouth, but soon a chuckle escaped. She broke into laughter, making her belly wobble, which struck her as even funnier. ''Okay, okay, I'm a hormone-addled preggo,'' she said between gasps. She wiped her eyes. ''Gimme a break.''

Tess smiled with fond amusement as she finished up, washed her hands and then set the doughnuts on the table. ''I brought some healthy stuff, too, but maybe you can ease up on the diet just a little bit?''

''Did you bring jelly?'' Beth sat up and worked her way through the contents of the bakery bags, piling the doughnuts on the plate Tess had brought over. "Ah, yes, you did! I've been craving jelly doughnuts all week. I do believe that my hormones and I deserve two or three of them. At least."

"I agree." Tess sat at the table. "So Randy's supposed to be back tomorrow?"

"Maybe sooner. He thinks if he pushes it hard today, he can drive home tonight, but I told him not to be taking risks if he's too tired. Even though I've been sort of uncomfortable lately, I don't think I'm having actual contractions yet. The doctor says it'll be another week yet, minimum. So I don't want Randy getting into an accident on account of me…" Beth had been chomping on a doughnut throughout her speech, but finally she stopped and considered what she'd been saying. "Oops. I didn't mean to—"

"Don't even," Tess said, forestalling the needless apology. "You know that bugs me when people think they can't say the word *accident* around me."

"Uh-huh."

"Accident," Tess said. She tore a bite out of a chocolate-glazed doughnut. "Accident, accident, *accident.*"

Beth's eyebrows bounced up and down. "Well, wow, you're in a mood." She looked at the doughnut feast spread between them. "Aha. Is this about Connor leaving town?"

"He burns me up."

Beth chuckled. "In more ways than one."

Tess made a face. "He did show up at the tournament last night. Won both of his games, too. He's in the semifinals with Cassia, DeeDee DeGroot and John the Scrabblenator.'' She shrugged. ''But what's the use? I have no idea if he'll even be in town for the last two games. I hate for there to be a default in the semifinals.''

''Yeah, that's what's got you peeved, all right.''

''That's part of it.''

''And the other part?''

Tess licked chocolate off her fingers. ''Do you think it's a bad sign when a guy does the big brush-off every time there comes a little hint of…you know…actual *feelings* to a conversation?''

''Not necessarily. That's just how some guys are.''

''Hmm.''

''Have you expressed any of these, like, actual *feelings* yourself?''

''Not exactly. But I've told him not to go. And I've hinted at…the other.''

''Sometimes the woman has to go first. You know how fragile men are.''

Tess grinned. ''Ain't they just?''

''And then there are the times when they don't say it, but they still show you how much they care. Like Randy. He didn't want to leave me any more than I wanted to be alone right now, but he made himself do it so me and the baby would be taken care of. Y'know?'' Beth sighed. ''Sheesh. That makes it real hard to stay mad at him.''

Tess put her chin in her hand and stared into the living room without actually seeing it. ''Connor's taking his grandpa out to the lighthouse today.''

"Ohh. How come you're not with them?" Beth rapped her knuckles against the Formica tabletop. "Crap! Because of me?"

Tess shook her head. "Nah. I figure it's a family-bonding thing. They don't need me there."

Beth peered into Tess's face. "Are you sure?"

"Yeah, I am. Besides, someone has to keep you from going into the delivery room with chapped hands and housemaid's knee."

Beth laughed. "You're such a friend. How will I pay you back?"

Tess picked up another doughnut, although the gripe session had lost much of its momentum. "I've always wanted to be a godmother."

"Sure, but how about a mother?"

"Um, we'll see."

Beth nodded knowingly. "I'll tell you one thing— I cannot wait to see you with crazy preggo-lady hormones." Suddenly she inhaled, scrunching her face into a sharp wince.

Tess dropped the doughnut and rose partway out of her chair. "What is it? A contraction? Should I call the doctor? No, Randy, right? I should call Randy first."

Beth shook her head, her eyes squeezed shut and her lips compressed. "Hold on. Wooh. It's gone." She rubbed her tummy, her face smoothing out. "Well, okeydokey. That was—*whew*."

Tess was jittery. *"Beth."*

Beth looked across the table. "What? Oh, don't get

all Butterfly McQueen on me. That was nothing. A little twinge. I'm to expect them, Dr. Jamison said.''

''But how can you tell a twinge from a contraction that's the start of labor?''

Beth rolled her eyes. ''Duh, Tess. Think about it.'' She spoke slowly. ''When they keep coming.''

''Still. Randy should be here.''

''I'll call him if I start getting contractions more regularly.''

''You mean you're *already having them?*'' Tess screeched, feeling the hair rise on the back of her neck.

''Gosh, calm down. It hasn't been that many. A couple yesterday, out at Gull Rock. One this morning, after Randy left. Jolted me right out of sleep, and I was having a very satisfying dream about starching the creases out of the Statue of Liberty's robe.''

Tess sank back into her chair. ''I don't see how you can take this so calmly.''

''Well, I did panic the first time I had one, a couple of days ago. I made Randy take me to the hospital in Marquette and it was so embarrassing when they told me I wasn't even close to labor.''

''Why didn't you tell me?''

'''Cause it was *embarrassing.* The nurses thought I was so cute, in an amusing, hormonal way. Anyway, you were preoccupied with Connor.''

''Hmmph.'' Tess felt as though she'd let Beth down. ''I'm here now,'' she said staunchly. ''Sticking like glue till Randy gets home.''

Beth gripped her belly like a basketball. ''We'll be

fine, you and me and Bump. First babies are almost always late. Everyone says so.''

Little comfort, as far as Tess was concerned, nor was she convinced that Beth was as relaxed as she claimed. Fortunately, Randy had promised to call home from the road. Tess vowed to watch Beth like a hawk for further signs of labor and be the first to the phone, particularly if she spotted Beth so much as wincing. Luckily, pregnant ladies weren't known for being fast on their feet.

CHAPTER FOURTEEN

THE AIR WAS SO HUMID it felt like wet flannel, but as soon as they neared the lake, a cooling breeze washed through the Jeep, sweeping away most of Connor's worries. He hadn't told Tess, but his grandfather's doctor hadn't been altogether enthusiastic about Sonny's trip to the lighthouse. But she hadn't forbade it, either. Not that Sonny—or Connor, except in extreme circumstances—would have listened, particularly when the doctor had admitted that Sonny was at the age where his health might fail in his room at the nursing home as easily as anywhere else. The only difference was access to medical help.

Connor had decided to take the risk.

"There she is," Sonny said as they turned onto the road that wound past the marina. He stuck his head closer to the open window and inhaled.

Connor didn't know if his grandpa meant the lake or the lighthouse, rising above the trees on Gull Rock. It didn't matter. Both were a vital part of the old man's blood.

"Hold on when we get to the turnoff. The road is rutted and my Jeep tends to bounce around a lot."

"Eh, these old bones are used to the jostling."

The Jeep rattled along the cool green tunnel of Gull Rock Road. When Connor glanced at his grandfather, he was sure the old guy was enjoying every bump. The gate to the mainland parking area—which was just a clearing near the shore—had been left open to accommodate the recent comings and goings, so Connor didn't have to stop.

The Jeep crested the rise of the clearing. Connor slowed. The road became steep and worn to hard gravel and rocks here, just before they drove onto the causeway.

Sonny gripped his cane with one hand and the edge of the door with the other. His blue eyes were fired with as much enthusiasm as Connor had ever seen him show. "Gun it, boy."

"Here we go." Connor didn't actually gun it, but the ride was hairy enough that they seemed to tear down the hill and across the causeway, with dust rising and gravel pinging off the undercarriage.

Sonny let out a whoop. So did Connor.

The wheels of the Jeep bit into the rocky path on the other side and sent them shooting onto the grounds. Connor swerved and braked, parking quite close to the cottage. The engine died, and at last they heard the familiar sounds—the swoosh of waves, the cawing birds, the flap of the American flag.

The flag had been the finishing touch. Every morning and evening during his summers at Gull Rock, Connor had helped his grandfather with the ritual raising and lowering of the flag. He'd found it stored in the basement, faded and somewhat tattered, and clipped it to a pole Noah had helped him raise as their final task before Sonny's homecoming.

Sonny stared at the hastily refurbished lighthouse. His jaw worked back and forth a couple of times, but he remained silent.

Connor cleared his throat. "Well, Grandpa, what do you say? You're home."

"Yup."

"I know it needs more work…"

Sonny nodded. "Looks good to me. Damn good."

Connor reached out and clasped his grandfather's forearm. "Let's take a look around."

He got out and circled to the passenger side to help Sonny from the Jeep. They moved slowly around the cottage to the point that overlooked nothing but the endless blue water. A simple wooden bench had been set where Connor remembered his grandfather sitting in the evenings, never tiring of looking across the great lake, watching the sun go down over the red ridges of the craggy shoreline to the west.

They stopped and rested, not saying much. Sonny took off his hat and soaked up the sun. Connor gazed at the blue-gray horizon, thinking it was good that he'd stayed for this.

Probably Tess was right about how far-fetched it was that he could be any help in arresting Strange. But that didn't matter. Any chance at all was worth trying for.

Tomorrow. He'd have to say goodbye to Tess.

Sonny stirred. "You think an old man can make it up t'the lantern room one more time?"

"It's safer not to try."

"Safe, huh."

"Mom told me I was to look after you until she got here. She and Dad are on their way north right now." Connor had called to inform his parents of the schedule as soon as he'd bought his plane ticket. Sonny wouldn't be left alone.

"Hmmph. Once Dorothy's here I'll never get the chance. She'll be fussing like a mother hen."

Connor had expected this. "There's no way, Grandpa. The staircase is narrow. There are too many steps." He'd have offered to haul the old man up on his back if there was any chance that Sonny would agree.

"You think I forgot? Thirty-nine years I was up and down those stairs. Longer than you've been alive."

"But it's different now."

"Well." Sonny clapped his hat back on, jutting his jaw as he gazed at the brick tower. "These legs might be old but they still work."

"And what if something happened? You could stumble or fall."

"I can think of worse ways to go."

"Think about your daughter then."

"Dorothy knows what a stubborn mule I am."

"And she's counting on me to be just as stubborn about saying no."

Yet Connor had to admit that he wanted to relent. It seemed right to him that Sonny should be able to decide for his own self if the arduous climb was worth the stress and strain upon his failing body.

Perhaps he was as foolhardy and stubborn as his grandfather, but Connor decided he was willing to take responsibility for allowing Sonny to try.

"GAD, TESS! I'm so sick of you watching me with that wary look in your eyes. I'm not a jack-in-a-box, you know." Beth kicked pillows off the couch as she swung her legs to the floor. "Even *if* I started labor, it would go on for hours and hours."

"I'm counting on that." Tess had spoken to Randy when he called and urged him to head home as soon as he could. He'd been in Sault Sainte Marie after making deliveries all along the eastern edge of the peninsula. He thought he'd be through by six-thirty, and it was a four-hour drive back to Alouette. If he drove the speed limit.

Should Beth go into labor, he'd still probably make it home in time. Nevertheless, Tess was determined to coddle Beth like a million-dollar Fabergé egg.

Beth hoisted herself up. "Let's get out of this place and go for a ride in air-conditioned comfort. The way I'm sweating, Bump might slip right out of me if I uncross my legs."

Tess chuckled. "Not in my car, okay?"

Beth switched off the fans and grabbed her purse. The little apartment was stifling, even with the windows open, but she and Randy were saving their pennies for a house of their own. "How about stopping at the Berry Dairy for one of their fruit slushies? That's the only thing that will cool me off.''

Tess was agreeable. The ice-cream stand was at the bottom of the Bayside hill. She could see the light-house from there.

They drove through town. A line had formed at the pick-up window. Tess went to stand in it while Beth waited in the car, chatting to passersby, listening to the radio and unconsciously stroking her midsection all the while.

Bump made Tess as nervous as a cat. Or maybe it was wondering how Sonny and Connor were getting along, she thought, looking across the road toward the lake. This time it was the lighthouse that was doll-size, like a little figurine that had been plopped among a stand of pipe-cleaner trees.

''Want to go and park by the marina?'' she suggested to Beth when she returned to the car with their frozen drinks.

''Hmm.'' Beth slurped through a straw. ''Why don't we just drive out to Gull Rock instead? Connor won't mind us butting in, will he?''

''Nope, but I'm not risking it. You'd get shaken up and then you really *might* pop like a champagne bottle.''

''Yeah, sure.'' Beth giggled. ''If shaking did it, hon, I'd've sent Randy downstairs to the Laundromat with a roll of quarters weeks ago.''

Tess drove out of the lot, keeping her eye on a pack of kids on bicycles. ''I do believe this pregnancy has sharpened your tongue.''

Beth pulled the seat belt across her body. "Yeah, well, then that's the only part of me that's sharp."

"And to think you used to be such a quiet child."

The town wasn't usually so busy, but they'd hit the late-afternoon hour when everyone was heading home from the beach or work, shopping for groceries, heading out for an early dinner, or simply going for a cooldown drive like Tess and Beth while they waited for the heat to break.

They parked by the marina and watched the arrival of a few sailboats. Beth put her drink on the dashboard and shifted around, at first saying she was restless, until the pain got to be too much and she had to wince.

"It's okay," she insisted when Tess asked if they needed to call the obstetrician.

"That's the second one today."

"Third, actually. I had a little twinge in the shower I took after lunch."

"Beth!"

"It's not time yet. My water hasn't even broken."

Tess checked her watch. "We're timing this from now on. And don't you dare try to pull a fast one. I want to know if your *eyelid* twitches."

"Scout's honor." Beth made a face as she wriggled deeper into the car seat. "I'm starting to think that Bump might come early after all. Maybe it was the jelly doughnuts."

"Let's find a phone and call Randy again."

"All right," Beth said meekly, and that was when Tess knew they were going to have a baby.

THEY STOPPED and rested every few steps, but eventually Sonny made it to the top of the lighthouse. Connor helped him over to one of the crates that had held the pieces of the lens, and when his grandfather dropped down with an exhausted sigh, he thought worriedly of the downward trip.

Sonny's face was chalky beneath the ruddy color that stained his gaunt cheeks. "Nothing to it," he said when he had his breath back.

Connor paced the limited space, wondering if he'd made another mistake. "Yeah."

Sonny was looking around the lantern room, his eyes gleaming with keen interest. "You've put the Fresnel back together."

"I tried. Don't know if I got it right."

"Help me up here, boy." Connor held his grandfather's elbow as he made a tottering circuit of the rounded room, examining the setup. "Not bad, not bad. Getting there."

"Since you're here, maybe you can help. Tell me what to do."

The old man's eyes narrowed. "Thinking of lighting this old thing up, eh?"

"I'd like to see it operational. Wouldn't you?"

"Guess so."

Connor lifted his hands, palms up. "You're the expert."

Sonny nodded, but before they could begin, he was distracted by gazing through the glass to the magnificent bird's-eye view. He raised his cane and tapped it against the glass. "There's the prettiest view for hundreds of miles. Priceless, isn't it, Connor?"

"Yes...but there are a few things I might trade it for."

"Eh?"

Justice for Strange's victims, Connor thought.

For his grandfather and the rest of his family, a little more time together.

As for himself...

What else? *A second chance to return Tess's love.*

THE AFTERNOON sped by, and before Connor realized it, the sun had begun lowering in the sky. He'd mentioned leaving a couple of times, but Sonny wasn't ready to budge. They hadn't done much besides go over the workings of the Fresnel lens and the weighted pulleys and clockwork mechanism that turned it, then made a slow descent and brief tour of the interior of the cottage.

Emmie had sent one of her picnic hampers over with Noah and they'd eaten at the kitchen table like old times, though Sonny's appetite wasn't particularly tempted. He mostly wanted to sit outside, dozing in the warmth as the waves washed the rocks. Each time Connor suggested calling it a day, Sonny put him off. This might be his last day, he'd said.

Connor had thought his grandfather meant his last day at the lighthouse. It wasn't until he knelt at Sonny's feet to rouse him for the walk to the Jeep that another meaning occurred.

Gently, he shook the old man's shoulder. "Grandpa. Time to go."

Sonny mumbled, blinking his tired eyes. "Did I dream? Am I here?"

"Yes, we're at Gull Rock. But the sun's setting. We have to go now."

"I want to stay."

"That's impossible. There's no electricity, no beds." Which was the least of it.

Sonny batted away Connor's hands. "Oil lamps. Always worked fine."

"The visit's over, Grandpa. Can you stand?"

"'Course." But he leaned heavily on Connor.

"Whoa," Connor said, grabbing on when his grandpa listed to one side.

"I feel dizzy," the old man croaked. He pulled against Connor's arms. "Let me sit."

Connor eased him back down to the chair placed up against the house in the shadow of the roof. He'd brought along Sonny's medication and fed him the pills on time, after lunch as directed.

He knelt to look into his grandfather's face. Sonny wasn't focusing as well as he had early in the day. But was that because he was dopey with sleep, or for another reason?

"Do you hurt anywhere, Grandpa? Arms? Chest? Head?"

"Just dizzy." Sonny lifted a hand. The cane fell to the ground. "My gut's upset."

"Okay. Sit still for a bit, let's see if it passes." The symptoms didn't sound like a stroke or heart attack, which was what Connor had feared. There were times the drugs his grandfather took for various minor ailments seemed to cause a dementia worse than the aches and pains they supposedly cured.

"Stay here," Sonny said, closing his eyes.

He slumped against the cottage wall.

Connor's worry became fear. He took Sonny's wrist, feeling for a pulse. It seemed unsteady.

Had the man passed out?

He touched his grandfather's cheek. Clammy. He started to lift an eyelid, but Sonny jolted from his stupor and shoved Connor's hands away.

"Mary Angela," he said, his eyes open but unfocused.

"Your wife's not here. She's dead," Connor said, feeling brutal but hoping the bluntness would reach the old man. "There's only me."

"Red hair." Sonny didn't seem to hear. "She's missing."

"Grandpa." Connor made his voice loud but calm. "Can you hear me?"

There was a long silence. Then, "I ain't died yet, boy."

Not yet, Connor thought, somewhat cheered by the caustic comment. *That* was the grandfather he knew.

What he didn't know was that if carrying his grandfather to the Jeep and putting him through the rough ride into town was the thing to do. It seemed that keeping him still and quiet was more important. But he had to get help—they couldn't stay out here all night. Even if that was what Sonny wanted.

Connor opened the back door of the cottage. "Sit still, okay, Grandpa? I'm going to move you inside. And then—"

He looked across the water to the bay, noticing how the water had deepened in color with the fading light. The town was so near. One distress signal and help would arrive within minutes.

A signal. Of course.

Connor dropped a hand over his grandfather's shoulder. "And then I'm going to get help."

"TESS! Tess, I think it's time."

Tess bolted awake, amazed that she'd dozed off on Beth's couch when she'd intended to be a vigilant watchdog until Randy got home.

Beth stood over her, wringing her hands. "The baby's coming."

Tess checked the illuminated dial of her watch. "What—what happened? Did you have another contraction?"

The sun had gone down, leaving dusky pink and purple streaks on the horizon. With no lamps on, the living room was dull and drab. Anxiety churned Tess's stomach, but she tried to ignore it. Beth needed her to appear competent and in control, even if she wasn't.

"Uh-huh." Beth held her belly with one hand, her shoes with the other. "It was strong. Woke me right up."

"Let's go then." They'd been in touch with both Randy and the obstretician's office off and on all afternoon and into the evening, keeping track of the progress.

"I really wanted to wait for Randy. But I just called him, and he's still seventy miles away." Beth's voice was reedy with worry. "My water hasn't broken, though. Maybe we should hold on a little while longer, to be sure—"

"No," Tess said firmly. "We should go now. There's no sense in putting it off. Sit down. I'll help you with your shoes."

Beth sighed with relief. "Okay."

"Um, do you think we should call an ambulance?" They were twenty miles from the nearest hospital. Normally that would be considered a short drive to a Yooper, but suddenly it seemed a long way to go on a country road with little traffic and sparse population.

And me driving, Tess thought as she tied Beth's sneakers. Her fingers started to shake.

"This isn't an emergency," Beth fretted. "I'm not sure if our insurance would cover ambulance costs."

"My treat," Tess said quickly as she stood and helped Beth up.

"No, that's okay. Besides…" Beth hugged her. "I have complete faith in you, Tess. There's no rush. We'll just take it slow and easy and we'll be fine."

"I could call someone to drive. Claire, Noah—"

"They're at his cabin, remember?"

"Someone else at Bay House, then. *Connor.*" She'd called there once, a couple of hours ago, hoping to find out how Sonny's day at Gull Rock had gone, but Emmie hadn't seen Connor all day.

Beth shook her head. "You can handle it, Tess. I know you can."

"Of course," Tess said, when she really wanted to call out the firefighters, the EMTs and Sheriff Bob for good measure. "Sure. Sure, I can."

"My suitcase is by the door."

Oh, God. They were really going to do this!

Tess took Beth's hand as they walked down the steps, not sure which one of them was trembling more. The Trudells' car was only a couple steps up from a junker, so of course they'd use Tess's. She'd gassed up earlier, and even had Jimmy Jarvi check her fluids. The trunk was equipped with emergency supplies. Unfortunately neither of them had a cell phone. Randy had taken his and Beth's, and Tess had never seen the sense in owning one, on the theory that everyone she cared about knew where to reach her at any time of the day.

She took a deep breath. "Beth, I don't want to scare you, but I really think we need to have a cell phone with us. Just in case."

"You're right." Both women glanced around the neighborhood, a mixture of commercial and residential buildings. "Mrs. Hallstrom, across the street." Beth pointed. "She has one."

"I'll run over." Tess waited until Beth got in the car, then raced to the neighbor's house, interrupting the Hallstroms in the middle of a sitcom. They were happy to surrender their cell phone, and even came over to wish Beth good luck. They were standing in the street and waving as Tess drove away.

"Oh, man," Tess said under her breath. "Here we go."

Beth smiled bravely. "It's gonna be okay. Bump's not coming for hours yet. And Randy will meet us at the hospital."

"After this is over, I'm going to look up your husband's boss and strangle him with my bare hands." The streets of Alouette were virtually empty. Tess clicked on the right-turn signal at the Berry Dairy, staring ahead at the road that led off into the dark, wooded countryside. Between here and Marquette there was little but forest. Anything might happen.

Her only comfort was that the sky was cloudless. No chance of a rainstorm.

"It's all right," Beth said softly. "Drive on."

Tess nodded as she rubbed her sweaty hands on her shorts. But then, as she placed them on the steering wheel and touched her foot to the accelerator, a flicker in the opposite direction caught her eye and delayed their departure. She hesitated, watching curiously as the light grew stronger in the purpled sky.

"*Look,*" she whispered.

Beth leaned forward. "What is that?"

The beacon shone across the water, flashing as the rotating lens atop the tower began to turn. "The lighthouse," Tess said, awestruck. A renewed faith and confidence surged to life inside her. "I'll be damned. Connor has lit the lighthouse."

CHAPTER FIFTEEN

Several weeks later

"LET ME HOLD Bump while you two eat," Tess said, sliding away her own piece of half-eaten blueberry pie.

Beth laughed as she handed the baby over. "We're calling her Burp now."

"By the time she's crawling, I'm betting the name will be Bump again," Randy said. He put two paper plates of blueberry buckle à la mode on the picnic table, then unstrapped himself from a baby backpack and diaper bag.

"One of these days we've got to start using her real name," Beth said. "Or I'll have a very unhappy thirteen-year-old on my hands."

"Lucia Madeline," Tess singsonged, smiling into the baby's sweet face. She'd found that she simply couldn't *not* smile when she looked at her beautiful goddaughter. A happy, cheerful child from the start, Lucia more than lived up to the meaning of her name.

Lucia, bringer of light, and *Madeline,* which meant "high tower." The night of Lucia's birth, when Connor had lit the lighthouse, was one that would go down in local history.

"Any sign of Connor?" Beth asked as she forked up a bite of her dessert.

Alouette was in the middle of its annual blueberry festival. The harbor park was filled with activity. Booths had been set up under canvas awnings, where craft items were displayed, photos taken, games played and every imaginable goody was sold, especially blueberry muffins, jam, pie, syrup and even blueberry-flavored cotton candy. Almost every kid that ran by had a blue tongue and lips. And some of the adults, too.

"He's not here yet," Tess said, cradling Bump. "The Scrabble final is supposed to start in five minutes."

Cassia Keegan was to be Connor's opponent. She was already in place at the table set up under a striped awning nearby, attended by a contingent from Bay House and her mother, who was packing enough supplies for a trek through the Amazon. While Emmie and Mrs. Keegan argued over the angle of the awning, the frequency of sunscreen application and whether or not sunglasses were required, Cassia calmly licked a blueberry ice-cream cone.

"Maybe you should have postponed the game," Randy suggested, "there being a death in the family and all."

"I offered." Tess kissed Bump's downy head. "Connor said no."

Addison "Sonny" Mitchell, eighty-nine years old,

had passed away four days ago in his bed at the lighthouse with all of his family in attendance. The funeral had been yesterday, and this morning Connor was saying goodbye to his parents and siblings as they departed for their homes. Tess had wanted to be with him, but he'd assured her he was fine and that he'd make it to the blueberry festival in time for the match.

She'd been prepared to support him fully, but Connor wasn't grief-stricken, only sorrowful. There was satisfaction in knowing that Sonny's last weeks had been spent at the lighthouse, where he was happiest. Connor had lived there with him, with the rest of his family coming daily so that every moment together was treasured to the fullest.

Tess had enjoyed getting to know Connor's family, but most of all she'd loved sitting with Sonny and Connor, all three of them working on the old man's memoirs of Gull Rock. His stories ran the gamut from wicked storms and capsized boats to the touching details of his love for Mary Angela and their family life in the keeper's cottage. Connor had announced a plan to see the memoirs published, and Sonny had gotten quite a kick out of the idea that he, who hadn't been able to read for so long, was to be memorialized in print.

The most frequently told tale of them all was of the day that Sonny had returned to Gull Rock. The old man never tired of hearing how his grandson had lit the beacon in order to attract attention and save his life. Never mind that he hadn't *quite* been at death's door—the small exaggeration made the story more dramatic.

On that evening, several people in town had noticed the light and quickly assembled a group to check into it. Ultimately, Sonny had been loaded onto a stretcher and hauled across the causeway by hand. He'd stayed in the hospital overnight, but had suffered no great damage.

Tess had been startled to run into Connor at the hospital that night. She'd been so consumed with her responsibility to Beth that it hadn't occurred to her to wonder why the beacon had been lit in the first place. She'd tried to tell him what it had meant to her to see the light—how it had given her the strength and steadiness to calmly drive Beth to the hospital, how she'd imagined that the lighthouse beacon was safely guiding her way.

"I see that John Kevanen is lurking," Beth said, lowering her voice. She nudged Tess, who was preoccupied with making faces at Bump. "The Scrabblenator's probably hoping that he can step in and take Connor's spot in the final."

Tess didn't even glance up. "Not to worry. When Connor makes a commitment, he follows through."

"Hmm. You've become awfully mellow."

Bump gurgled. Smiling, Tess reached for the baby's plump little hand. "Why not? There's nothing to fret over."

"So everything's great between you and Connor?" Beth prodded. The past few weeks, she hadn't gotten many juicy details out of Tess, who tended to smile a lot and drift off into her own little reveries. Which wasn't so different than before Connor, except that her imagination had been redirected, from intrigue and adventure to pure romance.

"Better than great," she said with a secretive smile.

The small crowd that had gathered for the Scrabble final began to stir. "That's him," they said. "Connor's here."

A smattering of applause greeted Connor's arrival. He was a local hero these days. Privately, he'd confided to Tess that what mattered most to him was the support he'd received *before* his reputation had been redeemed.

Not long after the lighthouse episode, when Connor was certain that his grandfather was getting the best care with other family in attendance, he'd left Alouette for a brief stay in New York. He'd canceled his contract with Scepter Publishing and provided the police with transcripts of his interviews with Strange along with all other research materials.

Meanwhile, Strange had turned himself in. His lawyer had declared that Strange had run only out of fear of being blamed for the recent disappearance. Days later and hundred of miles away the missing woman turned up—a runaway from a bad domestic situation.

Nonetheless, Strange was arrested for breaking his parole. A week later, police detectives involved in the ongoing investigation finally managed to put together a previous tip with details from Connor's materials. They believed the new evidence would secure

Strange's conviction for one of the other disappearances.

Connor had not sought any publicity for his part in the breakthrough, but word had leaked in recent days. Particularly in Alouette, where the locals were proud to claim him as a descendant of one of their own.

Tess was almost smug about the way it had all turned out, aside from a few sleepless nights when she hadn't known for sure what was happening or when he'd return. But even then, she'd been certain of her love. Come what may, Connor was forever one of *her* own.

"See ya, Bump." Tess kissed the baby's cheek and handed her over to Beth. "I've got a tournament to conclude."

"Break a leg," Beth said, waving Bump's hand at Tess.

"Good luck," Randy called to Connor, who lifted a hand in acknowledgment.

Tess met up with him in the middle of the crowd. He looked so good to her that her heart sometimes hurt with the hugeness of loving him. She hugged her arms around his waist. "How are you doing? Did your folks get off okay?"

"We're fine, all the way around. Mom and Dad send their regards. They would have stayed if they weren't so eager to get home. It's been a hard couple of weeks for them."

She patted his midsection. "You, too."

"I don't know about that." He smiled at her. "I'd

have to call it a case of the best of times, the worst of times.''

She nipped her bottom lip. ''Keep smiling at me like that, and I'll have to kiss you in front of all these people. And what kind of impartial judge would that make me?''

''Who cares?'' Connor said, and leaned down to smack her lips, making the doting onlookers laugh and cheer and call out a few teasing *''Woo-hoos!''*

Tess pulled away from Connor and called for attention from the crowd, embarrassingly aware of the blush that had worked its way up to her cheeks. ''Ahem. Well, as everyone knows, we've been playing the elimination rounds of the Scrabble Scramble over the past weeks. Today we have our celebrated final, pitting two excellent competitors.''

The crowd clapped.

Tess motioned for quiet. ''Let me introduce them before we begin. On this side of the board, we have our come-from-behind spitfire, Miss Cassia Keegan.''

Cassia clasped her hands like a prizefighter and shook them over each shoulder, bouncing up and down in her chair while she was treated to a rousing cheer.

''And playing opposite her is the pride of Gull Rock, Mr. Connor Reed.''

More applause. ''A man after her own heart,'' one of the wags called out to much laughter.

Connor waved, then bowed before Cassia, taking her hand in a gentle shake. The redhead grinned with pleasure.

Tess continued, "To your places, competitors."

They both pulled up to the table. With a flourish of her hand, Tess stepped aside. "And draw your tiles. May the best person win."

The game commenced with alacrity. Cassia made an impressive opening gambit with *vertex* for forty-eight. Connor played off the X for a reasonable score of his own. Then Cassia drew four vowels in a row, and they both hunkered down for a siege.

Soon the less enthusiastic onlookers drifted off in search of other amusements while the word freaks kibitzed nearby, keeping a close eye on the board as they rehashed earlier rounds. Mrs. Keegan darted back and forth with a water bottle, an umbrella, mosquito repellent. And Emmie was on hand with fresh blueberry muffins, should the players be in need of nourishment.

Tess strolled around the tent, keeping within earshot. Cassia was quite good, but Connor was almost sure to win, providing he drew reasonable letters. Of course, she might be prejudiced ever so slightly.

"Can't hardly take your eyes off him, huh?"

Tess started, whirling around. Claire Levander stood there, smiling, with her hands tucked in the pockets of khaki walking shorts.

"I—well, I'm the proctor. I have to watch—" Tess gave that up. "So, can you blame me?"

"Not at all. I'm the same way with Noah." Claire nodded across the park to the picnic tables, where another crowd had gathered. "Even when he's the hands-down favorite in a blueberry flapjack-eating contest.''

Tess laughed.

Claire said, ''When the prophecy came down, I guess Valentina granted you the brains while I got the brawn.''

''Don't tell me.'' Tess was surprised. ''You're not actually attributing this to the Bay House wedding legend?''

''I gave up fighting it. Noah and I are engaged.''

Tess grabbed Claire's hand out of her pocket. She wore a modest but lovely sapphire ring on her third finger. ''Congratulations! When did this happen? Where have I been that I didn't hear about it?''

Claire thanked her. ''Oh, you've had your head in the clouds, same as me.'' She looked at the ring, then tilted her head back, taking a deep breath of enjoyment. ''And it's nice up here, isn't it?''

Tess smiled to see such happiness. ''Well, perhaps I'm not quite as high as you.''

''But rising fast.'' Claire nodded indulgently. She excused herself to go cheer Noah on.

Slowly, Tess approached the game table. It was true—she was thoroughly besotted. But she was still waiting for Connor to acknowledge the same. With every gesture, every kiss, he showed her that he loved her. And yet he hadn't actually said so, at least not with the three little words she most longed to hear.

Connor looked up, winking when he'd seen that he'd caught Tess's eye.

She smiled noncommittally and leaned closer to ex-

amine the board. The man knew *furze* and *caliph,* but
he had trouble saying "I love you."

The contest was close. In the next few turns Connor
edged ahead. The onlookers murmured. Not many
tiles left. The end was near.

A triple-score square was open for Cassia, but the
best she could manage was a simple three-letter word,
mar, for twenty-one points total.

Connor surveyed the board, taking his time. Tess
edged behind him for a look at his rack. It was heavy
on the consonants, though he did have an S, which
was always beneficial.

The audience had grown again as word spread that
the game was close to the finish. A buzz of comments
followed Connor's next play. Instead of going for the
best score possible, he hung an R and Y off the end
of Cassia's *mar,* making *marry.* A measly ten points.

Marry, Tess repeated silently as she watched Connor draw an E and another S. How odd. There had
been much better words to play. She hoped he wasn't
throwing the game so that Cassia could win.

For her turn, Cassia used up five letters, not only
making a good score that brought her within winning
distance, but cleaning out the remaining tiles as well.

Connor's rack contained two each of the S and T,
plus H, K, and E. With a good placement, he could
secure the win on this turn.

Inexplicably, he put out just one tile, and his only
vowel at that, forming *me* off Cassia's original *mar.*
Calmly, he tapped the timer, making the turn official.

Four points.

Several onlookers gasped. In disgust, John Kevanen threw down his Scrabble dictionary and walked off, muttering about how much better he could have done.

Tess was stunned.

Connor had played the words *marry* and *me.*

Marry me?

That could not be a coincidence.

Cassia was scowling suspiciously as she examined the board. "You gotta be kidding me," she said, but she went ahead and played her turn, counting up nineteen points. She was ahead by six points now, with one tile remaining on her rack.

Tess scanned the available openings. Connor should still be able to win. All he had to do was play his higher-value letters in this turn.

The audience crowded closer, watching with bated breath as Connor casually picked up several tiles. He placed them on the board and a great buzz went up from the spectators. Tess couldn't see—Connor's arm was blocking her view.

Finally he pulled his hand away and slapped the clock timer.

And stood.

Tess looked at him, and then she looked at the board. *Tess.* He'd spelled out her name.

Marry.

Me.

Tess.

"Is that a word?" someone said.

"Not legal," came the whispered answer. "Proper name."

"I'm not challenging," Cassia announced. She set her final tile on the board and tapped the clock to win the game. There were a few hurried congratulations offered, but almost everyone was watching Connor and Tess.

He went down on one knee.

He took her hand.

A chorus of sighs went up from the crowd.

All the blood drained from Tess's face. She couldn't stop trembling.

"I love you," Connor said. "Marry me, Tess."

Her head swirled. Tears of joy blurred her vision. But the light shining in Connor's eyes was all the beacon she needed to make her way into his arms, falling against him as he rose, knocking them both into the table. The tiles rattled.

"Yes," she said. "Yes, yes, yes!"

They kissed to raucous applause.

"You lost," she whispered against his lips.

He hugged her tight. "Then how come I'm holding the prize of a lifetime?"

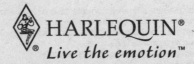

eHARLEQUIN.com

For **FREE online reading,** visit
www.eHarlequin.com now and enjoy:

Online Reads
Read **Daily** and **Weekly** chapters from
our Internet-exclusive stories by your
favorite authors.

Red-Hot Reads
Turn up the heat with one of our more
sensual online stories!

Interactive Novels
Cast your vote to help decide how these
stories unfold…then stay tuned!

Quick Reads
For shorter romantic reads, try our
collection of Poems, Toasts, & More!

Online Read Library
Miss one of our online reads?
Come here to catch up!

Reading Groups
Discuss, share and rave with other
community members!

For great reading online,
visit www.eHarlequin.com today!

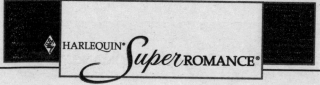

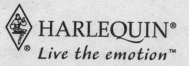

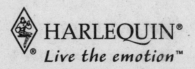